W•CLARK
PUBLISHING

SINCERELY, THE BOSS!

A Novel By

Wahida Clark & Amy Morford

Wahida Clark Presents Publishing, LLC

60 Evergreen Place

Suite 904

East Orange, New Jersey 07018

www.wclarkpublishing.com

ISBN 13-digit 978-1-944992-20-0

ISBN 10-digit 9781944992200

eBook ISBN 978-1-936649-11-2

Audio ISBN: 978-1-936649-08-02

Library of Congress Catalog Number

1. Urban, Romance, Suspense, Mafia, Italian, New York City, Crime, Street Lit – Fiction

Cover design and layout by Nuance Art, LLC

Book interior design by www.aCreativeNuance.com

Contributing Editors: Linda Wilson and R. Hamilton

Printed in United States

SINCERELY, THE BOSS!

Wahida's
ACKNOWLEDGEMENTS

All Praises is Due to the Creator. I am grateful to have had the opportunity to work with the Team of New York Times Best-Selling Partners. But this one goes to Amy Morford who was the first author to cross the finish line. She remained focused, exhibiting great discipline and kept to all of the deadlines given her. She was a pleasure to collaborate with.

Big-Big-Big, Special shout-out to the WCP Street and Home Team.
Wahida Clark
The Official Queen of
Street Literature

Wahida's

DEDICATION

This book is dedicated to all of the mystery/thriller/suspense/romance and more. . . To the readers around the globe.

Amy's
DEDICATION

This book is dedicated to my mother, Peggy-Jo Morford, who encouraged my love of reading at a young age and took me regularly to the El Dorado County Library to feed my habit.

Amy's

ACKNOWLEDGEMENT

I would like to thank my sister, Dana Morford, who through the years has always been my sounding board and editor on my many projects.

To everyone at W. Clark Publishing who assisted in the editing, proofreading, title and other miscellaneous things to make this book happen.

Thank You Nuance Art for designing a kick ass cover!

Last and not least: A big heartfelt thanks to the one and only, Wahida Clark, who encouraged, coached, and believed in me throughout the creative process of this project.

Prologue

Margo's phone rang, and she shrugged at Carol, as if to apologize for cutting her off. Secretly grateful to have an excuse this time, she saw it was Abby again and wondered if this was an apology.

"Hello, sweetie," she started but Abigail cut her off.

"Did you tell Dad that I wasn't in school?"

Margo could tell she was fuming. It seemed to be her daughter's normal state of emotion where Margo was concerned.

"I did," Margo confirmed. Abigail had been skipping school, and now she would blame her mother for whatever punishment David might dole out.

"I'm sorry, but I was worried about you." She had a million questions for Abby, none of which were going to get answered.

"I hate you!" Abigail screamed into the phone. "I hate you, and I wish you had just stayed in prison."

The line went dead. Margo let out a defeated sigh. She put the phone back in her bag and shrugged her shoulders at Carol.

"Kids!" she muttered to herself.

CHAPTER 1

The alarm clock blared and Margo groaned as she felt for the off button. She glared at the time, a whole four hours of sleep and it was time to start all over again. After a year of working three jobs, sleep was what she longed for. The dreams, however, were a different story. She rolled out of bed, and her feet hit the floor. There was no point in letting herself wallow in her current situation. She might not be an optimist, but if the last seven years had taught her anything, it was that she was as tough as nails.

Margo wrapped the towel around herself after getting out of the shower. Damn, if there was one thing she missed about her house it was taking a long, hot bath in her whirlpool tub after a long day at the office. Living at the motel sucked, even though she didn't spend a lot of time here. The plumbing was old, and showers were either scalding hot or ice cold. This morning, she had chosen frigid over third-degree burns and she was covered in goose bumps. She scowled at her reflection. The worry lines had become permanent recently. She checked her face for any other disconcerting developments. At forty-three, Margo knew that she still turned heads, tall and curvy, with long, auburn hair, and intense, green eyes that were still a distraction for men.

She rolled her eyes; she was a distraction for all the *wrong* kind of men. How long had it been now? No, she didn't have time for fantasy. Reality occupied all of her time, and there was little chance that Prince Charming was going to walk into the diner this morning and, between coffee and the check, offer to whisk her away.

Margo checked her uniform and her backpack before heading out. She would return sometime around midnight, almost comatose, and she would barely get undressed before falling quickly to sleep again. At first when she started this routine, she had told herself that working long hours would help her stay sane. Lately, she wasn't so sure.

She didn't have time to second-guess herself, and that was a blessing. It was three hours into the breakfast shift and the diner was slammed. Margo had waited tables on and off when she was a teenager, but had gone to college so these kinds of menial jobs would be forever in the past. If she could give her own children one piece of advice now, it would be to never say never.

Margo knew it was after nine, but not before ten, because she saw Sal walk in. He strode through the diner like he owned the place, and for all Margo knew, he might have. His dark hair was slicked back neatly; the touches of gray made him look even more distinguished. His suit was impeccable as always. He was the only man that she'd seen in the year she worked here who wore cuff links. She had realized shortly after meeting him though that it wouldn't have mattered what he wore; he exuded a quiet power, and he knew it. The other customers were quiet when he passed by, and he took his usual seat. He always sat in her section.

Her cheeks flushed this morning when she picked up the coffeepot and headed in his direction. She blamed it on the fact that he flirted with her; sometimes she blamed it on the fact that she couldn't remember the last time she had sex, but Sal's attention lately had made her long for a little romance.

"Good morning, Sunshine. How's my favorite customer today?"

She smiled when she saw him. She couldn't help it; he was contagious and had that kind of effect on her with that twinkle of mischief in his eyes.

"Wonderful, Cookie, and how's my favorite waitress faring today?"

His voice was gruff, and if Margo was honest, she imagined him calling her "Cookie" during some intimate moments.

"Great, you want the usual?"

He gave her those smoldering eyes and the look that kept her simmering lately. "If I can't get anything else . . ."

Their banter went back to the day they met, but the flirtation had become more heated lately, and Margo went in the back and eyed him from the kitchen. She had heard the stories; according to Vinnie, the line cook with a lazy eye, Sal was powerful businessman with ties to the Mafia. From her past dealings with the criminal element, she believed it. He was definitely a man who knew how to get what he wanted.

When she returned with Sal's usual, a glass of orange juice, two eggs over easy, and a slice of dry wheat toast, he stopped her. "Hey, Cookie, you're a smart girl, let me ask you something."

"Sure, Sal, anything." It was a lie; Margo was very good at dodging answers.

"What are you doing working here?" He looked around to indicate that the diner might not be a career choice for someone with ambition and half a brain.

Margo shrugged. "I needed a job. Help wanted sign in the window, five-question interview, I fit in the uniform, and voilà. Hired on the spot. Do you need more coffee?"

She was quick to change the subject. No matter how attractive Sal might be and how much they flirted, there were certain subjects that were off-limits.

Her section filled up again quickly, and Margo must have been in the kitchen when Sal left. When she went back to his table and found it empty, she couldn't help but feel slightly disappointed. Sometimes conversation with Sal was just about the only thing that made her smile all day. Under his coffee cup, he had left his usual ten-dollar tip and she folded the money and slid it into her pocket.

At noon, it was time to change and get to her second job. Thankfully, the Laundromat didn't require that she wear a uniform as ridiculous as the getup she wore at the diner. It was far too low-cut and showed way too much leg. Margo had complained to Vinnie.

"I'm not making enough money here to flash cleavage."

"Hey, think about how much less you'd make if you didn't." He had winked at her with his good eye, and she knew that the case was closed.

Jeans and a tee shirt were all she needed for her second job and the peace and quiet there gave her time to work on her third job.

Margo walked the ten blocks from the diner to the Laundromat. This was her only real free time of the day, and she would stop, grab a quick bite from the deli and one more cup of coffee. She had to remind herself to eat lately; she had lost enough weight over the last few years, and there was no point in getting sick. The cell phone in her backpack rang as she was chewing. Margo swallowed quickly. She didn't get many calls.

"Hello?" she answered, clearing her throat. "Hello?" she repeated.

"Hey, Mom." It was Abigail, her daughter who should be in school right now. Margo immediately wondered why she was calling her, what was wrong.

"Honey, are you okay? Are you at school?" Her sweet little girl had grown up way too fast and Margo would never forgive herself for the role she had played in all of that.

"No, I stayed home today." Abigail had just turned fifteen and had started lying a lot lately. Rather than call her on it, Margo decided to let it slide. The kids hated her enough right now.

"I kind of need some money." There it was, the reason for the call.

"Sure, Abby." It was her daughter's nickname from a long time ago, and Margo didn't seem to be able to stop using it, even though her daughter hated it now.

"Sorry, Abigail," she corrected herself. "How much do you need?"

"Like five hundred would be good."

It seemed like an awful lot of cash for someone her age and Margo's pulse beat faster as she thought of the possibilities.

"Can you tell me what you need the money for, honey?"

She was trying so hard to make up for the past, but it didn't seem to matter what she did. Her words and actions were always wrong. She hoped Abigail didn't catch on to her try-hard sickly sweet voice.

Abigail sighed loudly, and Margo knew that she had lost. Whatever the game was, she wasn't playing it right.

"Never mind. Forget it. I'll just ask Dad."

Margo had to calm herself every time the kids brought up David, and she held her breath before answering.

"No, I can help—" she started, but her daughter had already hung up on her. Margo looked at the time and shoved the last two bites of her sandwich in her mouth, drained the coffee, and decided that she would walk and talk.

She pressed David's name on her phone and waited for him to pick up. Her ex-husband was probably having a leisurely lunch somewhere with clients, drinking espresso and enjoying an overpriced meal in a trendy place with five-star food and service. The good life. The life they used to have together. Margo missed it. It had all slipped away so quickly.

Her call went to voice mail and Margo wanted to scream. Of course he would screen his calls, especially hers. "Hey, asshole," she started her message, "what the fuck does my daughter need five hundred dollars for? Do you even know what our children are doing all day? Do you know that Abigail isn't in school right now? Get your worthless ass home and check on the kids, damn it!"

She pressed end call and stood outside the Laundromat for a moment. Her heart was pounding, and her blood seemed to boil in her veins. No matter what she did, it wasn't enough for Abigail and Thomas, and it seemed like David could do no wrong. Margo had lost them long ago and sometimes she felt like it would have been kinder if she had simply died instead of having her heart broken again and again.

She went inside and waved at Carol, the heavyset woman who worked the mornings.

"You're not going to believe what happened," Carol began.

She always wanted to give Margo the blow-by-blow account of the people that had been in, the minutia of what had happened. Margo had learned long ago to just set up her laptop in the back and start typing. Carol seemed to have less to say to the back of her head.

"Uh-huh," Margo said. She barely pretended to be interested but that was enough for Carol. She was oblivious to whether Margo listened or not.

She waved good-bye as her coworker walked out the door. It was time to start her third job.

Margo had been writing as a freelancer over the last year, and it was the most lucrative job that she could find. In college, she always had her assignments written well ahead of their due dates. Writing had always come easy to her; she had a knack for it. Now she wrote term papers for spoiled college kids who would pass off her work as their own, that and anything else people wanted to pay her for. How could she blame people for a little plagiarism when she was a convicted felon?

CHAPTER 2

Sundays were the one day when she had a little spare time. It was her day off at the Laundromat. When Margo finished her shift at the diner, she headed to the nearest Starbucks to write. On her way out of the diner she glanced over at Sal's table and smiled to herself. He was a man who was predictable; he was always there at almost the same time Monday through Friday and never came in on weekends. She imagined that he and his wife had taken their brood to church.

He's married, Margo kept reminding herself, especially lately when his eyes had lingered on her décolletage and his look had suggested that he had continued to undress her from there. In fact, he'd been married to the same woman for almost thirty years; it was a matter of pride and nothing that he had tried to conceal.

"It's important for families to stay together, to have continuity and values," Sal had told her early on when Margo had asked. His expression had been serious and seemed to reiterate how committed he was. "Regardless of our difference my wife is important; she's the mother of my children."

"How many kids do you have?" Margo could picture Sal as many things but a father wasn't one of them.

"Five." He couldn't have looked prouder.

"Wow!" Her mouth opened unconsciously in disbelief. How could anyone afford a family that size anymore? Then again, Sal seemed to be quite enterprising.

"Well, I know what you do in your spare time," she had teased.

As she walked to the nearest Starbucks, she could clearly remember the look he had flashed her then. Sal hadn't said a word and none were needed. They both knew exactly what he was thinking.

Margo ordered coffee and found her usual table in the corner; she would sit here and block out the hustle and bustle until closing time. She had an article to finish and a new project to start, but her mind was still otherwise occupied, and she knew that her curiosity was going to get the best of her.

Just twenty minutes, she promised herself, twenty minutes online. She'd do a little reading; it wasn't spying, it was all public information. She typed "Salvatore Alonso Mazzillo" into Google and the screen came to life. Her eyes widened as she scrolled through the results; Sal was a man of many faces.

One of the articles was dated almost a decade ago. "Local Businessman Has Ties to Organized Crime." That looked promising. The picture was a profile of Sal, leaving the courthouse, smiling confidently, still dressed to impress. He had less gray in the picture, but he was every bit as handsome as he was now. Margo read the column quickly. Sal had been charged with racketeering and fraud, but the district attorney's case had been dismissed.

Sal was quoted as saying, "This is just another case of big government trying to strong-arm a regular guy trying to make a few bucks."

Margo smiled a little in awe; the man wasn't easily intimidated.

She continued to read. It was not his first skirmish with the law, and from the looks of things, wouldn't be his last either. Sal owned businesses all over town, from liquor stores, to strip malls. Margo figured this is why he could afford five children. She shook her head. There had been other cases, quickly brought and quickly dropped. The charges were all questionable and luckily for Sal, witnesses seemed to miraculously not show for court or changed their story in front of a grand jury.

In her past life, she would have dismissed him as a gangster and kept her guard up. He would have been a great client. Margo imagined that he probably kept his lawyers very busy, but the aura of danger that seemed perpetually around him, if only by reputation, would have been enough for her. She would have kept things strictly business.

After the last seven years though, Margo had learned that very few things were black and white. Life was a series of shades of gray, and rather than passing judgment on the man, she found herself even more fascinated.

Sal was at the diner Monday morning, and when Margo poured his coffee, she noticed that he seemed a bit distracted.

"You having the usual?"

"That would be great, Cookie."

There was no smile today, not even a lingering glance along her curves, and she couldn't help but notice the change.

"Something wrong?"

She bit her lip. She knew the moment the words left her tongue, she shouldn't have asked. Just because she had read a little bit about him did not mean that his life was an open book. She, of all people, knew how valuable privacy was.

"Business," he looked up at her. The lines on his face were more pronounced. "Always business. I have a legal issue that a nephew of mine is supposed to be handling . . ." Sal put his hands up. "Who knows!"

Margo had never seen him look anything less than confident. She recalled the articles from yesterday and was curious.

"Your nephew is your lawyer?"

"One of many," he exhaled slowly. "In this world, Cookie, you need a lawyer to take a piss." He smiled sheepishly at his own joke. "It took the dumb ass three times to pass the bar, and his aptitude still concerns me."

When she returned with his usual, she still hadn't let it go.

"Why would you give a job to your nephew if you don't think he's qualified?" Margo didn't think that he was the type of man to suffer fools lightly; she didn't even want to imagine what he would do if he were disappointed.

"He's family," Sal shrugged his shoulders. "You take care of family. Speaking of which . . ." he reached out and grabbed Margo's left hand, "who takes care of you, Cookie?"

His touch was gentle, but his hand was strong, and Margo knew that she wouldn't be able to pull away until he let her go, and she didn't want him to. She could feel the heat rising between them, and the sensation from his fingers around her palm had traveled up her arm and was coursing throughout her body. She had to stop this now before it got out of hand.

"Gee whiz, Sal, haven't you heard? Nowadays, women drive, vote, and work outside of the home," she scoffed and felt him let go of her hand. "I'm one of those liberated women who doesn't need anyone to take care of me."

The diner had almost emptied, and Sal was drumming his fingers on the table scanning the morning paper. His plate was empty, his napkin crumpled on it. Normally he would be on his way with a wink. The fact that he was slightly off schedule was alarming to Margo. It must be a bigger problem than he wanted to admit.

She brought the coffeepot, set it on the table, and for the first time since they had met, she pulled out the chair across from him. Sal looked surprised when Margo took a seat, but happily so.

"And to what do I owe this pleasure?" he asked.

"So tell me about the legal issue that your nephew is handling," She had cupped her hands together under her chin.

"Why? You been holding out on me, Cookie?"

She could tell that Sal wasn't used to being surprised often.

"Give me a shot, I haven't always been a waitress." It was all she'd give him.

Sal pondered this briefly, then she watched him lean in. She knew immediately that the legal problem was more than just a little worrisome. As he talked, her mind raced. It hadn't been that long ago, even if it was a past life. She listened intently, and when he paused for a moment, she put her hand in her pocket and pulled out her pen and ordering pad. She wrote down two lines quickly and tapped the pen on the table as she tried to remember the third.

"Is that all?" she asked Sal as she waited for it to come to her.

"That's not enough?" he grimaced. "What are you doing?"

He eyed the paper. Margo smiled as she remembered the last case number, wrote it quickly, tore the paper off her pad, and handed it to Sal.

"Tell your nephew to look these cases up. That will get the search dropped. After that, they've got no case; they'll have to dismiss."

The law knowledge from her past had not been lost. Margo felt more satisfied than she had in a long time. She had loved the law.

"So what does this legal advice cost me, Cookie?" Sal held the paper between two fingers, and Margo could see that he must have perked up because his eyes were focused on her cleavage rather than her face.

She got up and took his plate. She had overstayed her welcome and revealed way too much. "Oh, ten dollars is my going rate," she told him as she walked away.

A couple of weeks passed, and Sal kept to his usual routine and playful banter. Margo wondered what had happened with his legal situation and the information that she'd given him, but she wouldn't bring it up. No matter how much she might like him, there was a line, and she had already crossed it.

One particular morning Sal strutted in and was his usual cheerful self, but there was something more . . . He was grinning from ear to ear and waved her over to him.

"Can I get you the usual, Sal?" Margo couldn't help but smile at him; the man looked like a kid on Christmas morning.

"Yeah, yeah, Cookie." He wasn't as interested in food as he was in her this morning. "What time do you get out of here?"

Margo narrowed her eyes suspiciously. "Why?"

"Jeez, Cookie, it's called small talk. And it's a simple question." Sal's amusement laced his tone.

"Noon." Margo hurried away, her stomach lurched as she went in the back to pour him his orange juice. See, she had crossed the line, and now he wanted to know what she did outside of the diner. Even if she had spent a good deal of time fantasizing about Sal, it had now gone too far.

She gave him the cold shoulder the rest of the morning, and once the breakfast rush had passed, she looked over to see his chair was empty and sighed with relief. Margo had to remember that Sal was every bit the wrong kind of man for her. After everything that happened in her life, the last thing she needed was more problems or heartache.

It was almost a quarter past twelve when Margo left the diner. She was thinking about grabbing a salad to-go today when she heard . . . "Hey, Cookie, you're running late."

There was only one possible person that would call her that, and when she looked to her left, Sal was sitting in the backseat of a black Lincoln Town car that was parked near the curb. He was beckoning to her with a smile.

"Come on. Don't keep me waiting."

Margo felt the hair on the back of her neck stand up as she quickly accessed the possibilities. Any thoughts about her lunch were lost as she bit her lip and exhaled slowly in an attempt to act composed.

"Sal, I can't."

She shook her head. This was a dangerous man, a married man, a man that she could definitely picture fucking in the enormous backseat of his car, which was all the more reason why she couldn't get in.

"I've got to get to my next job, sorry," she shrugged.

"Margo Elizabeth Harris. Born on May 1st, 1972, in Brooklyn, New York. Parents John and Susan Harris." He was reading from an open file in his lap.

Margo gasped and froze in place. "How do you know my name, Sal?"

"I know all my associates' information." He looked at her briefly, and then looked back down and continued reading. "Scored 2,150 on your SATs and graduated in the top 5 percent of your class, even though you worked your way through college. Very good, Cookie."

She stared at him in disbelief, and their eyes locked.

Sal patted the leather upholstery. "Get in."

CHAPTER 3

The phone on the nightstand rang twice before her husband answered it. Early in their marriage Giovanna had become used to the phone ringing at all hours of the night, but as Sal's organization grew the calls had become fewer and farther between.

It was 1:47 in the morning and the conversation was brief. Her husband hung-up the phone and began to dress.

"There's been an accident. I need to go to the hospital," Sal said somberly. "It's Angelo."

"Is it serious?" Giovanna faked the concern in her voice.

"Yes, I'm afraid it is. I'll call when I know more. Go back to sleep," Sal replied as he left their bedroom.

No kiss good-bye, but there never was.

Giovanna wondered if Angelo had finally become too much of a liability for Sal. Angelo was four years older than Sal but had no ambition and a gambling problem. Angelo made good money, by the old neighborhood's standards, as a union ironworker, when he worked. When he was in-between jobs, he gambled and whored around.

Sal had paid off his debts over the years, but the last incident had escalated. He was into a bookie for sixty grand, and Sal had initially refused to pay it. The fingertips of Angelo's right hand had been cut off along with a promise of a bullet in his ear if payment wasn't received within twelve hours. Sal relented, but Angelo was forced into Sal's organization full-time. He had been doing side jobs for Sal as part of his retribution for the debt he owed, but now Sal owned him, and to his wife's distress, Angelo had no choice.

None of this information came from Sal himself. Sal had made it very clear within days of their marriage that her job was rearing his children and running the house. His job was to provide for his family, and how he did this was no concern of hers.

She would know nothing of Sal's business and indiscretions if she didn't have people on his payroll reporting to her. She smiled wickedly. Sal placed such a high value on loyalty, but little did he know how easy it was to bribe loyalty away from him.

Sal called early the next morning. "Angelo and Elena are dead."

"That's horrible." Giovanna asked, "What happened?"

"Car accident. It looks like Angelo swerved to avoid an oncoming car, lost control, and rolled several times. Elena was dead on arrival, and Angelo was dead at the scene."

Giovanna felt no emotion. "What about the boy?"

"He wasn't in the car; he's with Elena's sister," Sal answered.

"Thank goodness," Giovanna replied.

"He will stay with us," Sal stated.

"Of course," Giovanna responded automatically.

They hung up. Sal had funeral arraignments to make, and Giovanna needed to prepare for the boy.

CHAPTER 4

Her feet moved to obey him even though Margo kept shaking her head no.

"What do you want, Sal?" her voice trembled when she asked. If it had just been sex, there would be no need for a dossier. Suddenly she regretted flirting with him so much.

"Get in and we'll talk." His voice was authoritative, and Margo knew that he wasn't used to asking, let alone asking twice.

A driver appeared and opened the car door. She sat but kept one hand on the interior door handle. It seemed like it was only yesterday when she was surrounded by criminals and shady characters. She knew better than to let her guard down.

"How do you have all this information about me?" She looked at the stack of papers in the file.

"You were hired by McKinley, Patterson, and Conley right out of school, passed the bar on your first try." He winked at her. "Unlike my nephew, and on the fast track to be a partner." He closed the file and continued as if he'd already memorized what had been inside. "Your specialty was winning criminal cases using obscure case law, and your client list included a few business associates of mine."

"So you did a background check on me, Sal?" Margo tried to stay calm even though rage was building inside of her head. She had gotten herself into this, and she would have to use her brain instead of her cleavage to get herself out of it.

"What the fuck is going on? I don't have time for bullshit!"

"You were convicted of evidence tampering and perjury, sentenced to six years at Albion Correctional Facility, a medium-security woman's prison." Sal paused, "With no time off for good behavior. Who did you piss off, Margo?"

There was no sense in denying it. Whoever had done Sal's research had been thorough. Margo could only imagine what else the man knew about her.

She stuck her chin out. "How do you know that I pissed someone off?" Being this close to him was making her nervous for a variety of reasons.

"Oh, Cookie," he chuckled, "come on, you can drop the act with me. Of course you pissed someone off; a crackerjack lawyer could've gotten a much better deal if you'd really tampered with evidence."

Margo looked him in the eye. "Tell me what I'm doing here."

No more suggestive smiles, no more playing along, she would treat him like a client if that's what it took.

"I've got a business proposal for you." He leaned forward and tapped on the divider between them and the driver pulled the car out into traffic. Sal settled in his seat and remained silent for the rest of the drive. Margo looked over at him and started to speak several times, but stopped herself. When the car parked, she looked out of the tinted window. They were at an apartment complex.

"Come on, get out," he said.

Margo followed behind Sal and the driver. They were in a quiet upscale neighborhood and the building was older, but well-kept and rather nondescript.

Sal's driver pushed a key into a lock, the number 114 nailed into the wood hanging forlornly on the blue door. The three of them stepped inside. The apartment was huge, at least compared to her room at the motel. The living room had two new leather couches that faced a big-screen television on the far wall. The entire apartment was furnished.

"What is this place?" she asked as she walked around. To the right was a large kitchen and a hallway that must lead to the bedroom.

"This is for you if you like it."

Sal was leading the way down the hall. "Come on."

She couldn't help but wonder if this was all part of some sort of seduction when he stopped at the bedroom door.

"Well, of course I like it. Who wouldn't?" She noted that the mattress was king-sized, and she immediately pictured the two of them on it. Margo would not allow herself to make matters worse. She walked in the bedroom and took it all in.

"But tell me, really, what is this all about?"

"I need someone like you." He was all business; any trace of his normal lasciviousness had disappeared. "My businesses include many situations that require . . ." he was looking for the word, "a little finesse. Like what you did for me a few weeks ago. My nephew was able to handle my situation with the information you provided. So thank you." He cleared his throat and continued. "You would be working as a legal consultant. I know your law license was revoked, and you can't practice anymore; that's fine. I've got lawyers on speed dial. I need someone that can help with the case law, you know, the details."

"So . . . legal research?" Margo's mind was racing with possibilities, and she found herself intrigued at the idea. Waiting tables and working the Laundromat, even writing the college papers, had kept her busy and provided a meager income. But it was mind-numbing work and would continue to be.

"Yeah. Yeah exactly, legal research. Let's discuss details. The apartment and utilities are in a company name and included as part of your salary. In return, you will assist my attorneys and business associates as needed."

"I will put people who need legal advice in touch with you. You'll meet them in a public place of your choosing." He was quick to add, "Not here. You never know what some of these asshats do in their off time."

"Asshats?" Margo repeated with raised eyebrows.

Sal grinned. "Hey, just because you're acquainted with people doesn't mean you really know them, right? Even me, I don't know everything about the people who work for me or who I do business with."

Exactly. Margo didn't really know several of the people in her life, and it had come back to bite her. She should have investigated everyone as well as Sal had checked her out.

Sal continued, "Your clients will pay you directly for your expertise and will have agreed to the payment terms before they contact you. These payments are yours. Don't take any shit from these guys, and if anybody gives you a hard time, let me know."

He frowned and Margo could imagine what would happen to those clients stupid enough to cross him.

"Type up your notes for each client, and you'll send them to Lou. He works for me, and he'll contact you to work out the specifics."

"Joey, the briefcase," Sal called out, and the driver entered the room quickly, placed the leather briefcase on the bed, clicked the buttons, and opened the case for Sal.

"You'll need a couple of days to get yourself squared away. Check yourself out of that fleabag motel; quit the diner, the Laundromat, and your writing projects."

He looked her over and his dark eyes studied her face for a moment. Margo felt the familiar stirring inside that she had tried for too long to ignore, and she wondered if that too were known to Sal.

From the briefcase he handed her a cell phone.

"Clients and business associates will contact you on this phone. You only make client appointments Monday through Friday during normal business hours. No working on the weekends, understand?"

Margo was speechless and a little-light headed. Sal didn't wait for her reply. He flashed a mischievous grin.

"You're going to need a few days and some cash to get situated."

He handed her an envelope that was thick and seemed heavy. She peeked inside and realized it contained thousands of dollars, more money than she had seen in a very long time. Sal had reached in his pocket and brought out another wad of cash, slid the clip off, and counted out more.

"That's ten grand. After you check yourself out of that fleabag motel get a better laptop than the piece of shit you're currently using. Also, get yourself spruced up and go buy some clothes, Cookie. Something nice." He nodded to her tee shirt and jeans as if to say, "Unlike what you're wearing which isn't up to my standards."

"Show a little leg. You're too beautiful to be hiding your assets."

"So your clients would appreciate a little T&A along with their legal advice?" Margo's hands were on her hips, glaring at him in defiance.

Sal shrugged. “Hey, look professional but not like the stereotypical uptight corporate lady lawyer. Sex it up a bit and wear your hair down. You get more flies with honey now, don’t you?”

Margo couldn’t help but laugh. Sal was charming, even if the last thirty minutes had scared her, to say the least.

“This is a great offer,” she started. Her hand was damp on the envelope of money, sweating at the thought of being an employee of Sal’s. As interesting as it might be, as interested as she was in him specifically, it was overwhelming.

“I really appreciate what you are offering me, but I need to think it over.” She watched him look up at her and felt her pulse speed up as he looked her in the eye.

He cleared his throat. Obviously he didn’t give out job offers; he just told people what to do.

“Hey, Cookie, I understand. Six years in the joint . . . You’re probably a little nervous. But you don’t have anything to worry about; I would never let anything happen to you.”

Sal stepped closer and his hands landed softly on her shoulders. Margo shivered at his touch.

“I do need you to tell me right now, are you in or are you out?” he murmured, pulling her even closer. They were chest to chest and Margo’s nipples were pressing hard against him.

She swallowed the rising lump that had formed in her throat. In this moment, she knew this decision would determine her future—for better or for worse. She could only hope that she was making the right choice.

"I'm in," she whispered as she felt a wave of desire rush down the length of her body.

Sal's hands moved from her shoulders to her back and slowly cupped her round ass as he drew her closer. Margo was lost in his scent and his touch. She could feel his cock pushing up through his pants and suit jacket as his biceps flexed around her. It was far too easy for her to picture them naked together now and when she pushed her hips into him, Margo could feel that her panties were soaked all the way through.

"I better get out of here," he said without releasing her.

Margo realized she was holding her breath. Sal's look was tender when he added, "Before I get carried away."

"Important numbers are already programmed into your phone. I'm number one," he grinned.

Of course he was.

"Take care of your errands and call me if you need anything."

Joey was waiting for him at the door.

Of all the questions Margo had, when she would see him again seemed to be the most pressing.

"And, Cookie," Sal added before he slipped out the door, "don't be late again. It's bad for business."

CHAPTER 5

Margo had to admit that she was a little nervous as she waited. She checked her new watch again. Her first client was already ten minutes late. Apparently, Sal's sense of punctual timing hadn't trickled down through the rest of his organization.

The last two and a half days had raced by in a blur. First, she had handed her keys for the Laundromat to Carol, who didn't seem surprised at all.

"I could tell that you weren't going to stay here long," she said half to Margo and half to the television that she watched her entire shift. "You had that computer," she added suspiciously.

When she had handed her clean, folded uniforms back to Vinnie, he actually seemed a little sad as he asked, "Why are you leaving?"

"I got another job." She patted his hand; the man had hired her when she was down and out.

"I'm really grateful that you hired me. You helped me out a lot. I mean it."

He hugged her, and Margo patted his back. The man was a pervert and a sexual harassment lawsuit waiting to happen, but underneath it all, she felt he had a good heart.

"Well," he said, "I guess that means your gangster friend won't be coming in anymore."

Margo laughed. "Sal? I'm sure he'll be in like clockwork."

She did wonder who would wait on him and bring him the usual now that she wouldn't be here.

"Are you kidding?" Vinnie winked at her with his good eye. "He was only here to see you."

Margo thought about that statement and felt as if Vinnie might know something that she had been oblivious to all along.

She took Sal's advice to heart and had spent most of the next two days shopping. Her new wardrobe consisted of business suits her former company would have frowned upon. The skirts were more midthigh length than knee length, and her blouses were too low cut. After assembling her new wardrobe she had taken a hard look at her reflection in the full-length mirror in her spacious bathroom. She needed an update. Margo crinkled her nose at her reflection. Seven years of no makeup and little sleep had taken its toll on her appearance.

She made an appointment at a salon near her new place. When she stepped inside, Margo realized as she looked around that she hadn't been anywhere this posh in ages, maybe since before the kids. Even when she could afford this kind of treatment, between her ninety hours a week at the firm and trying to be as much of a mother as she could be, there had been very little time for her to get pampered.

"So what would you like to do today?" the impeccably made up and dressed young stylist asked as they both looked at her face in the mirror.

Compared to the girl, Margo felt like a washed-up has-been. Her face definitely didn't seem to match the clothes she had just bought.

"You know what, just something sexy, something that makes me look a little younger."

The girl nodded and smiled.

"It's been awhile," Margo said as she sank back in the chair and gave herself over to the girl.

Her ex-husband had never cared about her looks. David had always been sweet and for years, she thought he had been the perfect husband. Not too demanding and he was a good listener. He seemed to be proud of her work and at the fact she was so successful. When Margo listened to some of the office girls talk about their husbands and boyfriends—sexist pigs, lazy slobs, addicted to video games and porn—she was always thankful that she had been so lucky to have David.

For a long time, she had excused the fact that he didn't seem to ever be interested in sex. She was tired, he was tired, and the kids were demanding. But even before the kids, it seemed like David barely noticed if a month or two went by since they had last made love. Margo had tried everything. Lingerie, toys, she had even bought some porn that made them both blush; none of it had worked and the last two years of their marriage, they had been quietly celibate.

Margo closed her eyes as the girl worked her fingers through her auburn mop and marveled that she had been sexless really most of the last decade. It was crazy. No wonder being touched by Sal was enough to set her on fire. Just thinking about him made her tingle, and she wondered if their physical contact had left as much of an impact on him.

It seemed as if she'd been in the chair for hours when the girl finally asked, "Are you ready to look?"

Margo gasped when she stared at herself in the mirror. Her hair was shorter, straighter, she had highlights, and her face seemed brighter. She really did look younger; the circles under her eyes weren't even as noticeable.

"Do you like it?" the hairdresser asked anxiously.

"I love it!" Margo felt as if she was turning over a new leaf, reinforced by her new look. "I absolutely love it. I'm definitely going to need some makeup too."

"I'll be happy to help you with that as well," the girl said.

It had been so long since she'd bought anything for herself. She could get used to being pampered, and she was done with looking like a dowdy old maid.

Margo checked her watch once more. Her first client was twenty minutes late now. She'd give him a few more minutes before she called Sal. Margo was really just looking for an excuse to talk to the man that she couldn't stop thinking about. The blouse and the skirt that she'd worn today, the heels, hell, even the new, skimpy underwear she had on were, if she was honest with herself, all just in case Sal paid her an impromptu visit at some point during the day.

A young Hispanic man wearing a wife beater tank top and baggy jeans stopped at her table and asked politely, "Are you Miss Margo?"

"Yes, I am." She looked at his bare arms, full of tattoos, and saw that he had a neck covered in gold chains. "Are you Eddie?"

"You can call me Cruz. That's what everyone calls me."

The man didn't look like he was much more than eighteen, but he already had a rap sheet of a career criminal. But it wasn't her job to be maternal or pass judgment.

She looked at him sternly and said, "I will call you Eddie, and Eddie . . . ," she was going to pass Sal's advice down to the young man, "don't be late again. It's bad for business."

Eddie swallowed hard and touched the cigarette that he had tucked behind his ear.

"Sorry, Miss Margo," he mumbled. He obviously found her a little intimidating, and she wondered what Sal had said about her.

She got the yellow legal pad out and nodded at him. "Sit down and tell me about your situation."

The boy told her the story. It was a story about a girl, as many good love stories were, Margo contemplated. It was just that this girl was a drug-addicted stripper with a temper who had started a commotion in their apartment one night when she had smoked too much meth.

Margo nodded as she listened, stopping him occasionally with one finger. "Now what did the officer say?" She took notes the whole time and caught herself clicking the end of the pen back and forth when he paused.

"Is that it?"

Eddie seemed to be searching his memory, his face frowning as he did so. Margo hoped that at least in this instance, he had been very thorough.

"Really, Eddie, if there's anything else you need to tell me, now's the time. It doesn't matter if it's something illegal." She had lowered her voice; the boy had to trust her.

"Nope, that's everything, Miss Margo." He nodded, proud of himself, as if he had just passed a test.

"OK, then from what you have told me you have nothing to worry about, Eddie," she said.

She picked up her coffee cup and took a delicate sip.

"The police took advantage of the situation, and your lawyer will be advised about precedent. You and . . ." she searched her notes for where she had written the girl's name down.

"Kandy, with a K," Eddie informed her. He lit up just saying her name despite the problem she had created.

"You and Kandy with a K need to take it easy and keep it down at night. Your neighbors must be tired of the partying and the noise. You really don't want to repeat this in the future." Margo raised her eyebrows at him like a mother. She couldn't help it; the boy was young enough to be her son.

"No, Miss Margo, we won't," he assured her. "Is that it?"

He appeared anxious to leave, and Margo assumed he needed to smoke that cigarette behind his ear.

"That's it, Eddie, for now." She watched as he stood and pulled out a wad of folded bills from his inside pocket.

"That's good, right, Miss Margo?" he asked. She quickly scanned the money and removed it from the table.

"You're good. Now behave yourself," she told him before he walked away.

She looked through her notes and realized that she really had missed practicing law.

Margo followed up Eddie's appointment with two white clients who, she guessed, were pushing thirty, but trying to appear younger and hip. One tall and thin, the other was short and stocky. Both wore oversized shirts, baggy jeans, and pristine ball caps representing sports teams. They came together, and when the stocky man had started to fill her in on the details, the thin man had interrupted. Margo put her hand up.

"No, I need to hear everything he has to say first, and then we'll get to you."

Twenty minutes later, the cell phone that Sal had given her buzzed and she said, "Excuse me, please," to the two men who still couldn't agree on a minor detail. It was Sal. She pressed her index finger to her lips for quiet.

"Hello."

She pictured his face as soon as she answered, and then she remembered vividly what it felt like to be in his arms. She was immediately weak in the knees.

"Hey, Cookie, how's it going?" he was talking loudly, as if he was outside.

"Good, I'm with clients," she added. Margo wanted Sal to know that she was taking the job seriously.

"I know, I can see you," he told her.

Startled, she peered out the window near her table. There was Sal, standing outside the Lincoln Town car, nodding at her as he hung up. Margo couldn't decide if she was more flattered or apprehensive that he was keeping such a close eye on her.

Sal entered the coffee shop and walked straight to her table; he took one look at the two clients and waved them away with a flick of his wrist.

"Why don't you two take a break?"

It wasn't a suggestion, and both men knew it. Margo watched as the two wannabe gangsters moved quickly from their seats and kept their heads down as they shuffled away.

"So everyone just follows orders for you, is that it, Sal?" She had been left to her own devices for so long that she didn't know how she felt about being one more employee doing his bidding.

"Basically," he nodded, and then smiled at her. "Your hair looks great."

She felt herself blush and wondered if he'd notice the rest of her makeover.

"Thanks." She glanced over at the two men that hadn't been able to get their story straight yet. "Those two, I'm still sorting through the details."

"Knuckleheads. Don't worry, it can't be that complicated." Sal's eyes had moved down to the front of her blouse which revealed more than her waitress uniform had. "If they had a brain between them they might be dangerous."

Margo concentrated on acting professional. She flipped the page back to Eddie's notes.

"Eddie's case is open-and-shut. The cops overstepped their bounds; I'll have the case information over to Lou later today."

Sal leaned forward toward her, and Margo wasn't sure if it was just her breasts or the continuation of the chemistry that was palpable between them.

"I knew you'd be an asset, Cookie. Can't let talent like yours go to waste."

He made eye contact again, and Margo caught herself imagining what it would be like to kiss him. His lips were full and expressive, and he had a dimple on his right cheek when he smiled.

"What are you doing this weekend?" he asked her.

She was caught off guard by the question, and then realized she had the entire weekend to herself. Even when she was with the firm, she usually worked on Saturday and often at least part of the day on Sunday. She knew exactly what she was going to do and told him. "Sleep in my new bed in my new apartment."

For the past year she hadn't been able to get more than five hours a night, if she was lucky, and thought of stretching out and not being a slave to the alarm sounded like heaven.

He made a face. "Sleep? You'll sleep when you're dead. What is a good-looking single girl like you doing home on a Saturday night?"

Margo knew he knew she had children. He had to. He had known her SAT scores, for God's sake.

"I really had no social life before prison. I was a mother and a wife when I wasn't busting my ass trying to impress the pricks I worked for." She felt sad hearing herself say "was" as if somehow she wasn't a mother to her kids anymore.

"Well, tell you what, I'm going to take you out Saturday night."

It wasn't a suggestion or a question, and Margo wouldn't have said no if it had been.

"We'll have a nice dinner, a few drinks, you'll relax, and you can sleep on Sunday."

Had this been the reason that he had stopped by? Did he want to see her as much as she wanted to see him? Or was he just managing his business investment?

"What should I wear?" She hadn't had a date night since before she'd stopped having sex with her husband.

"Clothes," Sal said as he stood up. "Anything. You look great in that suit, by the way. I'll pick you up at eight."

He motioned to the two men that they could return to their seats before he left. Margo watched as the black car pulled out and drove away.

She'd never told him where she was meeting clients. Just how close of an eye did he have on her?

CHAPTER 6

Rather than spend her Saturday in bed, Margo had spent the day shopping for things she didn't normally shop for. She had found the perfect dress, and then continued shopping until she found the perfect shoes to accompany the dress. At 7:30 p.m., after finishing her hair and makeup, she almost didn't recognize this person who had been primping for the better part of two hours.

She needed a little something to take the edge off so she poured herself a glass of red wine as she waited for Sal. It made sense that she was nervous. She was out of practice and actually, she had never had much practice to begin with.

She had lost her virginity at seventeen to a boy who was a year younger than she, and looking back, she had felt that it was more a thing to get done than an experience she had enjoyed. She was the last of her girlfriends to be deflowered, and she had started to feel like even more of a social outcast than she suspected she already was. The first time with the boy lasted all of two minutes. She had kept track of the time on his car stereo. She blamed it on nerves and fucking in the car, but over the next three months as they continued to widen their horizons, she had never enjoyed it much more than the first time.

In college, she had been far too busy to waste time on a boyfriend. Between working full-time and taking a full class load, the few hours that she had leftover were mostly spent studying, and later, writing short pieces for her school's law review. There had been a lover here and there, a one-night stand, a couple of awkward dates that ended with her spending the night. There was even a frat party where she had gotten horribly drunk and woke up in a strange room missing her underwear. She had always considered herself lucky that she didn't remember any of what had happened that night.

Then she met David, and he had become a lover almost by accident. She remembered their third date; the one that everyone said was when it was socially appropriate to have sex. Too late and you were forever just friends; too early and you were a slut. David had brought her back to her apartment and kissed her gently at the door, and Margo had almost let him go back to the car. Being friends with David would have been acceptable. He was sweet and dreamy, smart and poetic; sexy was never one of the adjectives she used when thinking of him.

Instead, she had grabbed his arm and said in a low, husky voice that she had thought was seductive, "come inside," and kissed him all the way upstairs to the bedroom. Margo had taken the lead from the beginning, and when she had taken off her shirt and bra, David had looked almost frightened. She had pushed him back on her sagging mattress and continued kissing him while her nipples were pressed against his chest. She could feel it rise and fall quickly, almost as if he was in a panic.

That had stopped once she had his pants down and worked her hand into his underwear. David had a nice cock, one of the better penises that she had seen, although she had to admit that the total was only six, so she was no expert. He had been a nervous lover, and she felt his hands tremble when he touched her thighs. Margo thought it was another sweet thing about him, that he had wanted it to be good, to be special.

He hadn't climaxed after almost thirty minutes inside her that night, but she experienced her first orgasm ever. When he had stopped thrusting and lay beside her, he had apologized.

"I'm sorry, it usually takes me awhile."

She had kissed him and whispered, "Don't apologize. You feel so good inside me."

Margo had continued kissing him in a soft line down the center of his body until she reached his dick, still wet from her remnants. Up to that point, the boys she had slept with always tried to push her head down on their erections, something that they wanted and didn't mind demanding whether she felt like it or not. David simply sighed when she touched him from root to tip with a feather-light touch of her tongue.

Margo had looked up at his face on her pillow and saw that his eyes were closed as she took him all the way in her mouth. Working her tongue along his hard, silky skin, she wrapped her lips tight and felt the tip of his cock hit the roof of her mouth. His precum tasted like her, and he smelled like soap. He made soft, contented noises as he raised his hips and rocked back and forth against her bed.

David warned her, “I’m going to come,” as if he expected her to release him to spurt all over his belly, and normally, Margo would have, but there was something about having him inside her that she enjoyed far more than she ever expected. She pulled up to the head of his cock and sucked every sticky, salty drop from him and listened to him moan and felt his smooth body spasm until he was empty.

The knock at the door interrupted her walk down memory lane and she quickly took the last sip of her wine. She shook her head unconsciously. It was hard to believe after everything that had happened over the last few years that she could even remember a time when David had seemed sweet.

She would not allow herself to continue. All thoughts of David were banned for the evening. Tonight was a new beginning she promised herself, her hand on the door handle. It was a new night and a new man.

“Cookie!” Sal was all smiles, and the first thing she noticed was that he wasn’t wearing a tie, and his shirt was open at the collar. When he grabbed her and pulled her close, his scent was all around her, and Margo ran her hands down his back and felt the line of muscles that ran down him under his shirt.

"Jesus, you clean up good." His hands cupped her voluptuous ass under the black fitted dress, and she bit her lip so she could hold back the moan that was caught in her throat.

"Hey, are you saying I didn't look good in that smoking waitress outfit?"

Margo had to get back to their usual banter before she lost every bit of self-control.

"You always looked good because you're a beautiful woman."

He let her go and opened the door for her. His car was parked outside, and Margo saw Joey in the driver's seat. It seemed odd to have a third accompany them on a date.

In the car, she was nervous. She updated him on the clients she had seen over the past couple of days. She felt like she needed to prove her worth.

"I know you're smart, Cookie. I knew that early on in the diner. It's a gift I've been blessed with." His eyes were twinkling when he smiled at her. "In my line of business it's all about finding the right people."

"Your line of business?" Margo asked. Was he referring to organized crime specifically?

"My business." He opened his hands, spreading his arms wide apart like he was demonstrating his wealth of talent. He seemed to mean all of it.

"Everything. It's all about finding the right people. Without the right people, in the right places, a guy like me would be yesterday's news. I would have never made it on the streets."

"Did you grow up here?" She was trying to envisage him as a child, running around a backyard playing, laughing, carefree.

"Came here from Sicily when I was five."

Sal reached out and took her hand gently. Margo watched him as he told her the story.

"My parents didn't speak English, and they came to America with no money and mouths to feed. I'm one of six kids. My father did his best to support his family, but it was tough, and money was scarce."

"How could anyone take care of that many kids?"

Margo was amazed by the idea. She knew she wouldn't have been able to do it. She couldn't even handle her own two.

"In the old country, it was what people did. Here, it's different."

Sal had five children himself. Margo wondered what it was like to have so many siblings. As an only child she often wished she had a brother or sister just for the sake of company.

"I had to learn to hustle when I was a kid, to help out the family. Once I learned how to make money, I wanted to make more. I didn't need history or science, I needed to work."

"You didn't go to college?" She didn't know why she asked. Perhaps it was because she had worked so hard to get through college, but the idea of Sal not even reaching that stage struck her as odd.

"College?" he chuckled, "I didn't finish the eighth grade. I was helping the old man in our neighborhood who ran numbers. Once I was making fifty dollars a week there was no turning back."

"Did you ever wish you had stayed in school?" Margo had loved school. As a kid it had been an escape for her. She was encouraged and validated by her teachers. She knew from an early age that education would be her means to a better life than her parents had chosen.

"Nah, it wasn't for me, too many rules. I'm more of a hands-on learner," he smiled. "But my kids are a different story. No dropouts. Four college graduates so far, and my baby girl is a freshman at Penn State." Sal beamed when he talked about his kids.

Margo was stunned. "Your kids are adults?"

Sal smiled. "Yep, four of them are out of the nest and completely on their own. Three are married and have given me five beautiful grandchildren combined."

"But you're not old enough to have five grandkids," Margo stated in disbelief.

Sal chuckled and placed his hand on her knee and winked at her. "Started young, Cookie."

She couldn't believe that she didn't know this. Then again, why would she? Their routine banter at the diner never got personal, and she had been sure to keep it that way. He had been a customer she looked forward to seeing, but he was a married customer who was off-limits and way out of her league.

She imagined that he was a protective, stern father, and it made her smile. Her parents had always been too wrapped up in their own problems to have known what she was up to most of the time. If she hadn't been a good kid, she could only imagine what might have become of her.

"What about your kids?" he asked her. "They going to college?"

Sal knew all of the details, and some of those details were hard for her to talk about.

"I'm sure Abigail and Thomas will both be going when it's time," she said.

There was no more sidestepping his questions with sarcasm or ambiguity. She knew it was all in the folder.

"Do you see them?" he asked, and Margo thought that he probably knew that answer as well.

"My going to prison was hard on them; they didn't visit when I was incarcerated so now . . ." Now what were they, strangers? Margo hardly knew what to say when she talked to them on the phone.

"We're still working on that."

He must have sensed it hurt to discuss her kids. She felt him squeeze her hand affectionately.

"You're doing the best you can, Cookie, and they might not know that now, but they will later."

She wrapped her fingers around his strong, solid hand, and they were silent until the car parked.

"We're here; you're going to love this place. Best linguine and clams you ever had in your life."

He got out first and waited for her to slide across the seat. He watched her every move, her dress riding up and showing off her lovely legs.

The restaurant was dimly lit with oversized leather booths, a huge wine list, and decades of ambiance. The waitstaff was attentive, and the owner came over to chat with Sal and personally check on their meal. The night went by quickly, and before Margo knew it, it was almost midnight, and they had eaten and drunk and talked and laughed as if they'd known each other for years. Her sides ached from laughing, and when they finally made their way back to her apartment, she looked over at him and realized how great it was to have a friend again. She had spent so much time over the last few years alone that she almost didn't realize how lonely she had been.

Margo didn't have long to contemplate that thought because Sal was walking her to her door and she was unsure about what would happen next. What were the rules now? Was it still three dates or you were a slut? If you slept with a married man who was also your boss, you were a slut no matter how many dates? Was sleeping with him even what she wanted to do? She felt that they were just getting to know each other, that they had just become friends.

As she fumbled with the keys, she felt him running his hands down her waist to the bottom of her short dress.

"Can I come in, Cookie?"

Margo opened the door and murmured, "Isn't this your apartment?"

Sal followed her inside and grabbed her by the wrists, turning her around to face him.

Inches apart, she was overwhelmed. His body against hers, and his eyes told her everything that she needed to know about what he wanted, and she forgot about all the reasons why this shouldn't be happening.

"This is different, Cookie. I like you."

They were almost kissing as he spoke. She could feel his breath on her face and neck, and she shivered.

"Meaning that you don't usually like the women you sleep with?" She was nervous and her voice was barely above a whisper.

"Meaning I don't want to fuck up a good thing." His hands were back on her ass, and he was pushing himself against her. "Even if that means I don't get to rip this dress off you."

Margo knew it was too late to stop herself. She could feel her hands in his hair, and it was just a moment until his lips were on hers. Her mouth opened as soon as they touched, and Sal's tongue teased the bottom of her upper lip. Margo heard herself sigh when his tongue slipped inside and explored hers. It had been so long . . . *too* long. When had she kissed like this? It felt like Sal was devouring her, and when his hands reached the top of her zipper that ran down the back of her dress, she wanted it off immediately.

He never took his mouth off her. The dress fell to the floor in a heap at her feet, and Sal's tongue continued its exploration along her bottom lip, his teeth nibbling her there until Margo was trembling for more. He backed her slowly down the hall to the bedroom and once inside, he closed the door behind him.

Sal picked her up and set her down in the center of the mattress. He pulled away, then was on top of her, on his knees as he took his jacket off. "Damn, Cookie, you feel exactly like I thought you would."

Margo reached up to touch his chest as she watched him unbutton his shirt. The hard muscles finally revealed, she writhed her hips under him as her fingers finally felt his skin, an intoxicating combination of velvet over steel. "Why Cookie?" she asked.

"Because the minute I saw you," he hovered over her, and kissed her neck from top to bottom, "I knew you would be warm and soft, just like a tasty cookie right out of the oven." His mouth continued to meander down to her collarbone, and she felt Sal reach underneath her with one hand as he quickly unhooked the black lace bra.

He stared at her breasts for a moment. "God, you're so beautiful," he murmured and Margo let out a cry of sheer want as his tongue lapped in a slow circle around her pointed nipple. She pushed her hips against him as he drove her crazy, sucking on her flesh with his lips, grazing her with his teeth. She had never felt anything like this and every nerve was on fire.

"Oh my God, yes, Sal, what are you doing to me?" she whispered as he made his way down her body. Everyplace he kissed her tingled, and with every touch she gasped and felt the twinge of pleasure between her legs.

"What I wanted to do since the first day I saw you, Cookie."

He reached down and flipped her heels off, caressing her legs, his fingers moving up the tender skin on the back of her calves to her knees. When he finally reached her inner thighs, she shuddered as he came closer and closer to her mound.

Margo watched Sal bow his head and kiss her over the soaked panties. His lips were hot, and she moaned under his touch.

"You're so wet, Cookie." Sal slid his tongue along the ridge of her fabric and tasted the sweetness that was pouring from her core.

She was almost on the verge of tears. Margo had bottled up her sexual needs for so long, and now she felt like she would explode.

"Please, Sal, please." She reached down to tear her panties off, but he stopped her, holding her hands in both of his.

CHAPTER 7

"Let me, Cookie." Sal was taking the lead, and Margo stopped and felt him slide the last of her clothes down her legs. He threw the panties over his shoulder before burying his face between her legs with a deep sigh.

He kissed her lips from top to bottom, hard, closed-mouth kisses that made her ache for more. She spread her legs even wider, giving him everything, and when he licked her softly from her opening to the tip of her clit, Margo felt the spasm shake her from head to toe.

Sal slid a finger inside as his tongue continued to taste her. She was so wet; she could hear the slippery noises coming from her as he worked back and forth with first one finger and then two, his tongue making her clit flutter. She'd never been so lost; she'd never been so close to the brink of losing control, and her cries grew louder and louder with each touch.

His fingers moved faster and deeper as he held her clit between his moist lips, sucking on her harder as if he had to have all of her. Ravenous, he wouldn't let her go, and Margo could hardly breathe, the waves of her pleasure rode down her body, and she couldn't help but yell his name when her orgasm came like an electric shock.

"Yes, Sal, yes!"

He responded by burying his fingers deep inside her as she came and trembled and pushed up to meet his face. She soaked him and shivered under his touch like she had never known she could.

Sal withdrew his fingers and kissed her soaked, bare lips softly as the waves died down, his hands wrapped around her hips. He felt every quiver and listened to her gasp for air.

"Cookie," he sighed as he lifted his head and stared up at her.

Sal's face was wet with her. She could see the droplets on his lips and chin. "Even better than the clams," he said with a smile.

He was unzipping and in a moment, he had taken off his pants. Margo reached out to touch the huge bulge that protruded from the front of his boxers. She could feel his cock jolt in her hands. She slowly traced the outline of his round head, and then up and down his thick shaft, running her hand down to caress his heavy sack.

"You're making me crazy, you know that." She watched him throw his head back as he rubbed himself against her hand. "I can't wait any longer . . ."

"Fuck me." She reached inside and pulled his enormous dick out, holding him in her hand as drew him down to the bed. "I want you inside me."

Sal was finally naked on top of her, and she realized that it was what she'd always wanted. All the glances, all the flushed cheeks, the ache she had inside—it had been months of foreplay, all leading up to this moment. He kissed her again—a hot, insistent kiss, thrusting his tongue into her as he teased her slowly with the wet tip of his cock, brushing her lips and rubbing it against her opening. He moaned into her open mouth when he drove the full length of his erection deep inside.

Margo cried out. She had never been so filled. He was all the way inside her in one push, and she trembled as he moved back and forth.

"Sal, yes, fuck—yes!" She reached around his waist and felt his ass flexing with every powerful thrust as she dug her fingers into his flesh and felt her hips rise to meet him.

She felt the pleasure mounting the harder he fucked her. Looking in his eyes, she saw all of his pent-up want for her there. He met her gaze, and she felt her heart melt. No man had ever looked at her like that before. No man had ever felt like this before. His hands gripped her tight as he rocked back and forth, every line of his body flexing as he pumped his hard cock deeper and deeper into her core.

Margo let herself go, and the orgasm exploded through her, oozing out of her onto the bed, and as she clenched her wet walls around Sal's impressive girth, she knew she would come again.

"Sal," she panted, bit her lip hard, and the sound of their bodies slapping together grew louder as he increased his tempo, "I'm coming." She could barely speak as she reached her third climax of the night with a scream.

He thrust faster as she pulled him in. Margo felt his cock tense, and he raised up and let out a roar as he let go inside of her. She felt the rush of his orgasm, filling her, buried deeply and with every spurt, he thrust once more. Finally, Sal sank down to the pillow, his face in her hair. He panted as the last of his release entered her. Margo's hands slid up from his ass to his back, and they held each other as their hearts beat in sync.

She closed her eyes and thought that she could stay just like this, feeling every inch of him wrapped around her and inside her, consuming her, possessing her. Margo couldn't help but sigh when she thought this is what they meant, this was what other women were always talking about, their obsession with the idiot men in their lives. If this was what making love was all about, she had never known it until now.

"What's with the sigh, Cookie?" Sal slipped out of her and rolled onto his side, one hand underneath his head. He was glowing as she imagined she was.

"Just thinking," she ran her fingers down his face and felt the line of sweat run down his cheek. "That was amazing."

"That was just a taste of what's in store." His strong hands kneaded her flesh, "Wait until we know each other."

The thought that sex could be better than this was incomprehensible at this moment and she sighed with her contentment. "I'd say you know me pretty well right now."

Sal pulled her close, and Margo rested her cheek on his chest. His hair there was damp and scented of his cologne. She ran her fingers slowly down his abs to his pelvis. It seemed so right, this place on his chest seemed to be made for her to rest her head. His gold chain had a heavy, circular pendant on it that had moved back and forth as he made love to her. She touched it now.

"I never knew you wore a necklace." She had noticed he didn't wear a wedding ring.

"I always have this on. It was blessed by a priest; it's my good luck charm." He was serious, and Margo thought this was a new side to him.

"Can I ask, do you really believe in that stuff?" She would have guessed he believed in muscle and intimidation. "Good luck charms?"

"What do you believe in, Cookie?"

No one had ever asked her that before, and she wasn't prepared to answer. "I don't know," she said.

There was a time when she would have thought that hard work and a little bit of luck had a hand in her life, but after the prison sentence, she couldn't let herself give up and think that fate had taken her there.

"I think you have to make your own luck."

"You haven't been very lucky for a while then," Sal whispered in her ear.

Margo sighed. A year had gone by since she'd been out of prison, and the situation with her children hadn't improved at all; maybe it was even worse.

"Sometimes I think I'm being punished for something. That's why I worked three jobs at the same time; total exhaustion eliminates time for self-pity."

"Bullshit, Cookie." Sal shook his head. "Like I said before, you pissed someone off."

Margo wondered if Sal knew about Jay Cook, the man who had worked hard to see that Margo was never lucky again. Again, she remembered the thick folder on Sal's lap; he probably knew more than she did.

"Jay Cook. That's who I pissed off," she said.

She would never forget the look on his face the day that she had won the tax evasion case that had earned the firm over ten million dollars in fees and had won her boss's admiration and gratitude.

"He hated me. We started about the same time at the firm, but I was on my way to be chosen as the next partner."

She could clearly, see him in her mind storming into her office and slamming the door so hard that the wall had shaken.

"So he was jealous, outsmarted by a woman and all that." Sal did know more than he let on.

Margo nodded her head and said, "Yeah, he was always a misogynistic asshole; slept with clerical help, the interns, the female clients, wives of clients. He was a walking hard-on."

Jay had hit on Margo nonstop for the first few months he worked there. It didn't matter to him that she was married and not interested.

"But he couldn't conquer you," Sal finished.

"God, no, not me. I couldn't stand him."

Jay was exactly like so many of the kids she had known in law school . . . rich kids, there to party on Mommy and Daddy's money, knowing that they had a cushy job waiting for them after graduation. He never took anything seriously while she put in fifteen-hour days and sweated every detail.

"So how did he make the charges stick?"

"He had a witness, this girl." Margo recalled the girl on the stand. She must have been in her twenties, but she looked all of sixteen. Her hair had been in a ponytail, her white blouse buttoned tightly at the neck. She really had been the perfect witness; the jury ate up her innocent routine.

"I never knew her, I had never seen her before that day in court, and by then, the damage had been done and it was too late."

"Only one witness?" Sal asked.

"It was enough, along with some other bullshit thrown in for good measure."

It hadn't helped that the whole firm had switched allegiances so quickly. Overnight, Jay was a hero and Margo was a conniving bitch who would do anything to win.

"Couldn't you reopen your case?" he asked.

"Yeah, with new evidence if I could disprove his witness . . .," she trailed off.

It wasn't as if she hadn't fantasized about doing exactly that the first few years she'd been in prison. She would fall asleep at night and plan each step that she would take to exact her revenge. But six years in prison was like a lifetime. Basic survival and maintaining her mental stability became her focus. It was what she had control over on a day-to-day basis. The problems of the outside world slipped further away with each day she was incarcerated. The fire she had early in her sentence for justice and revenge was slowly distinguished over time. Prison changes a person. Their hopes, their dreams, their fears, their beliefs, she had discovered.

"Why aren't you doing that then, Cookie?" Sal looked her in the eye and saw her brow furrow and face harden.

"What difference does it make now, Sal? I've lost six years of my life, well, seven really, and my kids hate me. I can't fix the past, I can't change it."

"They don't hate you," he tenderly stroked the side of her face. "They're just kids; they don't understand."

"They know that I went to prison. The whole time I was there they never visited. They didn't want to see me."

Now there was an insurmountable distance between them, especially with Abby, and she feared that Thomas would eventually follow his sister's lead.

"Do you know that for sure they didn't want to see you or are you just guessing?"

Margo realized the wheels seemed to never stop turning in Sal's head.

"David told me that they didn't want anything to do with me. Then he quickly divorced me under the pretext it was in the best interest for the kids."

"So your ex-husband told you they didn't want to see you? Your kids confirmed this?"

Margo's mind began to race. Why hadn't she ever questioned that before now? "Holy shit," she looked over at Sal in disbelief, "you think that fucker lied to me?"

"Ex-husbands will do crazy things, Cookie," he kissed her hand. "I think you should talk to your kids though."

Margo nodded her head yes, thinking about the conversation. She needed to know what they had been told, and suddenly, the thought that David had been at the center of all of this and had played both sides against the middle made her heart harden. If he had done this to her, there would be no forgiveness for him.

"I'm going to use your shower, Cookie. I'll be back in a minute."

Sal was up and she heard him go to the bathroom and turn the water on while she was lost in the memories that had been haunting her for the last seven years. Sal was right, it wasn't bad luck and it wasn't a punishment. She knew in her gut that Jay had instigated the tampering case and conviction, but what if something even more insidious had been at work? What if she could get her life back? Was that even possible?

It was a quick shower and Margo watched Sal return to the bedroom. He was dressing, and she bit her lip. She wasn't going to ask. She was not going to be a weak and clingy . . . what? What was she? She wasn't sure and before she could stop herself she heard herself ask, "Can you stay the night?"

His eyes were warm and his expression was tinged with sadness when he answered, "No, Cookie, it's late; I've got to get home."

His boxers and pants were back on. He pushed his arms into the wrinkled shirt, adding, "Sunday is family day."

Margo chastised herself for even asking. It was clear. Sal didn't belong to her; he wasn't going to spend the night now or probably ever. She was just a mistress. She wasn't sure how she felt about this. How was she supposed to feel about this? She was in unfamiliar territory.

Sal sat on the bed once he was dressed and asked, "Did you have a good time, Cookie?"

Her body was exhausted, but her mind was racing. Margo wondered if she would stay up all night no matter how much she craved rest.

"I had an amazing night, thank you."

He smiled and kissed her forehead quickly. "You deserve to have a good time and nice things, Cookie. Call your kids tomorrow, OK?"

As usual, it wasn't a request and Margo nodded her head yes.

She never even heard him close her door. She had closed her eyes and when she opened them, Margo realized she had slept for almost twelve hours.

CHAPTER 8

It was 3:21 a.m. when her husband slipped into bed beside her. He made no effort to be quiet, but he never did. He smelled of a fresh shower, one of the many indicators she had learned over the years that he had been with one of his whores.

Marriage hadn't slowed down Sal's appetite for women. Giovanna married Sal with her eyes wide open and wasn't naïve enough to expect him to become magnanimous after a shotgun wedding ceremony. He was already set in his ways.

Sal's reputation was well-known in the neighborhood as a lady's man. He was handsome, cocky, and all of the teenage girls gushed and chattered about what a catch Sal Mazzillo was. Over the years Giovanna watched one girl after another primp and preen in their best attempts to get Sal to notice them, but Sal had no interest in silly girls.

Rumor had it that he lost his virginity at thirteen to Mrs. Crenshaw who gave him a hands-on education as often as she could about the female anatomy. When Mr. Crenshaw caught wind of this he took the issue to Sal's mother. Sal handled the allegations by badly beating Mr. Crenshaw for burdening a woman with a man's issue. He also took a cut of Mr. Crenshaw's weekly pay and continued to fuck Mrs. Crenshaw whenever he wanted to. Mr. Crenshaw looked the other way as did many of the other husbands in the neighborhood after Sal branched out and made rounds servicing all of the attractive, married women.

Giovanna had done her homework on Sal. He had started hustling at age seven. By the age of nine he had quit school and was supplementing his father's factory wages to help make ends meet. He was tall and had always looked older than his actual age. He also carried himself with a confident swagger.

The old man who had run the neighborhood for years for the DeLucca family was rumored to be skimming off of the top and running side deals. The person who took this information to the DeLucca family had firsthand knowledge and touted the importance of loyalty and trust in business and partnerships. It was the same person who murdered the old man and took over the neighborhood.

With the blessing of the DeLucca family, Salvatore Mazzillo slit Renzo Spatzi's throat in the bathroom of Ruthie's Pasta and Pizzeria while his wife and kids ate their family-style meal.

Renzo Spatzi was found in a pool of blood with his dick in his hand. No witnesses, no suspects, and no effort put into solving the case by New York City's finest. No outrage from the neighborhood as most people kept their opinions to themselves and justified the violence with canned responses such as, "street justice" or "live by the sword, die by the sword."

By the age of seventeen Sal had taken over the neighborhood. He was ambitious and maneuvering to make a name for himself. He ran the neighborhood with an iron fist and dealt swiftly with those who doubted him, crossed him, or betrayed him. Within six months Sal had drummed up new business ventures and doubled the profits for the DeLucca family.

Giovanna had no misconceptions about Sal. She knew he was ruthless and would do whatever it took to be successful. Sal was not as complex as many made him out to be. He was, actually, very simple. He had come from nothing and craved money and power. Rich, powerful men attracted women. She had known women would always be readily available for him to indulge in his primal sexual appetite. It was a fact she accepted when she decided she was going to lure the catch of the neighborhood in marriage.

CHAPTER 9

There was no time like the present and when Margo pressed David's name on her phone, she imagined his smug face and immediately felt the anger building inside of her. How could she have been so blind? She was grateful for Sal pointing out the obvious.

"Margo, how are you?" he asked when he answered.

Polite and clipped, her ex-husband would not spend any more time speaking with her than was absolutely necessary.

"Great," she was obviously being sarcastic, "I'd like to speak to my children, please."

"Hold on." She heard him whisper, and Margo imagined that he was holding the phone out to each of them, with their heads fiercely shaking no.

Thomas finally spoke. "Mom?"

"Thomas, honey." She smiled, he was eleven now, but he was still a sweet boy, and she knew no matter how far apart they had drifted that he was still tenderhearted.

"How are you?" she asked.

"I'm OK. Abigail doesn't want to talk to you." He was the more honest of the two as well.

"That's fine, I understand that she's mad at me." Margo was willing to take the hit this time, but she was drawing near the end of her patience. "Hey, can I ask you a question?"

"Sure, Mom."

"Is your dad standing there?" Margo asked.

"No," Thomas replied.

Margo paused; she had nothing to lose at this point.

"When I was in prison, did you and your sister tell your dad that you didn't want to come see me?"

He had only been four when she went to prison, but she hoped he remembered something—anything.

"Well, I don't really remember when you left, but Dad always went to visit you. We wanted to come and see you, but Dad said he couldn't take us."

Her kids really believed that David had come to see her regularly?

"Do you remember why Dad didn't bring you?" Margo asked.

Thomas was eager to reply. "He told us that kids weren't allowed to visit prisoners. But Abigail looked up the prison's visiting rules online and found out we could go as long as we were accompanied by an adult. Abigail asked Dad why he was lying to us, and he said that you didn't want to see us because it would make you sad and make it harder for you to do your time."

Margo closed her eyes. Her children had missed her. Her poor babies had spent those years thinking that their mother had turned her back on them when she had been dying inside a little every day in their absence. Her heart sank.

"Did Daddy come to see me a lot?" She would play along with David's charade for now.

Thomas sounded confused. "Yeah, he was there three times a week, Mom, don't you remember? On Saturday, Monday, and Wednesday, every week, he was there."

David had only been to prison three times in six years, and never again after she had signed the divorce papers. What exactly had the bastard been up to three days a week for six years that he had to lie to her children about?

"You know, Thomas, I want to ask you something else. Did you get any of my letters, sweetie?"

Her first year in prison she had written them diligently. She poured her heart out telling them how much she loved them and missed them. Mail call came and went and Margo's cell mate got mail from loved ones on a regular basis. Nothing ever came for Margo.

David refused to accept her collect calls, and Margo suspected he was intercepting her letters to the kids, but she continued to write them anyways. She wrote to them less as the years passed by, but she always sent letters for their birthdays and holidays. If they had received any of her letters they would have known how much she loved them and thought about them.

"What letters, Mom?"

Her son had no idea what she was talking about. Her anger was throbbing inside her; the vein in her forehead beat like an incessant drum as she reviewed all of the little details again and again. There was no other possible explanation other than David had turned her children against her, kicking her when she was already down. He might be the father of her children, but to her, he was the enemy.

Margo resolved that she wouldn't put them through any more turmoil until she had gotten to the bottom of this. She changed the subject quickly, forcing herself to sound happy and cheerful while she talked to Thomas.

"Tell me about school, honey."

"It's good, Mom," he started and she tried to follow along, but her mind kept wandering back over the years . . . David's face when he told her that the kids were scared to visit and scared of her. The smirk he'd had when she pushed the signed divorce papers across the table to him. When had it all started? It seemed like convenient timing that he was able to take her out of the picture so easily thanks to Jay and his vendetta.

Were the two working in tandem to take her down or was it just a happy coincidence? How could David, her husband, the man that supposedly had loved her from the beginning . . . How could he just have been lying in wait to strike when the opportunity arose?

There was a pause in the conversation and Margo said, "Really?" as if she had been listening.

Thomas continued and Margo thought she needed to treat both instances like a case, not just her criminal case, but her husband as well. Sal was right. She had pissed someone off, and she wondered if she hadn't overlooked David as a possibility.

"I got to go, Mom. Dad is waving at me." Her son sounded sad to hang up. "It was nice to talk to you though."

"Sweetie, it was wonderful to hear your voice. Please tell your sister that I said hello. Can you do that?"

"Yeah, sure, Mom." Thomas was whispering, and it sounded like he might cry.

They exchanged good-byes and the thought of her boy crying pushed her over the edge. Margo paced furiously, going over events and details meticulously in her mind. She took out a legal pad and a pen. She was long overdue. If she were her own client, she never would have given up on herself like she had.

The first thing she had to do was to write it all down, like a deposition. She would accurately record the chain of events in chronological order and review all the information.

Hours later, her hand was aching when she took a break and drank a glass of wine. Her stomach growled, and she looked at the time. With the legal pad on her lap, she ate a sandwich as she went over it again. It was dark outside when she finished, and now, Margo realized what she needed to do was very clear. She had a plan.

At the very end of the document, she wrote a name at the center of the page and circled it. For the first time since she could remember, she felt alive. She had a purpose, had direction, and she had hope. She might have been all wrong about the good luck charm stuff. Maybe Sal was on to something. The pendant around his neck might have meant nothing; it might not even have been blessed by a priest, but it was something to believe, something to inspire hope.

She changed for bed and crawled under the covers that still smelled of last night's coupling. A trace of Sal's cologne was on her pillow and when she closed her eyes, she could almost feel his lips on hers, the taste of his mouth, the feel of his skin against hers, his strong hands that seemed to have much more knowledge of all the tender places on her body than a first time lover ever could have known.

She was somewhere between sleep and waking when she touched herself between her legs and continued to whisper his name as if he were there until she reached an orgasm. As she rolled over, she wondered if Sal had thought of her at all that day, and if he had, did he miss her as much as she missed him.

Monday was getting off to a busy start. It was only noon, and she had already met with two clients and a third one was on the way. Margo had told herself to stop checking her phone to see if she had a missed call from Sal. He wasn't the kind of man that checked in, and she wasn't going to let herself turn into a needy, codependent woman. Besides, she thought, he probably knew exactly where she was right now so if he wanted to see her, he would. He was calling the shots in this relationship, and she needed to remember that.

The third client was a tall man with sandy blond hair. He was younger than she, but it was difficult to tell his exact age. He had a laugh line or two, but his eyes were bright and youthful.

"Miss Margo?" he asked before sitting down.

"Yes . . . Marcus?" She smiled and extended her hand.

He took it. His grip was strong.

"It's a pleasure to meet you," he said. "Do you need another cup of coffee?"

Margo was surprised. He wasn't the typical criminal element that had come to her so far. He was wearing a dress shirt and tie, no backward cap, no tattoos on his hands or neck, plus he had manners.

"Yes, please, that would be great." She watched him get up and noticed the muscular frame under the expensive shirt and silk tie.

"Cream and sugar?" he asked.

"Yes." Margo sighed as she watched him walked away. He had an incredible ass, and she found herself staring far too intently. Her cheeks were hot as she caught herself. What the hell was she wrong with her? She'd just had the best sex of her life and every time she thought about Sal, her pussy twitched in response.

But Sal wasn't a boyfriend, she reminded herself. This was not a typical relationship. He had a wife at home and a brood. A wife that he still probably fucked on a regular basis. Margo wasn't so stupid as to think otherwise. After all, he was a man; a smart, intuitive, powerful man, but nonetheless, a man.

When Marcus returned with the coffees, she took out her notepad and started to ask questions. She did not have time or the emotional resources to get involved with this man, or, frankly, any man . . . including Sal.

After writing out her case notes, she vowed to herself that her spare time, from here on out, would be spent clearing her name until she had what she wanted . . . what was owed her.

CHAPTER 10

The car was parked at the end of a deserted dead-end street. If anyone could have seen through the tinted windows, they would have seen two heads, very close together. It would have been easy enough to think they were kissing, but they were only talking . . . for now.

"So, what do you think of her?"

"She's different." There was a long, thoughtful pause. He wasn't one to come to quick conclusions; he had discovered long ago that appearances couldn't be trusted.

"It's hard to say, but she's smart, educated, and older. She's definitely not the usual type." He didn't want to elaborate on the past, and he didn't have to.

There was a sad smile and a nod. Giovanna always knew when there was a new girlfriend. They never lasted very long, but it was a distraction. There were whispers and innuendos amongst personnel and changes in schedules and patterns. It had always been this way, but her patience was starting to wear thin.

Giovanna sighed. "Sometimes I think you deserve better."

"What do you mean?" He took her hand and curled her fingers around his palm. "I hate when you talk like this. It sounds like you're giving up." He sounded worried, as was his tendency.

"Sometimes, I wish I would. Maybe we would both be better off." The path she had chosen had been hard. At times it had almost been unbearable. Planning revenge since the age of fifteen had taken its toll; containing her hate had been a daily struggle, and the exhaustion was unmistakable.

"Shh, don't talk like that. The wait is almost over. We're so close." He felt her relax and could feel her breath on his face. He inhaled her perfume and made no effort to stop himself. The lips were familiar and always hot and sweet. He knew he would smear her lipstick, but she would just have to fix it later.

"Dammit, I want you," he confessed, his voice husky. She knew him like no other woman ever could. They shared an unspoken bond, an unspoken trust. She controlled him, and they both knew it.

"Are you asking me or telling me?" she replied coyly.

"I need you, and I fucking want you," he responded with authority.

Her arms opened, and he instantly melted into her soft, warm flesh. The lipstick would be gone quickly, and that was the least of it. Her hand effortlessly found its way inside his pants and withdrew his pulsating cock. He looked up and noticed that the rear windows were already covered in steam from their breath, and they had only just begun.

CHAPTER 11

The last few months had slipped by in a blur. Margo was busy, busier than she ever could have imagined from making appointments on the fly. She had to admit, when she signed on for this wild ride, she really had no idea just how much of the criminal element in this city Sal was involved with. Days had quickly turned into weeks, and now she knew why he had told her to only make weekday appointments. Her phone never stopped ringing.

She had always loved her job, but now, even with the sometimes scary and questionable clientele, she was never sure what each day would bring, but she loved her work even more. There was something rebellious about it, a fuck-you to the system that had screwed her over and wreaked havoc with her life. Margo was using the same rules that had brought her down to help criminals stay free, and last week when she had met with Sal for lunch, she had told him that she felt a little like Robin Hood.

"What do you mean, Cookie?" he asked, running his fingers gently down her open palm.

His touch was intoxicating, and now she found herself enthralled with the man, probably dangerously so, but there was something so necessary that was fulfilled in the hours that they spent in between the sheets at her apartment.

"I mean, this is street law. I'm really helping to screw over the system, and the system is a shitty deal for people who can't afford a top-dollar attorney."

Margo felt good about herself and her work. Her life had a purpose again, and that was all thanks to the man who had picked her up out of the breakfast shift.

"Yeah, Cookie, for the rest of us who have to make a living however we can, the system is always a problem. You're doing good work."

Sal didn't give out many compliments, and when he did, it meant something.

"Which is why I've got a bonus for you." He reached into the inner pocket in his jacket and pulled out a fat envelope. "A little profit sharing."

Margo had learned over the last sixty days to never open an envelope where prying eyes or anyone with a camera phone could be watching.

"So you working on your own case, Cookie?" he asked, his eyes on hers, meaning that he was more interested than he sounded.

"Yeah, it's coming along slowly."

After the first day of furious writing, she had been adding here and there to her notes, but the weekly grind left her tired with little time to pursue her ideas beyond the notepad.

"I'm still putting it together." She watched him lean forward, and her heart beat faster. Margo wondered if he would kiss her right here.

"You're smart, Cookie, you'll figure it out." He smiled, only inches away from her lips, but he got up from the table and was about to leave. Sal was always aware of other people, other people who might be watching him and what he was doing. He hadn't gotten to where he was by being impulsive or careless.

"See you Saturday?"

It was a question, but Margo never considered saying no.

Saturday night had been sensory overload. It was as if the more sex they had, the more she wanted, and this morning when she woke up, naked, she could smell Sal in the sheets and just that alone was enough to make her close her eyes and run her hands over her body. When she was in the shower, she noticed a red mark above her right nipple. Upon closer inspection, she realized it was from his teeth. She ran her finger around it, remembering in detail what it felt like with his mouth clamped on her, his body above her, his hands constantly roaming, caressing, and teasing . . . His cock buried deep inside her, and Margo gasping for more.

Sunday was reserved for family and Sal was predictable. Today she would hear nothing from him or from clients. The cell phone would be silent until Monday morning. Margo had decided to use her quiet Sunday to go find Jay's witness, Megan Dittmar.

Margo had three addresses, and her plan was to start at the closest and go from there. She had used private investigators when she worked at the firm and had never needed to do her own leg work. She assumed that Sal probably knew a guy who knew a guy, but she wanted to do this herself. It was personal. She wanted to look the girl in the eye who had brought her world crashing down around her, and ask her why.

The first two addresses turned up no results. She had to take the subway, and then a cab to get to the third address. When the cab stopped in front of an old rundown brownstone, Margo took it in. Gang symbols were spray painted everywhere, at least half the windows were boarded up, and all of the windows had bars on them. Tires and garbage littered the sidewalk and stoop.

Margo asked the cab-driver, "You sure you've got the right place?"

The building was dreadful and looked uninhabitable.

"Lady, I've been driving a cab in this city for thirty years. I know where I am."

The fat man turned around and barked out, "I could have told you twenty minutes ago this wasn't a neighborhood a nice woman like you would want to go to."

Margo sighed. She was dressed casual but regardless, she stuck out like a sore thumb in this part of town.

“You getting out or what?” the driver asked as he eyed her in the rear-view mirror.

“Yeah, I’m getting out,” Margo said with more confidence than she felt.

“Keep the meter running. I’ll be right back.” Margo was out of her element and wasn’t about to get stranded in this part of town.

“I wait here and you don’t pay me?” the man snorted. “Yeah, I’ve never heard that before. You pay me now,” he pointed at the meter, “thirty-one dollars, lady, and I’ll wait for you.”

She pawed through her purse and handed him a twenty-dollar bill. “You want the rest, plus more, you wait for me,” she said with authority. She had picked up a thing or two from Sal’s street smarts.

She got out and slammed the door behind her, not waiting for any negotiations from the fat man. Back in the day, the old Margo would have politely paid him and hoped he’d wait for her. The old Margo did whatever was expected and played by the rules, but that Margo had spent six years in jail, rotting away for something she never did. The old Margo was in the past, and the new Margo wasn’t taking shit from anybody.

Inside the building Margo climbed two flights of stairs and quickly found the apartment she was looking for. She knocked on the door and after a few moments heard feet shuffling. She sensed the person on the other side of the door was looking through the peephole.

Margo took a step back from the door. "Hello, I'm looking for Megan. Megan Dittmar. I'm an acquaintance of hers. Hello? I'd like to know how she's doing."

No response. The old Margo would have left defeated, but the new Margo wasn't going anywhere.

"Hello, hello? I know someone is in there. Please open the door and speak to me. Hello?" Margo was pounding on the door with her fist by now.

A man's voice rang out, "Okay, okay, hold on."

Multiple locks clicked and churned before the door opened as far as the security chain would allow.

A man peered out and snarled, "What the hell you want, lady?"

"I'm sorry, sir, I don't mean to bother you. I'm looking for Megan Dittmar," she smiled politely.

The door closed momentarily. Margo heard the security chain being removed this time. The door opened wide, and the man stepped into the threshold. He was as broad as he was tall. His head was shaved bald, and Margo recognized the teardrop tattoo on his upper cheek from prison.

"What you want, lady? You're bothering my mom, so that means you is bothering me." He smiled viciously at her, his grill catching the light.

Margo looked past him and saw an old woman, small in stature, wearing a worn house robe and slippers. She quickly assessed she wouldn't get anywhere here with a tough attitude.

"I'm looking for Megan Dittmar. I have this address as a place she lived."

The man gave her the once-over, "You, 5-0?" he tilted his head and smirked. Obviously, the man had no respect for law enforcement.

"No, hell no," Margo waved off the suggestion. "My name is Margo Harris, and I used to be an attorney."

"Megan in trouble?" the big man narrowed his eyes. He had just admitted that he knew her. At least Margo was headed in the right direction.

She shook her head, "No, sir, Megan's not in trouble. I just had a couple of questions for her about someone we used to know."

"Megan comes here when she's in trouble."

Margo was no Nancy Drew sleuth detective, but she had her first real lead. She was in the right place, and the man had indicated that maybe little Miss Perfect was not what she had seemed on the stand.

"Megan is a good girl, but she's always getting mixed up with assholes."

Margo could relate and raised her eyebrows and nodded.

"The last one fucked her up real good; she had to go back to rehab."

"Drug rehab?" Margo could feel the wheels turning in her mind now. Perfect witness-now-drug addict. She would get ripped apart on the stand.

"Yeah, some dickhead she was mixed up with got her back on meth."

Jay definitely qualified as a dickhead.

"Do you remember if his name was Jay?" Margo was jumping inside with anticipation, but she doubted it was going to be this easy.

The big man seemed to be searching his memory and shook his head no.

"Nah, his name wasn't Jay. He has a street name like a wannabe pimp or something."

"So Megan stays here sometimes?" Margo was not going to give up that easily.

He shrugged. "She comes and goes, but we haven't seen her for a while. The rehab didn't work too good." The man looked genuinely sad.

"Do you know where she hangs out?" Margo tried to sound nonchalant, but it was getting more difficult.

The man rubbed his bald head and sighed. "She's more than likely on the streets. I'd check down by York and Sixty-Fifth Street, you know, the strip."

It was an area known for drugs and prostitutes.

"OK, sir, thank you very much." Margo turned to go. The sooner she got out of this neighborhood, the better.

"Hey," the man called out to her, "you find Megan, tell her Z says to come home."

Margo looked back and saw the old woman clinging to the big burly man. She nodded. "Will do."

She got back in the cab with her mind racing. What were the odds that a drug-addicted prostitute could be found? What if she couldn't be found? What if she was dead? Margo couldn't imagine that girls selling their bodies in exchange for a quick fix lived long enough to collect Social Security.

"Can you take me to York and Sixty-fifth?" she asked the cabdriver.

"Lady, I take you wherever you want, but you pay me first." He pointed at the meter. Margo silently passed him two twenties and sat back as he pulled into the street.

"What do you want to go there for?" he asked, looking at her from the rearview mirror.

"It's a long-ass story," she sighed and was silent the rest of the ride.

CHAPTER 12

Monday was always a busy day for Margo. Clients who were arrested over the weekend had to stay in county lockup until they were arraigned and released on Monday morning. They typically showed up at the designated location wearing wrinkled clothes, smelling like they hadn't showered, and looking like they hadn't slept.

Margo was studying the boy sitting across the table from her. He was only nineteen, and he couldn't look more scared. Despite his bravado, it was all just an act. Two nights in jail had been enough for him to have the shakes ever since he sat down.

"Scott, I'm going to help you, but you've got to be smart." She tried to smile but looking down at her notes, there wasn't much to smile about.

"Miss Margo, I can't go to jail." He was scratching his face continually, and she had met enough of them now to know that he was in need of a fix.

"I'm going to cut a deal, Miss Margo, tell them whatever they want to hear, whatever it takes." He scratched himself violently leaving a red mark. "I got to take care of myself."

"Scott, listen to me. You don't want or need to make a deal." She wondered what had happened in lockup over the weekend. Had he been threatened?

"Your case is difficult, but you'll have a good lawyer."

Sal had a team of lawyers, mostly relatives or friends. He had been burned by big firms so he stuck with people he could trust. His lawyers weren't necessarily great, but they were hustlers. They fought for their clients and were happy to have the information that Margo fed them.

"Nah, Miss Margo, I don't even care about this bullshit. I'm telling you that I can't go to jail. I won't make it in there." His eyes were wild with fear.

Margo lowered her voice and leaned in toward the boy trying not to inhale his body odor. "Listen, Sal is your boss. Sal takes care of his people, right?"

"Man, fuck Sal," the boy was far too loud, and it wasn't something people thought, much less said. "Where was that motherfucker when I was getting treated like a bitch this weekend?"

"What happened in lockup, Scott?"

Having been in prison Margo knew a thing or two about the brutal violence and rape that happened on a regular basis.

The boy's eyes were glazed. He shook his head back and forth. "I ain't going back, Miss Margo, that's all I am sayin'. You can tell Sal that too."

The boy stood up and slammed his chair into the table and strode out of the coffee shop.

By the end of the day Margo hadn't heard from Sal. He usually checked in at some point. She was already home when her cell phone rang. She couldn't help but smile when she saw his number on the caller ID.

"I was starting to worry about you," she told him when she answered.

"Cookie, you don't ever have to worry about me. I'm an expert at taking care of myself," her lover chuckled. "Run me through your day."

She ticked off the list; everyone but Scott had simple cases. Illegal search and seizures, reasonable doubt, triumphed-up charges, or other dirty tactics by the cops that would get their cases dropped. But she had to admit that Scott had her worried.

"He told me he'd make a deal to get out of doing time."

"Hmm, that's interesting. Do you think it will come to that?" he asked.

Margo paused before answering, "Honestly, I think they have him dead to rights. He was careless, and I couldn't find any loopholes in his story. It doesn't help that he ran and fought with the arresting officers."

She took a sip of her wine. "He's pretty freaked out. I think he was threatened and raped in county."

Sal changed the subject. "What about your case, Cookie? How's that going?"

Margo had walked the strip peering at faces and asking women in various states of undress if they knew Megan. The women gave her blank stares and no information. Margo had called it a night after a tall, well-built black man with large diamond studs in both ears and a lot of gold chains around his neck had approached her.

"You a cop?" he asked.

The man was definitely a pimp. Margo had glanced at the even larger white man with tattoos covering his neck that sat in the driver's seat of the Lexus that the black man had come from. Margo was out of her element and possibly putting her safety in jeopardy.

She had postured before replying, "No way, just looking for a friend. She's not around, so I'm outta here."

Margo had walked quickly in the other direction and looked back over her shoulder once to see that the man was still eying her.

Sal was curious. "So the fat man, Z, he told you she was hooking . . . Does he know that or is he just guessing?"

Margo remembered the sad expression on Z's face and absentmindedly bit her lip.

"No, he seemed genuine. He missed her and wished she would come home."

"I see." Sal was quiet for a moment. "Well, Cookie, what are you going to do next?"

"I'm going back out early Saturday morning, hitting the shitty hotels around the strip and see if anything turns up."

Earlier seemed safer than later and maybe she could catch a break. She knew the odds were against her, and she doubted that Megan used her real name on the street.

"The problem is if she's strung out, she might not remember anything from seven days ago much less seven years."

"That's just one of the problems, Cookie."

Sal was probably several moves ahead of her and Margo had grown to respect him for his intellect as well as his prowess.

"I tell you what, Thursday, don't make any appointments after two. I may have a lead on Megan."

Margo wondered what Sal had up his sleeve. She was curious, but she knew better than to ask. Sal never revealed his hand until he was ready.

Margo opened her day planner and looked at the scribbled calendar she had been keeping. She had no appointments lined up yet for Thursday.

"Not a problem." She made a large X on Thursday afternoon. "Am I meeting you here?" She was always anxious to be alone with him.

"No, Cookie, I'll find you and pick you up." Tonight, Sal seemed to be all business and Margo had told herself long ago that she should be too.

Sal was predictably early. Thursday at 1:55, Margo saw the Lincoln Town car pull up and park. She had already packed up her briefcase, knowing that he would be on time. She slid in next to him and was greeted with a smile.

"Cookie, you're looking more and more gorgeous every time I see you." Their legs were touching and Margo felt the chemistry between them rising as her nipples hardened.

"Thank you, Sal." She never took Sal's compliments for granted, and she loved the attention.

Sal turned to his left and ran his fingers through her hair and caressed her face. He pulled her near and kissed her, leaving her breathless. Sal's scent had an intoxicating effect on her. She heard the low moan that escaped from her as she rubbed her body against him. Margo shuddered as his hands traveled down her sides and stopped at the hem of her skirt.

"I've been thinking about you all morning, Cookie," he whispered as his fingers started the slow slide up her legs, under the skirt, tracing a line along the lacy edge of her stockings.

His index finger rubbed against her damp panties.

Her cheeks were flushed, and she could feel the heat between them.

"Ah . . . , I was thinking about you too." She was already breathing hard, and she parted her legs to give him access to anything he wanted.

"I can tell." He flashed her a wicked smile.

If she had thought the first night was mind-blowing, it had only gotten better. Sal had been right. The more they knew each other's bodies, the hotter the sex had become.

"Please, Sal," she whimpered and looked him in the eye.

"Sorry, Cookie, we can't," he whispered.

He removed his hand from under her skirt. "We're almost there, and I want you focused."

Dammit! He had so much self-control. Margo had waited years for sex—really, all her life when she thought about it. No one had ever fucked her like Sal did, but today was apparently about business not pleasure.

Margo sighed and pulled her skirt down in frustration. She composed herself before asking, "Where are we going?"

"You'll see soon enough, Cookie."

The car came to a stop and parked. Sal exited and waved her out. Margo looked around and realized they were in a deserted industrial area.

She walked in silence with Sal toward the entrance of a large warehouse building that looked as if it had long been abandoned.

They entered the dimly lit building. Their feet on the cracked concrete floor echoed loudly in the heavy silence that surrounded the large, open space.

It took a few moments for Margo's eyes to adjust to the lighting before she saw two men that she didn't recognize standing beside a table. A figure appeared to be slumped over on the table. As they got closer, Margo realized the figure was a woman with long, matted brown hair spilled out. Her arms were crossed underneath her, and she seemed to be asleep.

"Cookie, meet Megan Dittmar," Sal gestured to the sleeping figure in the chair.

"Holy shit!" Margo felt adrenaline surge through her. Sal had found Megan. She realized she should never underestimate Sal's reach. She wasn't sure if she was more frightened or fascinated.

"Wake up, Megan." Sal stood behind her and yanked her by the hair, pulling her head off the table.

"Bring Miss Harris a chair," Sal told one of the men standing nearby, and Margo watched as he scurried to follow directions.

"I can't work right now, I need some sleep," Megan mumbled, slurring her words. Margo noticed she had a fat lip and her front teeth were bloody.

"What happened to her?" Margo felt a chill travel down her spine. Sal was a gentleman; he wouldn't strong-arm a girl . . . would he?

"Lots of bad things happen to girls on the street." Sal let Megan slump back to the table with a groan. "Lots of scum and undesirables on the strip."

Margo couldn't believe the difference between the woman here at the table and the girl Jay had put on the stand. If time had altered Margo, it had ravaged Megan.

Margo wondered if Jay was responsible for her decline to the absolute bottom that she appeared to be at now.

She felt no pity toward the girl. She was angry and wanted answers.

"Hey, Megan, you need to wake up. I'm going to ask you a few questions." She patted Megan's hand.

The woman raised her head halfway and slurred, "I been up all night."

"Yeah, I'm sure you have," Margo replied sarcastically. "This won't take long, and I'll get you something to eat when we're done."

The woman raised her head at the mention of food. "I'm hungry."

Her eyes seemed to be permanently glazed over. The girl that Jay had known was gone, and Margo wondered if she could ever come back.

"Just answer my questions, Megan." Margo paused and took a deep breath. "Do you remember me?"

"Never seen you before, lady," Megan's head bobbed, and she scratched her face. "Never seen any of you," she gestured with one shaky hand across the room.

"Blaze is going to be pissed when I'm not out later and he can't find me. You don't want to piss him off."

Margo figured that was her pimp, remembering the tall, black man that had scared her a few nights ago.

"Don't worry about Blaze," Sal told Megan. "I've taken care of him."

Margo was quickly putting it all together now. The thugs that came to see her ran with other thugs. Sal had a street network. Through contacts, Sal had found Megan through her pimp.

"Megan, do you remember testifying in court several years ago?"

The woman snorted, "Yeah, I been in court a few times."

"This wasn't about you being in trouble. It was a criminal case. They asked you a bunch of questions about a lawyer named Margo Harris."

Megan's expression was blank.

Margo continued, "Do you remember a man named Jay?"

There was a glimmer of recognition there. "Yeah, I remember that asshole."

"Why is he an asshole? What did he do?" Margo was tense; it felt as if her whole life hung in the balance of this junkie's memories.

Megan rubbed her lips back and forth, a sign that she was coming down off of God-knows-what.

"He got me hooked. I never did drugs until I met that prick." Megan seemed to know how far she had fallen.

"I never had anything before I met Jay. He bought me nice things, took me places, gave me money, and made life easy. He introduced me to cocaine and got me hooked. Then he threw me out. No place to live, no money, no blow, no nothing."

It explained what had started her slow road to the strip.

"Megan, why did Jay take care of you and give you money?" Margo hoped it was as she suspected.

"He told me if I was a good girl, if I said what he told me to say, he would take care of me. I would be his girl, and I would never have to worry about money again. I thought he loved me."

Megan absent-mindedly picked at her face and head. Margo saw the track marks and assorted bruises on her arms.

"Megan, did you lie for Jay when you were in court?" Margo felt like her head was going to explode. She fought the urge to shake the girl and scream—"You lied and ruined my life!"

"He told me it wasn't a lie, it was justice." Megan was awake now, and it was obvious she needed a fix. "You're that lady, right?"

"Yes," Margo narrowed her eyes at Megan. "I'm the lady you put in jail for six years."

"Fuck, I'm sorry." Megan couldn't look her in the eye, but Margo doubted that was remorse as much as her inability to focus.

"If I had known Jay was playing me I never would've done what he wanted."

She had been very young and very gullible. Margo could imagine how easy it had been for Jay to manipulate her.

Margo was relentless. “So you’re telling me that you lied in court because Jay promised to give you money and take care of you, is that right, Megan?”

Megan’s demeanor suddenly changed. Her face hardened, and her lip snarled at Margo. “You ask a lot of fucking questions, lady. Why should I keep answering your questions? What’s in it for me?”

Sal shook his head no and interrupted. He held onto both sides of the table and leaned in toward Megan. Margo looked at his face and saw the cold stare he gave her.

“We’re not here to negotiate with you. So here’s what is going to happen, Megan. You’re going back to rehab. You’re going to get cleaned up, stay clean, and get your shit together.” He frowned at her. “No checking out, no running, and no relapse. If you fuck up, our next chat won’t be so friendly. Do I make myself perfectly clear?”

Even in her needy state, Megan could hear the underlying threat and nodded, quietly whispering, “Yes, sir,” loud and clear.

Sal maintained his stance. “Once you’re off the drugs, I’ll help you get a job and keep you off the streets.” He grabbed the back of her head once more to keep her eyes on him. “And then you’re going back to court and tell them that you lied.”

Her eyes filled with tears. “I’m sorry I lied, I didn’t mean to hurt nobody.”

Sal let go of her hair and nodded in the direction of the two men. “Get her outta here and get her something to eat before you take her to St. Joseph's." It was a private hospital with a wing for rich rehab patients.

Margo and Sal were silent until the men and Megan were gone. The sound of the door closing behind them echoed through the empty space.

"So Jay got her to lie and got her hooked on drugs to make sure that she'd never be a reliable witness again." Margo knew that Jay hated her, but it seemed like a lot of trouble to go to in order to get her promotion.

"Sounds like that was his plan, Cookie." Sal put his hand out to help her out of the chair. "She's going to be in rehab for a while, but I'll keep tabs on her."

"You have people working for you in the hospital, Sal?" Margo wondered if there was anyone in this town that didn't somehow work for him.

"Cookie, you just worry about reopening your case with her new testimony."

His arm was around her waist, and they walked in time to the door, then climbed once more in the backseat of the car, their legs touching. As much as Margo wanted him, she couldn't stop thinking about what had just happened. She felt Sal's strong, solid hand wrap around hers.

"We're here, Cookie." She must have been lost in thought the whole ride and when Margo looked up, she saw her apartment complex. Sal had brought her home and the desire that had palpated through her body just a few hours ago resurrected.

"You want to come inside, Sal?" She could vividly picture him naked and on top of her.

"Not tonight, Cookie. I've got a few things to take care of." He sat back and dismissed her. Not even a kiss good night.

His self-control really was amazing.

CHAPTER 13

Scott, the kid who had left after threatening to turn state's evidence, hadn't returned her calls, and on Friday afternoon, Margo left another one.

"Scott, it's Miss Margo." All of the clients referred to her as that, and she had found that she had started using the name as well. "This is my fourth message. I'm getting a little worried about you, and I'd like you to call me as soon as you get this. You have my number." She pressed end call and made the next call to his attorney.

"Miss Harris, how are you?"

The attorney was a slick, fast-talking defense lawyer that she had known professionally in her past life.

"I'm great, Mr. Kaplan, how are you?"

They exchanged pleasantries for a few minutes before she asked him, "Have you heard from Scott Bollin?"

"Bollin, Bollin . . .," the lawyer was searching through papers on his desk; Margo could hear him in the background.

"The kid was arrested for possession, intent to sell, amongst other things."

How could he not remember the skinny boy who scratched himself constantly?

"Oh yeah," Mr. Kaplan recalled him. "I haven't heard from him."

"You haven't heard from him either?" Margo was quickly reviewing the possible scenarios in her head. "Is he in protective custody? Did he make a deal?"

"I have no idea, but I doubt it."

Kaplan was hiding something. The man knew more than he was telling and although she didn't blame him for protecting his client, it still pissed her off.

"I'm sure he changed his mind about that," Kaplan assured Margo.

When they hung up, Margo couldn't help but wonder why Kaplan would think the boy changed his mind. He had been adamant about it before slamming his chair and storming out. What would change between then and now?

It was Saturday night and instead of anxiously awaiting the time she would spend with Sal, Margo's mind was obsessed with Scott Bollin. She hadn't let it go and couldn't stop picturing his face, his wide-eyed look of horror when he had told her that he wouldn't go back to jail.

She remembered the same sickening fear coursing through her. Margo had spent the first night on her bunk in the ten-by-ten cell, a tough-looking Hispanic woman occupying the bunk below, snoring loudly. Margo wondered how the woman could sleep. How was she ever going to sleep here? The prison seemed to come alive at night.

Her cellmate was a Hispanic woman in her late fifties with silver hair. Her name was Esperanza.

"Just call me Essie," she had told Margo.

"What do you go by?"

"Margo," she had told the heavyset woman. "Just Margo."

"OK, Margo, so you want to be my girlfriend or what?"

Essie was holding her hand. Margo swallowed hard and did her best to maintain a polite posture and not pull away.

"No, I'm sorry," she shook her head and mustered up some false bravado "I'm not a lesbian."

The woman let out a hearty cackle and let go of her hand.

"Don't be naïve, sweetie. I'm not a lesbian either, and neither are most of the bitches in here," she nodded to indicate the rest of the inmates. "But in here, it's a power trip. You're fresh meat. You need protection."

"Protection from what?" Margo had heard stories about jail, but she had never known that the same held true in a women's prison.

"From whomever; inmates, guards, staff; trust no one. Take my word, it's a fucking jungle in here."

Essie was twelve years into a life sentence for murdering her husband. Margo figured she must know the ropes and be familiar with how the game was played.

"So what's in it for you?" Margo's voice had barely been above a whisper.

Essie winked at her and smiled a little. "Good girl. You catch on quick. You take a look at my case and help me with my appeal. In return, I'll keep you safe. I tell the home-girls that you're my bitch, and they'll leave you alone."

It wasn't a secret that Margo was an attorney. Her case had been smeared all over the papers and local news.

Margo took Essie's offer, and it was a deal that had saved her life. Margo was sure of it. Essie had made the six years bearable and had kept her out of trouble and safe. She knew from seeing what happened to other inmates that her time in prison could have been much, *much worse.*

When Sal rang her doorbell, she still hadn't rid herself of the memory, and her smile must have looked forced.

"Cookie, you all right?" Sal asked as he entered her apartment.

"Yeah, I'm fine."

She would be. There was no way that she could think of anything but Sal's touch and the physical sensation of him once they were in her bed.

"I'm just a little worried." She watched as he hung his coat and approached her.

Sal's hands were on her, his strong arms clasping her to his hard body. His cock was already a stiff pole in the front of his pants and Margo gasped when he rubbed himself against her in the silk negligee.

"Worried about what, Cookie?" His warm breath was on her face.

"Worried about that kid, Scott." She bit her lip. "The one who said he'd make a deal. He hasn't returned any of my messages, and Kaplan hasn't heard from him."

"I wouldn't worry about him anymore, Cookie." Sal's eyes flashed for just a second, and then his mouth was kissing her neck. "He won't be calling you back. He's Kaplan's problem now."

He was walking her backward down the hall to the bedroom, and she briefly wondered if Sal had taken care of the problem himself.

Once he pulled the lingerie off, there were no more worries, no more thoughts of any kind other than the aching hunger that Margo felt inside for Sal and knowing that he could fulfill her in ways she'd never dreamed possible until now.

"My God, Cookie, your body is amazing."

She was on the mattress, naked and breathless. Sal was undressing quickly, and she watched intently.

Shirt off, pants down, she sighed when his hands kneaded her skin and his lips found hers, parted and wet and eager for her mouth.

"I want you," he told her as his lips moved slowly down her neck, his fingers pulling her stone-hard nipples, and then tracing the soft curve of her breasts.

"Sal, how do you do that to me?" Margo gasped and pushed her hips up to meet his. She was soaking wet, the rivulet of her want dripping down her inner thigh, her knees weak from the thought of him taking his pleasure with her.

"Do what, Cookie?" He was sinking slowly to the floor in front of her, and she felt his kisses burn down her sides to her hips as he made his way to her mound.

"Make me want you so bad." Margo was panting and parted her legs for him and watched as the man kissed her softly along her lower lips. "I've never felt this way before."

She had never told him how little sex had sustained her all this time.

"Good, Cookie, just relax and enjoy."

He teased her with the tip of his tongue as he looked up from his position, kissing her once more . . . before devouring her.

Margo cried out when he lapped her from her tight opening to the tip of her hard clit. The man had an uncanny knowledge of her body, and she found herself craving more every time he left. He licked her in a slow circle, and she could feel herself swollen and hot. He would drive her absolutely crazy until her juices were running out of her, bringing her to the brink of her release, and then keeping her there with his steady, sweet rhythm on her body.

"Sal, you're driving me crazy." She could barely speak, and she clutched the bed behind her for balance, thrusting up. She heard his lips sucking on her sensitive skin, and she quivered. His tongue kept its maddening, perfect tempo. It was as if Sal knew how she touched herself, as if he could see how she would run the vibrator over the very place that he seemed to be so enamored with. He drank from her, gulping down her essence, and he let her clit go only to touch her with the tip of his finger while he licked the damp skin of her inner thighs.

"God, you're going to make me come." She rocked back and forth as his tongue slid up to her thumping clit and she watched the back of his head as he buried his face there in her southernmost parts and consumed her. The sound of her wet pussy meeting Sal's exploring tongue got louder and louder, and she felt the first spasm explode as she began to climax.

"Sal, yes!" her hands were in his hair, and she pumped her hips as every wave of pleasure reached down her body and shook her. She said his name again and again with every stroke of his hot tongue on her shuddering clitoris, and he took every drop of her orgasm, and Margo knew that this was only the first.

Her head sank into the bed, and her body relaxed. Sal rose from his knees, his face wet with her sweetness, and he smiled, pulling her to him in the center of the bed.

"I love the taste of you, Cookie."

He must because it was a necessity . . . every time Sal's mouth was on every inch of her and every time, she found herself brought to a new level of ecstasy.

She reached between his legs and stroked his huge dick through his boxers. "I want to taste you," she whispered and started to make her way down his body, kissing his skin, his scent was all around her, and it was making her want him even more.

Margo pulled the boxers off and watched as the thick length of him bobbed up to greet her.

"I think you want me to taste you too," she said playfully. She looked up at Sal, his head on her pillow. If it were possible to look any more pleased, she couldn't imagine it.

"Yes, I do, Cookie," he exhaled hard and he told her, "I want to watch you."

She ran her tongue along his wide, engorged head and listened to him moan with desire as she licked the puddle of precum that waited for her. Moving her tongue down under the thick ridge under the tip she tasted every bit of him and sighed as she opened wide to take him inside her mouth.

"You're so fucking sexy, Cookie."

He pushed up and the head of his cock touched the roof of her mouth before she even took half of it. She cupped his heavy sack and kneaded it softly, pulling on his testicles as she moved her mouth down on Sal's enormous cock.

"Jesus, yes, that's so good," he murmured, and she looked up and met his gaze as she opened her mouth wider to take in more of him.

"I don't want to come in your mouth, Cookie. Get on top of me." She bobbed her head up and down, ignoring his request.

"Come on, Cookie, I mean it."

He tugged at her shoulders and for the first time since they met, Margo didn't do as he requested. She sucked him harder and slower, her tongue bathing almost the full length of him as she took his shaft to the top of her throat.

"Damn," he panted, thrusting into her mouth now, pushing back into the mattress and rising up to meet her lips. He was driving his cock in and out of her mouth.

"Get on my cock. I want your juicy pussy on me."

Margo couldn't wait anymore, and she purred as she slid up his body. Holding his cock tightly at the base, she felt impaled as he plunged deep inside her with one hard movement.

"Fuck me, Cookie. Take all of my cock."

He pulled her close, and her breasts were sealed against his chest, their mouths open and joined, her hair falling down around them as their hips met and retreated.

"Sal, yes, you feel so good . . ." she whispered in his ear.

He was pounding her from below, gripping her hips and filling her to the very bottom of her core.

"Cookie, you're perfect," he groaned, clenching his jaw.

She knew from watching him over the last two months that he was on the brink of letting go deep inside her but wouldn't let himself until she had her second orgasm on his throbbing dick.

She sat up and moved her hips faster, up to the tip, down to the bottom of his shaft, her eyes on his face, the drops of her first climax were gone and she shivered as he pushed her to the next. This man knew her body, every inch of her. He had memorized her skin, her curves, and the places that when touched made her purr.

It never ceased to amaze her that she had gone for so long without any idea of what ecstasy could be. When she tensed up, he knew she was ready to come. She clenched around his erection before crying out his name once more.

"Cookie, oh fuck, I'm coming."

He met her stroke for stroke, and she could feel him exploding inside, bursting with his pleasure and pushing long, hot ropes of semen up into her core. Margo collapsed, her damp forehead pressed against his heaving chest. She continued to shiver with each sweet wave of her orgasm as her insides drank him down in gulps.

They would lie like this until they caught their breath, kissing softly between sighs and sometime in the next hour, Sal would get his second wind and roll on top of her and fuck her even harder and longer the second time than he had the first.

Margo wondered what it would have been like to know a younger Sal. She couldn't imagine that he'd be more virile than he was now, but a chuckle escaped her when she pictured him in her mind's eye.

"What's so funny, Cookie?" he asked, his breath coming slower now.

"Just imagining that when you were younger, you must have been quite the ladies' man."

Who was she kidding? She knew that women were all over him now.

"Yeah, maybe," he shrugged. "I like women. But most importantly," his expression was serious, "I like you."

Margo had been very stern with herself about keeping her emotions in check. He was married, and he was married for life. A devout Catholic, she knew that he honored his commitments to family above anything else, and whatever this was, as much as she thought about him and could easily picture something more, Sal was off-limits.

"I like you, Sal." She murmured against his shoulder, moving her lips up his throat. "Very, very much."

They made love again and when he kissed her good night, he asked, "When are you going to see your kids, Cookie?"

"Soon," she promised.

Abigail and Thomas hadn't completely warmed up to the idea yet, but she wouldn't give up.

"Make sure you do," he pulled on her bottom lip with his teeth, and then smiled at the sigh that came from her.

"You're beautiful. I bet you look like an angel when you sleep."

He would never know, would he?

CHAPTER 14

Things had never been the same since her father died. She was nine years old and her entire world had been turned upside down. Her mother cried non-stop for the first month and had no money to pay the bills. They were eventually evicted from their apartment and shuffled around to various relatives. Giovanna did her best to help out by looking after her three younger brothers, but she was scared. She missed her father terribly and worried that the generosity of relatives would only last so long. The thought of being completely homeless and hungry was terrifying.

A year later they were financially okay, but things were worse, much worse in Giovanna's opinion. Her mother had married Dino Rossi who was a widower with two small boys. They moved into Dino's small house and became a blended family. Dino had insisted on legally adopting her and her brothers, and her mother made no objections.

The man her mother had married had alarmed Giovanna from the beginning. She saw through his charming exterior and insincerity, but her mother had waved her off, clearly annoyed that her defiant daughter would be so bold as to complain.

"He's a good man and don't you dare ruin this, Gia."

Her mother used to be beautiful and vibrant, but now it seemed as though the mother she knew was fading quickly before her eyes. It was alarming. It was as if time was moving faster for her than anyone else.

Giovanna should have been grateful for a roof over her head, but she wasn't. She hated Dino Rossi. She hated having two new brothers that she had to help out with, hated that Dino demanded she call him Daddy, hated that she had been forced to take his name, and mostly, she hated how she would catch her step-father staring at her in ways that made her very uncomfortable. Giovanna kept her mouth shut and did her best to keep her distance from her step-father, which was nearly impossible in the tight quarters they lived in.

She had been eleven and in the bathtub the first time. With so many children in the small house, the bathroom was usually her only refuge, the only place she was ever alone. Gia's eyes were closed and she floated, pretending that she was far, far away, on a warm and sunny beach in California, staring at the ocean. Better yet, in the ocean—anywhere but here. The lock on the bathroom door was broken and when the hinges creaked she screamed, "Get out," covering herself quickly before she turned to see which one of her siblings was the offender.

It was him. He didn't get out. Instead, he closed the door behind him, and when she saw his face, she knew the panic that kept rising up inside her every time she caught his eye was true and real. She had known. Why hadn't her mother?

when she pushed back. "My little girl likes that," he observed, and it was then that she stopped instantly. He knew it was wrong, and Giovanna thought he must be the devil for doing this.

He sat on the edge of the tub, his pants were unzipped, and he announced in the same soft tone, "Now it's your turn to touch your daddy." He pushed her small hand through the front of the zipper and closed her fingers around the pounding flesh that was waiting for her inside.

Her step-father held her hand and moved it up and down, faster and faster until he stiffened and closed his eyes. She felt the hot stickiness cover her hand, and when he released her, she took her hand away quickly and smelled the metallic scent that the white substance left on her hand. It was the same scent that was rising from his open zipper, and she knew that whatever he had just done, it wasn't something that he should do with his step-daughter.

"Wash your hand, little darling," he told her. "And if you say anything to your mother, anything to anyone, do you know what will happen? I will leave your worthless mother; you and your brothers will have nothing and nowhere to go. You will end up living in shelters and on the streets." His eyes were hard. "You know what happens to little girls like you who live on the street, don't you?"

She shook her head. She didn't want to know either.

"As long as you're a good girl, you'll never have to find out. Daddy's girl will keep our secret." He kissed her forehead once more as he zipped his pants, one lingering finger traced a circle around her tiny nipple.

He had trained her well. Not only had she kept his secret for years, but many others. She was an encyclopedia of secrets.

CHAPTER 15

The next morning, Margo flipped through the newspaper as she sipped a huge cup of coffee. It had become her Sunday morning routine, bathing in the idea that she had a full twenty-four hours to do absolutely nothing. The year of three jobs had taken its toll, and she had just recently felt as if she'd caught up on her sleep. It made a difference; her mind was once again sharp as a tack.

She paused at a headline that made her stomach flip.

"SUICIDE BEING INVESTIGATED."

Underneath the bold print, was his name, "Scott Bollin, 19, was found dead at a local construction site. The coroner has not confirmed the cause of death but first responders have indicated that the Bollin committed suicide. Bollin was recently arrested for drug trafficking; therefore his death will be investigated for foul play."

Margo read the rest of the details quickly and took a deep breath. She knew in her gut the boy was in over his head. She knew it when she met with him, and she knew it when didn't return her calls.

Had she played a part in Scott's death? The hairs on her arms were standing at attention as she remembered the conversation she'd had with Sal. She had told him that Scott was going to cut a deal. Now he was dead. Had Sal given an order to guarantee Scott wasn't ever going to be able to tell anyone anything?

Sal was her lover and her mentor, but for every kindness he showed her, she wasn't sure if she wanted to know what kind of cruelty he doled out to others. He ran his organization carefully and was a hands-on kind of boss who kept his finger on the pulse at all times. She sensed the fear he instilled when clients came to visit her. The thugs treated her with the utmost respect and courtesy, and she had always known that it wasn't her presence that had inspired it. It was the thought of Sal and what he might do if they weren't on their best behavior.

He had a whole file on her life, tucked away somewhere, his to peruse whenever he found the time. She had a couple of spots she liked to see clients at. He always knew where she was. He obviously had someone keeping tabs on her. She had tried to convince herself that it was no big deal, but now she wondered how much of that was him protecting her and how much of it was to protect himself.

She put on a sweatshirt despite the warm temperature in her apartment; she was chilled to the bone. Margo knew a lot, probably much more than most in Sal's organization. Despite his kindness and generosity, would Sal ever let her go if she wanted to leave?

Margo rocked back and forth holding her arms around her chest. Why did she attract the wrong men? Was it a pattern? Had she been set up for failure as a child? Even her seemingly perfect husband had turned out to be evil.

An hour had gone by quickly and Margo looked at the time. She actually had plans today. She was meeting her kids for lunch at a restaurant near their house.

Margo sighed. There didn't seem to be any point in dwelling on Sal one way or the other right now. She might be falling in love with him and that presented a whole other set of problems by itself.

Abigail and Thomas were a few minutes late, and Margo waved at them from the table she had gotten in the corner. Abby looked pissed off already, but her son was smiling from ear to ear. He rushed to greet her with a hug.

"Mom, I missed you." His arms were around her neck and Margo realized that he was so much taller than the last time she had gotten a hug from him.

"I missed you too," She kissed his forehead and looked over at Abby, "both of you, very much."

Abby slid into the booth and watched mother and son with a smirk. "So if you missed us so much, where are you? Why don't you ever see us?" She raised her eyebrows at Margo, waiting for an answer.

Margo exhaled. Her daughter reminded her of herself, and she would make a formidable attorney someday if she had any desire to do so.

"That's a good question, Abigail." She would try to get into the habit of addressing her daughter by the name she preferred. "And I owe you an apology, both of you, actually. Your father didn't want us to see each other, and I needed to take some time to adjust to not being in prison.

I had to find a job and just get used to taking care of myself. I'm sorry that I didn't make more of an effort to reach out to you sooner."

"What do you mean, Dad didn't want you to see us?" Thomas asked.

"Well, your dad got full custody of you because I was in prison. When I got out, he thought it would be best to not disrupt your routine. I wanted to do what was best for you two, so I went along. But I love you guys, and I've missed you so, so much. I want to see you two and work on getting to know you again." Margo was doing her best to speak well of David.

"Dad's gone all the time, so you could come over whenever you want," Thomas smiled at her.

"What do you mean your dad's gone all the time? You mean at work?" Why would David leave them up to their own devices? Teenagers needed even more supervision than they did when they were younger.

"He's busy, and he doesn't want to be home with us." Abby rolled her eyes at both of them. "It's not like I want him to be at home anyway. He's a total asshole."

"Abby, don't talk about your father like that." Margo made a face, secretly agreeing with her daughter about her assessment of David.

"Abigail," Abby reminded her with a snarl.

"Sorry, Abigail," Margo forced a smile.

The kids started their stories to catch her up on their lives. Margo found it interesting; they had both changed so much on the outside, but were both very similar on the inside.

Thomas had always been the sweet, sensitive one, the peacekeeper, and he still was. Trying to include Margo in the little things that she had missed for so long, the boy was what Margo had always thought was the best of both her and David. She knew David far better now though and wondered where he got this almost bottomless well of tenderness and compassion.

Abigail was sullen and sarcastic, a typical teenage girl, but she had always been intense. She was the brilliant one, the precocious one who had been light-years ahead of her peers, but she had also never been the one who wanted to be held or sit in Margo's lap. Fiercely independent, Margo had always been amazed at what Abby could do without her, and now, she could see that her daughter needed her even less, but she hurt nonetheless.

"Do you have a real place to live now?" Abby asked her.

"Yes, I do," Margo told them about her new job and new apartment, keeping Sal out of the conversation. She kept things light.

"So when do we get to see where you live?" Thomas wanted to know.

"Would you like to come over?" she asked him, their fingers were entwined on the table, and Margo looked over at her daughter as she regarded them both with disdain.

"Yeah, if Abigail comes," he looked over at his sister with a hopeful expression.

"Whatever. We'll see," Abby curled her lip, but Margo couldn't help but notice that there was a bit of curiosity in her eyes.

They talked about having a sleepover in the not-too-distant future on their way back to David's house. Margo was holding Thomas's hand, and when they were less than a block away, she felt Abby grab her arm.

"Mom, something is up with Dad," she said. All traces of her previous snide attitude were suddenly gone and she noticed that her daughter stared toward their house with a worried expression.

"What's going on with your dad?" Margo had her own theories, but the kids had lived with him for the last seven years. It wouldn't hurt to hear their side of the story.

"I don't know, he's been acting strange for a while." Abby shook her head as if she wasn't sure how much to tell Margo, "And I hear him talking on the phone late at night, sometimes yelling."

"Well, maybe he's fighting with his girlfriend." Margo had wondered why he hadn't remarried long ago. He was still attractive; there had never been a shortage of women who were interested in him, even though he had seemed oblivious to it most of the time.

"Please," Abby snorted, "like he'd ever get a girlfriend." She laughed, and Margo couldn't help but chuckle.

Her daughter was right; David probably would still be waiting to have sex with her if she hadn't taken him by the hand that night.

The three of them hugged, and Margo felt relief, happiness, and sadness all at once. It had been so long since she'd felt that she even had a family. Sal had been right. Seeing her kids weren't just important for her state of mind; it was a physical necessity.

Margo was lost in thought on her way home. David's behavior from the day of her arrest hadn't made sense, and Margo had given him the upper hand for too long. He'd fooled the kids into believing that he'd been visiting her three days a week for six years. But that was a complete lie. So what exactly had he really been up to during that time?

At first she had suspected he had a girlfriend. She could almost respect him for lying to the kids if that was the case.

No, Abby was right, as Margo reviewed the details over in her mind. David wouldn't be sneaking off to some lover's hideaway. There would be no reason to keep a girlfriend a secret at this point. It was something else, and she was going to catch him in the act.

In the morning, the first order of business she handled was calling Sal. It was out of character for her to call him.

She always waited for him to call her, but she had some questions for her employer that couldn't wait.

"Good morning, Cookie, how was your Sunday?" If he was surprised to hear from her, she couldn't tell.

Margo knew he'd be available to take her call. He was an early riser and put in long hours. It took a lot of time to run an underground empire.

"Good, Sal, how was yours?"

Sunday was the day of the week that he was off-limits to her and the thought of him and his wife smiling at each other from opposite ends of the table, surrounded by their offspring, was an image Margo tried not to think about too often.

"Good, Cookie, always nice to spend time with the family." He was waiting for her to get to the point.

"I was wondering if I could take a few hours this afternoon for personal reasons."

Margo knew David was a creature of habit. For six years he had lied about what he was doing on Mondays. She was going to assume he hadn't changed his routine and was still up to whatever the hell it was he was up to.

"Of course, Cookie, do what you have to do. Got a hot date?" he asked.

She wondered if he were teasing. "Sal, wouldn't you know if I had a hot date?" She kept her voice playful, but she had to assume the man was always several moves ahead of her.

"I don't spy on you, Cookie," he cleared his throat.

Margo wondered if he called it something else.

"Can I ask you another question?" She closed her eyes and saw the newspaper headline. If she'd ever pushed the boundaries before with Sal, this was going to be above and beyond. "What happened to Scott Bollin?"

"Who?"

Now he really was lying. Margo knew that Sal had a memory like an elephant. He remembered everyone's name, exactly what they were supposed to do, and where they were supposed to be.

"Scott Bollin, the boy who came to see me after he had been arrested. Talked about making a deal," she was giving him the details, playing along. "You told me not to worry about him calling me back. Well, he's dead. I saw the article in the paper. The cause of death is under investigation."

Sal was silent for a long time, and she knew she had crossed a line.

"Sal?" she asked, waiting for him to say something.

"I'll see you in a bit, Cookie," he told her and hung up on her.

Margo realized that once again, Sal must know where she was without any help from her. She looked across the coffee shop and scanned the faces, wondering which one of them was watching her.

CHAPTER 16

In less than thirty minutes, her lover was sitting across from her. Margo watched as his gaze crept down the front of her blouse.

"Gorgeous tits, Cookie," he whispered before focusing his attention back to her face. "Now, what was this you were talking about on the phone?"

She kept her voice low as she asked once more, "Scott Bollin, he's dead."

Sal sat back in his chair. "It's sad when someone dies so young." He didn't look sad though. "Their whole life ahead of them." His arms were bent and his hands tucked behind his head.

"Exactly." Margo bit her lip. Sal exuded strength, power, danger, confidence, and an animal magnetism that made her want him in ways she couldn't rationalize. Jesus, how could she be so turned on at this moment?

"Does his death have anything to do with me telling you he was talking about taking a deal?" There, she had done it. She had put the question out there.

"You know what the most important thing in the world is, Cookie?" He looked Margo in the eye. "Loyalty. That's it. More important than brains, money, luck—hell, it's even more important than love. Without loyalty, nothing else you have in the world fucking matters. It all goes to shit if you don't have loyalty."

Margo let the words sink in, and her stomach tightened as she processed them. Scott had spent a weekend in jail being sexually violated and had threatened to do whatever was necessary to protect himself against that from ever happening again. Sal took swift vengeance against disloyalty.

"Okay," she nodded and took a deep breath. "I hear what you're saying. But what happened to protecting the people who work for you?"

"Cookie," he leaned in placing his hand over hers. Her heart thudded at his touch, and her body coursed with delight. "You know that I would protect you, don't you?"

She bit her lip. "I know, Sal, but . . . well, I feel guilty."

"You've got nothing to feel guilty about, Cookie." Real affection burned in his eyes for her, and she felt herself melting under his gaze.

"If you have a rat in your kitchen, it's your job to call me. It's my job to come over and get rid of the rat so you're safe in your own home." Sal raised his eyebrows. "Doing the right thing isn't always easy, but you were just doing your job. And I gotta do my job."

Margo couldn't help but smirk a little. The rat reference was clever, and its parallel meaning had not been lost on her.

"Your right, Sal. I'm sorry."

Sal held her gaze. "Don't be sorry, Cookie. Just promise me that no matter what you read or what hear about me, you'll remember that I do protect the people that I care about."

"I know," she agreed.

"Promise me," Sal insisted.

"I promise." In that moment Margo said it and meant it.

There had already been a few instances where she had seen his muscle move mountains, and she knew that for as many sins that he committed, he made as many miracles occur as well.

Whatever he might do, whatever he might be, he had plucked her out of a monotonous existence and had given her opportunity, security, fun, and hope. Margo could have loved him just for that. As it was, she knew that there were other feelings in that mix.

Sal sat back in his chair, adjusted his cuff links, and winked at her.

Damn he was smooth. Margo couldn't help but smile. She wished he would take her back to her apartment and fuck her senseless. She needed to get out of her head for a little while and being in bed with Sal worked every time.

"So, Cookie, what's on the schedule for today?" Sal asked making safe conversation.

"I'm going to find out what David is up to today," she blurted out.

Sal raised his eyebrows. "You call me if you need anything." Margo knew he was a busy man, and while she didn't know what he filled his days with, nor did she want to, she also knew that if she needed him, he wouldn't let her down.

She was still debating Sal to herself in her head when she found herself parked across the street from David's house. Margo had rented a car for the occasion, and she tried to remember the last time that she had driven. In the city, public transportation was the easiest way to get around, and she had gotten used to it since she had gotten out of prison.

It hadn't crossed her mind to buy a car. Thanks to Sal, she could afford to purchase and maintain a vehicle, but it was an expense she preferred not to have. After being in prison, and then living on next to nothing she had a new perspective on what she needed and what was really important in life. Her current income was more than enough to keep her comfortable when she compared it to her expenses, and she had a healthy nest egg saved up.

Margo had rented the car because she had no idea where David was going and figured it would be easier to tail him in a car rather than a cab.

She had arrived about thirty minutes before she figured he would be leaving to go wherever it was that he had religiously gone to for the last seven years on Monday. David was a stickler for being on time, and she kept a close eye on the door as she waited.

There he was. Her ex had on a coat with the collar turned up and a hat. The brim down low, covering his forehead, and he would have been easy enough to miss, but she recognized the coat that she had bought him ten years ago and watched as he hailed a cab.

Margo pulled into traffic and followed the cab, keeping a safe distance but staying close enough to navigate the lights and turns. They ended up on Maple Street heading east. She wasn't familiar with the neighborhood, but she knew it was a mix of new, up-and-coming art galleries and theaters and run-down, gang-controlled blocks of duplexes. She watched as the cab stopped in front of what looked like a theater. After he got out of the cab, David seemed to check over both shoulders before entering. Whatever he was doing, if this was his Monday routine, he was still paranoid after all this time. Margo took it as a bad sign.

She parked, turned the car off, and tapped her nails on the steering wheel. The name of the theater was "Trademark." Margo had never heard of it, but that meant nothing. She was sadly out of touch with what was cool and always had been. David was always much more trendy than she had been. She had envisioned him meeting someone outside of his location, wherever it was, that would have given her some kind of clue as to what it was that her ex-husband found so much more interesting than raising their children. As it was, she wasn't about to sit outside a theater for however long it would be.

Margo had no choice. She was going inside. It seemed odd that he would spend this much time at a theater, but she had to admit to herself that it had been a long time since she'd really known her husband.

Once she was inside, she was met by a handsome man wearing only skintight leather pants and no shirt, "Hey, sweetie, are you lost?" he asked her, curiosity in his eyes.

"I'm not sure." Margo looked around and took in the scenery. There were posters all over the dark walls, men in various states of undress, in each other's arms, men kissing; the last one she noticed directly behind the young man was a man performing fellatio on his knees. "This *is* a theater, right?" She watched as he smiled.

"Yes, sweetie, we are," he chuckled. "We show movies too."

"And what else?" She felt like she should whisper. She definitely didn't belong here.

"Sweetie, are you looking for someone?"

Margo assumed that this wasn't the first time that the doorman had dealt with a woman snooping around.

"I am." Her hands were clammy, and her mind was starting to kick into overdrive. "What really goes on here?"

The concern on his face was genuine. "Sweetie, this is a sex club. Men come here to hook up." He was trying to break it to her gently. "With other men," he added as if it was necessary.

"No women, I guess." She felt stupid even asking, but it was her last attempt to excuse David's behavior.

He sighed and his eyes softened. "Well, every once in a while a woman comes in, looking for her man. I'm guessing that's what you're doing?"

"He's not my man anymore." She shook her head. It was all coming together. It made so much sense. Why hadn't she realized this years ago?

"Sweetie, if he comes here, he never was." The bare-chested young man looked genuinely sorry as if he too understood what pricks men could be.

"I can't believe him." She had to get out of here. Her kids were home alone while David came here to hook up with miscellaneous strangers.

"Sweetie, believe me, I know what you're going through." The young man rolled his eyes. "I was just with this guy, he's a regular," he added, and she assumed that fraternizing with the clients was frowned upon, "so I should have known. Anyway, we've been on and off for almost a year, and then suddenly he dumps me. Find out he's got a wife and kids at home."

"That sucks," she mumbled politely.

She tried to console herself; she hadn't been with David for years, so it wasn't as if she was sharing him with all the other men that he would come into contact with in a place like this.

Or had she been? Would she have known?

"Better luck next time," she nodded and smiled at the gorgeous doorman.

"You too, sweetie," he winked at her as she turned to go.

Margo was filled with rage and disgust when she got back in the car. How could she have been so blind? Of course David was gay; it explained his lack of interest in her, why he had never initiated sex. It had always been her pursuing him. The kids were no accident; she had planned and worked on getting pregnant. Once she had stopped being the aggressor, he seemed perfectly content to bypass any romance at all. Hell, he was probably relieved.

She started thinking about the first time again. He hadn't been able to finish when they had made love, and it hadn't been until Margo had gone down on him that he was finally able to let go. Had he closed his eyes and thought of a male lover while she sucked his dick? The longer she thought about it, the more times she remembered that the performance had been repeated. Except for when they were trying to get pregnant, David had only achieved an orgasm with her mouth.

Margo suddenly felt sick to her stomach. She opened the car door quickly, leaned out, and threw up. She was shaking from head to toe and gulping down air. It had all been a lie. Why didn't he tell her from the very beginning? The bastard. She could have easily been his friend if he had just had the courage to tell her that he preferred men. Now, after all this time, two children later and he was sneaking around to live his lie. She hated him. She hated him more than she could imagine hating anyone.

She was physically ill and wasn't sure she could drive. Who could she turn to at a moment like this? Sal. It was frightening how quickly she had come to rely on him. With no other options, she called him.

"Hey, Cookie, what happened?" Her lover's deep voice was in her ear, and it was an immediate comfort.

"I found out where he goes, what he does." Margo sounded as dismal as she felt. "Have you ever heard of the Trademark?" she asked Sal.

He sighed. "So he's gay."

"How did you know?" Was everyone in on the secret but her? She wondered how many other people besides the men that he met for trysts here knew about David's status. Had they all been snickering behind her back the whole time?

"Cookie, I own the theater."

Of course he fucking did. It was seedy and dark and illicit dealings went on there, so it only made perfect sense that Sal would be involved.

"It used to be a brothel back when I bought the place. Tried to turn it around, make it a regular bar but the gays kept coming back. Guy who runs the place is nice enough, and hey, their money is green."

"Well, that's where David has been coming." Margo heard the defeat in her voice as she said the words out loud. "For years now, he lied to my kids that he was visiting me in prison, when in reality, he was sneaking around getting his rocks off at a gay sex club."

She wasn't sure if she was going to throw up again. She opened the car door, the phone pressed to her ear as she took low, slow gulps of air.

"Cookie, where exactly are you?" For once Sal didn't know.

"I'm across the street from the theater. I rented a car," her pulse was throbbing so hard in her throat that she wondered if she might pass out.

"Stay there, I'm coming to get you," he told her.

Thirty minutes later Sal appeared, just like he said. He opened the car door slowly and took her by the hand, the other arm around her waist; he walked her to the Town car and once inside, held her close as she broke down.

"It's going to be all right, Cookie," he whispered into her hair as she sobbed hysterically. His shirt was wet from her eyes and runny nose before she was finally able to stop. When she peeled her face back, she noticed the smeared marks that her mascara and eye shadow had left behind.

"I'm sorry, you're a mess. I got make-up on your shirt." She was embarrassed by her behavior, but she was unable to compose herself as more tears followed. Sal grabbed her and held her tight.

"Cookie, I don't give two shits about my shirt. What I care about is you. Cry as much as you need. Let it out, just let it all out." He held her and rocked her back and forth.

The most comforting man she'd ever met was also the scariest. That conflict was something to be settled another day. The fact that he was married and she wished he wasn't was, also a problem that she would have to face later. Right now, she needed this, to be wrapped up in the safety of his arms, her head on his chest. There was nowhere else she wanted to be.

CHAPTER 17

At Sal's insistence Margo had reluctantly agreed to meet Marcus and his lawyer in court at 8:45 a.m. She checked her phone and saw that it was now 8:50. The hall was packed with people. She scanned the crowd until she spotted Marcus. She walked over and took a seat next to him.

"Have you seen your attorney?" she asked him.

Marcus looked good; he was in a tailored suit, his blond hair slicked back, and his face was relaxed, as though he didn't have a care in the world. He looked as if he could be the expensive lawyer rather than the client.

"No, I'm starting to worry," he grimaced but when he turned to look at her, she saw a flash of dimples when he smiled.

Margo almost sighed. Not only was he handsome, well-mannered, and far classier than the typical client, he also had cute dimples.

"So what exactly do you do for Sal?" She almost whispered the man's name as she glanced at the people loitering nearby.

"What exactly do *you* do for him?" he shot back playfully.

He was smart. Margo realized he really didn't know her either.

"I'm sure you know I used to be an attorney." She felt sad for a moment, looking around at the people in the crowded hallway. She could pick them out easily . . . the attorneys, they were bent down, thumbing through stacks of papers, talking to clients in low voices, patting a back here, shaking a hand there.

Working for Sal had given her the opportunity to feel as if she was useful again, as if she was using her brain, but she couldn't deny the fact that she was working for a criminal enterprise, and sometimes it was difficult to justify. She tried not to think about it too much.

Marcus nodded. "Here comes Resler."

The lawyer rushed over to his client. "I'm sorry, so sorry. Got delayed in traffic." He didn't even acknowledge Margo.

Resler herded Marcus into the courtroom, and Margo followed behind. "Take a seat. I've got to check on something." Resler made a beeline toward the bailiff.

Margo remembered Resler as being a so-so attorney. He was arrogant and operated by the seat of his pants. Margo wondered why he was representing Marcus. Sal could afford better.

Marcus leaned over and whispered in Margo's ear. "What are you now?"

"What am I now?" Margo replied, confused by the question.

"Yeah, you said you used to be an attorney. What are you now?" He flashed a flirtatious smile.

“I asked you first,” she replied. Two could play this game.

“You should know what I do.”

What an ego on this guy, Margo marveled. She had meet with him for a whopping forty-five minutes, and she should know his life story?

“Oh yeah, why is that?” Margo played along.

Marcus paused with a dramatic flair. “I’m your newly elected local state senator, and as a responsible taxpaying, voting citizen, you should know that.”

Margo was momentarily speechless. Sal had his hands in politics.

She quickly recovered from her initial shock and jabbed back, “Just so we’re on the same page, Senator, one, how responsible I am depends on who you talk to; two, I’m a convicted felon, so I’m not allowed to vote; and three, you assume I pay taxes.”

Marcus threw his head back and laughed. “You’re all right, Margo, I like you.”

“All rise.” The bailiff had entered the room and the hundreds of conversations that had been in progress paused as the officer continued. “The Honorable Judge Mahoney presiding. Please take your seats and wait for the judge to call your case.” The bailiff paused at the center of the room while two hundred people sat almost simultaneously.

Conversations resumed and Marcus leaned over. "Just so you know, I won't hold your inability to vote against you."

It was Margo's turn to laugh out loud.

The judge used his gavel to get everyone's attention. "First preliminary hearing is U.S. Bank versus Mazzillo. Are the attorneys here?" The judge looked over his glasses.

"Here, Judge," Resler called out as he furiously scribbled something before handing it to the bailiff.

The plaintiff's attorneys were present and chomping at the bit.

"Are the parties ready to continue?" the judge asked. Margo looked up as Marcus rose from the seat next to her and joined Resler at the defendant's table.

Margo sank back in her chair and studied Marcus. He was confident, smart, and handsome. Sal was a genius. She'd bet Marcus's political climb had been well planned for a very long time. With Sal's connections and money behind Marcus, the plan had been successful.

There was a team of lawyers at the plaintiff's table, and they seemed to be conferring with each other, foreheads almost touching as they flipped through papers. It was a power play that big companies pulled trying to intimidate the defendant into a plea bargain to avoid the cost of a lengthy trial.

"We're ready, Your Honor," the lead lawyer for the group called from the table.

The charges against Marcus were breach of contract revolving around failure to comply with access laws on a commercial property Marcus's company owned.

The team across from Resler started off strong presenting damaging facts to the court.

Margo had told Marcus he had nothing to worry about after they had met at the coffee shop. But it was clear to Margo where things were headed. Resler was unprepared and obviously hadn't looked at Margo's crib notes that Lou had sent him.

Margo sighed as she feared Marcus's well-greased political career was in jeopardy.

She reached into her briefcase and quickly flipped through her notebook. She found her notes on Marcus's case and copied the case number she had written down. This was the difference between the unknown and a cleared name. She, of all people, understood that distinction and wished that she had an ally working for her when she had been sitting in Marcus's chair.

Margo continued to write. She figured she'd better explain anything that wasn't obvious since she had no confidence in Resler and no idea how stupid he may be.

"Your Honor, we'd like your permission to call our first witness to the stand," the lawyer for the other side called out.

Margo felt a surge of adrenaline, and she wrote faster. This case should have never gotten this far.

Marcus was family. Not only was he family, but he had been groomed for big things. A guilty outcome was not an option for the man, not this one.

She tore the piece of paper from the notebook and made her way to the front until she was standing directly behind Resler. She tapped him on the shoulder. He turned around, and she offered him the folded paper. The arrogant prick held up a plump hand and waved her away, dismissing her like a small child.

Marcus leaned over and whispered something to him.

Resler turned around again. Margo leaned forward and hissed, "Use it," as she handed him her notes.

Resler unfolded the paper and began to read.

Margo looked over at the team of attorneys. They were cocky, smirks all around the table. They thought they had a slam dunk and were mentally already celebrating.

Margo returned to her seat. All she could do now was watch it play out.

The judge looked over and asked, "Is there a problem, Mr. Resler?"

"No, Judge." He never looked up. "But I've just been presented with some new information. If the court could indulge me and just give me a moment."

There was a rumble in the courtroom, and Margo looked around. The courtroom was full. She realized the media was sprinkled in with the onlookers. They were here to report on Marcus's case. She hadn't realized how much was riding on this case until right now.

Resler stood and addressed the court. "Your Honor, I'd like to move to dismiss."

"Based on what, Mr. Resler?" The judge looked annoyed.

"Sidebar, Your Honor?" Resler was all smiles and had a new found confidence that he lacked just moments ago. He was still holding the paper that Margo had given him.

Margo clenched her fists in her lap. She was nervous. Decisions like this could either make or break a career.

Resler and the team of lawyers from the other side walked to the front when the judge said, "Approach the bench."

The judge turned off the microphone that was attached to his podium. The whispers grew louder, and the expressions of the other attorneys quickly dissolved, smug melted away, and anger and dismay were reflected on their faces.

The judge waved them all back to their places, and once the team had finished shrugging at one another, the judge asked, "Mr. Cartwright, do you have any new evidence to present at this time?"

The man who had been so confident just moments ago now appeared as though the wind had been knocked out of him. He sat when he addressed the judge. "No, Your Honor, not at this time."

Judge Mahoney didn't look too pleased either, but there was no other choice. "Then I am dismissing all charges, and Mr. Mazzillo," he glared at Marcus for a moment, "you are free to go."

The courtroom sprang to life. It was as if everything had been put on pause, and now, someone hit the play button. Margo watched as Marcus held his hand out to Resler who shook it heartily at first, and then grabbed Marcus by both shoulders and hugged him. The two were all smiles as they turned to walk out of the courtroom.

Marcus stopped and looked at Margo, waving her over with a dimpled smile. "Come on, we need to celebrate," he yelled to her over the chatter.

The crowd jostled the three of them, and when Margo heard reporters start to blurt questions to Marcus, she ducked into the shadows and moved away from the commotion. She prayed that no one recognized her. Even though her case had been a long time ago, she didn't want to risk her tainted past interfering with Marcus's bright future.

She watched him artfully answer questions and dodge bullets. She realized he was a natural politician. He was cool under pressure and answered questions without really giving answers. He worked the crowd, flirting with the women and referencing sports terms with the men. Margo shook her head in wonderment; people probably either loved him or hated him. She thought in that way, he was probably very similar to Sal himself.

Marcus had finally broken free from the circus around him and waved her to him. He put his arm around the back of her shoulders. "You should be taking all the credit for this." He flashed her the dimples once more, and Margo found herself blushing.

"Oh God, no," she shook her head. "You don't want my face or name associated with yours."

"Hey, I like your face," he elbowed her. "Besides, if you weren't here, Resler wouldn't have pulled this off on his own."

Margo leaned into him and whispered, "Well, now you know, that's what I do."

"I can see why my uncle respects you so much." Marcus gave her a sideways glance. "He talks about you, you know."

"Really?" Margo did her best to sound casual, but this information made her morning. She didn't know why it was so important to her that Sal thought about her. Maybe it was really getting to be too emotional on her end; there was no good outcome for her when she thought about it.

"Well, yeah, that you work for him, how smart you are." Marcus paused, he sounded a little sheepish when he added, "How much he likes you."

"We work well together." Margo wasn't going to reveal too much. And her response wasn't a lie, it just wasn't the whole truth. There was much more to it, but it was hardly appropriate to discuss with his nephew.

"He's always had a girlfriend, you know, someone on the side he spends time with." They walked down the courthouse steps in unison. "I think it's an old-school Sicilian thing."

"Having a wife and a mistress?" Dammit! She had put it out there, what she really was to Sal. Margo instantly regretted it.

"Yeah, you know, the wife is for marriage; family is very important." Marcus was part of the family, he would know.

"And the mistress?"

The other woman. The one that saw him on Saturday nights and fucked him until the wee hours just to watch him leave and go home to her.

"The mistress is for pleasure," Marcus shrugged. "But you, I think it's more than that."

They were on the sidewalk now and had stopped in front of a black Lincoln Town car. "Is this Sal's car?" she asked him.

"No, it's mine."

Like uncle, like nephew she supposed.

"Hop in; I'll give you a ride."

She remembered the first day when Sal had caught up with her on the street, on her way to the Laundromat. He had changed her world in an hour. For some reason, she felt like it was about to change again. It was like déjà vu to be in the backseat with Marcus. He had slid in beside her and sat close, too close for his own good considering that he knew the relationship that she had with his uncle.

Margo tried to move away. Was it paranoia that made her wonder where Sal or his spies were at this moment, or was it only logical? She assumed someone from his crew was in the courtroom and had relayed the outcome in real time. Of course, Sal would be watching the case closely. Marcus was not only a politician that Sal had in his pocket, he was family.

"Where are you going, Margo?" Marcus didn't seem concerned at all, and he seemed totally comfortable with the fact that their legs were pressed together as well.

"To the coffee shop on Sutter and Ninth." This would save her the trouble of hailing a cab, she told herself. It would have been silly to say no. She had to get to work, and Marcus had a car sitting there.

"So can I ask you something?" Marcus was probably used to women just melting under his gaze, his charm, and his looks would make him practically irresistible. Then there was his family name too. "What do you see in Sal?"

She laughed. "Are you kidding? Why am I going to talk about him with you?"

Not only was Sal her employer, but he was her confidant and lover. Marcus was a handsome boy with dimples.

Case closed.

"Come on, I'm curious." Marcus touched her hand, running the tips of his fingers down her skin, stirring every nerve along every inch as he did.

"Why him? I mean, I guess it's a power thing, right? Women like the fact that he can take care of them."

Margo hated that Sal took care of her. She had never before depended on a man in her life, and there was no denying it, she was in Sal's debt.

"There's the power thing. I was in a pretty bad place when he and I met."

Hate it or not, Sal's power had turned everything around for her. The comfort she found wrapped in his strong arms when everything overwhelmed her was soothing and intoxicating all at the same time.

"But it's not just that, he's sexy too." She smiled. The boy had dimples, but he was missing the raw, animal heat that his uncle exuded.

"Really? I'd never noticed." Marcus was teasing her.

She rolled her eyes and laughed. "Well I wouldn't think that you'd see it, but ask any woman. Sal's got sex appeal."

Marcus leaned in closer, and the dimples were almost touching her face. "So do you, Margo."

Just like his uncle, his eyes were moving down the front of her blouse that Margo suddenly felt was open far too low. Marcus's eyes lingered before he whispered, "You are so sexy."

His mouth was on hers. It started as an innocent, closed-mouth kiss, almost sweet, and Margo tried to pull back, but he was insistent. His tongue caressed her top lip in a slow, wet embrace. She shivered and found that her hands had reached out to touch the back of his head and pull him closer. His pulse was throbbing in his throat. She could feel it under her hand as her fingers moved along his neck.

Alarms were sounding off in her head to stop. This was Sal's nephew, and this was wrong. Marcus continued to explore her mouth with his tongue while a hand had found her ample breast and began to rub and tease.

She heard herself gasp with pleasure and knew things were out of control. It was all too much and happening too quickly. She couldn't pull herself away, and she feared if he made a move to have more of her she would be unable to say no, and all she would do was say yes over and over.

Her cell phone buzzed. Work beckoned, clients probably waiting for Miss Margo to fix things for them. Again, it pulsed next to her and thankfully snapped her back into reality.

She pulled away from Marcus, and he groaned. Their mouths parted, and she could see the desire in his eyes, the look that was unbuttoning her quickly and ravishing her totally. Once more the phone buzzed. She looked at the caller ID, whispering, "It's your uncle."

She knew that her eyes were expressing the terror she felt in her heart, but her voice emoted happiness. "Good morning, Sal."

"Hey, Cookie, I hear you made it to the courthouse this morning."

Margo wondered where her lover was. "I did."

"Yeah, well I also heard it was a good thing because you saved Resler's ass and the senator's neck."

Margo smiled. "It was pretty crazy, but it's all good now." It had been a long time since she'd been part of a swift victory in a courtroom, and it felt good.

"You know that Marcus is my nephew?" Sal asked her.

"I just learned that this morning." There was never a point in lying to Sal, but she knew that she would never volunteer what had just happened seconds ago with Marcus. "I also learned I should address him as Senator." She raised her eyebrows at Marcus, and he smiled.

"Yeah, he's got a lot to live up to. I've got high expectations for him." Sal sounded as if he was thinking of Marcus fondly at that moment.

"I've actually got some news for you this morning, Cookie." It was never just a social call; Sal was always thinking about business.

"Okay, do you want to discuss it now or wait?" She expected the news to be about a client, or maybe there was another Mazzillo family member dancing too close to the line.

"It involves some pictures, Cookie." He paused and let it sink in.

"Shit," she groaned. It had to be David. Whatever else it was that he was up to, Sal must have proof.

"Are you sure you're up for it?" he asked.

"No . . . yes . . . Shit, not really . . . but I need to see them," she mumbled. "I'll be at the coffee shop in about ten minutes."

"Which one, Cookie?"

"Grinders."

"I'll be waiting," Sal told her before hanging up.

Margo sighed and leaned her head back against the seat. She closed her eyes as she thought of all the possible scenarios that Sal's people had captured on film. He hadn't been her husband for a very long time, but that didn't make it any less humiliating.

CHAPTER 18

Sal didn't look surprised when Margo exited out of the back of his nephew's car. It registered with her for just a moment that Sal could, very easily, know everything that had just happened between her and Marcus on the ride over. She couldn't deny the thought sent a chill down her spine.

"Did my nephew thank you?" Sal greeted her with open arms that she gratefully ran into. Regardless of Marcus's good looks, his charm, his undeniable sex appeal, compared to Sal, he was just a boy.

Margo had her arm around Sal's solid bicep as she grinned at Marcus. "Yes, he did. He has very good manners, just like his uncle."

Sal opened his hands and looked very pleased. "What can I say? He's a good boy." Turning to Margo, he told her, "Get in the car, Cookie, I'll be back in a minute."

She watched from the backseat of the Town car as Sal approached Marcus, his hand clasping the young man by the shoulder and their foreheads almost touching as they spoke.

Margo couldn't help but wonder if Sal wouldn't sense the kiss and the heat they had just shared. The man was uncanny in his ability to ferret out the truth.

The two parted, and Sal returned to the car. They were silent as they watched Marcus drive off.

Sal reached for her hand and brought it to his lips. “Thank you, Cookie.”

Margo blushed. “For what?”

“That was a close call this morning. Thank you for being there and saving everybody’s ass.”

She reveled in the praise from her mentor and lover, but she played it cool.

“It’s what I do, what you pay me for.” She shrugged her shoulders. “But do us all a favor and stop using Resler. He’s a fucking idiot. And a sexiest pig,” she added as an afterthought.

“Yes, ma’am, consider it done.” Sal held her face and softly kissed her on the lips.

The kiss was tender but over quickly. It had no passion and held no promises, yet it made her tingle with anticipation. How could she have been so stupid and weak with Marcus?

Sal pulled an envelope from his jacket’s inner pocket. “Are you ready to see these, Cookie?” he asked her.

Margo shook her head. “No, but when would I be?”

She had been stewing about David and his secret other life since following him to the theater. She felt as though she’d played the fool for far too long.

She reached for the envelope, and Sal handed it to her. “You really didn’t know he was gay?” he sounded incredulous.

It was something she had been asking herself too. Analyzing every look, every word, she was mentally exhausted from replaying their entire marriage over and over again. "You know how they say the wife always knows?"

"Of course," Sal nodded and Margo remembered that he had a wife at home that he hid things from as well.

"Well, I swear to God, Sal, I'm the dumb wife that had no fucking clue." Some investigator she was.

As she pulled the pictures out and studied them one by one, the images were forever burned into her mind. David didn't have a problem getting it up for other men.

"Oh, Jesus." Margo was a mess the deeper she got into the pictures. Her heart seemed to race faster and faster with each successive image. David on his knees, David on his back, David in the middle of a tangle of bare, muscled flesh.

"How did you get these?" she whispered, her stomach starting to churn as she vividly saw exactly what her husband had enjoyed and preferred.

Sal's arm was around her shoulder. "I know a guy who knows a guy." It was his standard answer when he didn't want to give her one.

"There's more Cookie. Your ex has bigger problems than his sexual preferences."

"It gets worse than this?" she shook her head in disbelief, "Well, besides lying to me and his children all these years."

"David's in trouble financially." Sal's sources, so far, had always been extremely accurate. "He's in over his head, way over his head."

That didn't make sense. David had always been responsible with money. Margo had been the breadwinner in the marriage, but David made good money. It was one of the few things that comforted her in jail, knowing David could provide without her and that her kids would be all right.

"Is it drugs?" she wondered aloud. With all of the other lies, why not?

"I'm not sure where his money is going, but it's not to drugs or gambling. Whatever he is up to, he's paying in cash, and it's been going on for a while. He's going to be in the red in a matter of months. You do need to figure out what's going on. You owe it to your kids." She knew how important family was to Sal.

Margo stuffed the pictures back into the envelope and turned to look Sal in the eye.

"What should I do?" She bit her lip. David was in debt up to his eyeballs and leading a secret life. He was suddenly not the good parent that she had hoped for. The legal system would not be kind to her if she tried to get custody. In the eyes of the law, an ex-felon working under the table was still far worse than a broke, closeted homosexual.

"Talk to him, use the pictures to your advantage. It should be easy for you to find out what he's up to, Cookie."

Sal's strong hands were suddenly on her waist, sliding down her thighs over the skirt, just to push the hem up so that he could explore her underneath. His mind was already off David and on to her curves and fleshy inner thighs.

"You're so sexy, Cookie. I don't know how any man could live with you and be a homo."

Margo closed her eyes and pressed her head back in the seat as Sal's insistent fingers reached the top of her thigh-high stockings. She was wet, and his touch was the one thing that could make everything temporarily melt away into oblivion.

"Sal, God, you know you make me crazy." She gasped as he ran his finger along the edge of her panties.

He whispered in her ear, "I love how juicy you are for me." He pressed against her crevice as his fingers explored her. Sal had always had an uncanny knowledge of her body and the longer they were lovers, the more amazing it had become.

"You have to stop teasing me, Sal. If you can't finish what you start, it's not fair to get me worked up." Margo meant what she said, but she secretly hoped he'd abandon his self-control and fuck her right here in the backseat of the Town car.

Sal removed his hand from her skirt. "I wish I could take you somewhere, Cookie, but I'm already late for a meeting."

There it was, business before pleasure.

Margo sighed. It was clear where she ranked in his world. She hadn't accepted it yet; she wasn't sure that the mistress ever could.

His dark eyes were studying her face, and no matter how imperceptible her mood changes may be, Sal always seemed to know what she was thinking.

"You going to be okay, Cookie?" He touched her cheek affectionately.

She didn't really have a choice. "Yeah, I've just got to buck up and talk to David."

"No, I mean, you and me." Sal had never brought up the nature of their relationship. Their pillow talk was reserved for stories, and she seemed to have known from the beginning that she should never ask.

"Our situation bothers me a little." It actually bothered her a lot. Margo had grown up to believe in the sanctity of marriage and the fairy tale of happily ever after. She had never even considered cheating on David.

"I guess I'm just an old-fashioned girl." She almost laughed at herself, it sounded so cliché.

"Cookie, you *are* an old-fashioned girl, and it becomes you." Sal kissed her hand softly. "You're a good woman, the total package. If things were different . . ." he meant his whole world . . . if he hadn't been married forever, if he didn't have a shitload of kids and a whole conglomerate that depended on family, "I'd make you mine in a heartbeat."

She found it almost impossible to ask, but she had to. She needed to know, she needed to hear the answer.

"So what does that mean for me?" She had grown accustomed to their Saturday nights and the fantasies about their elusive happy ending coming to fruition, somehow, against the odds.

Sal was struggling to answer her. "Cookie, you're free to do what you have to do."

He couldn't claim her, and she saw the wistful expression on his face. "And when you meet some nice guy and want to settle down, I'll be happy for you. But," he pointed at her, "he better be fucking nice and treat you like a queen, like you deserve . . . not like this," he waved at the envelope, looking for the right word, "excuse of a man."

Margo felt like she had just physically been kicked in the stomach. A part of her wanted to cry, but she held back the tears. She had come to rely on her resilience, and she would continue to do so.

"Your plan sounds really nice, Sal, but I doubt it's going to happen. I'm a little too old to be waiting around for Prince Charming."

She got out of the car and walked inside the coffee shop. The pictures of David were tucked away inside her briefcase. Margo would take Sal's advice and use the pictures against him. David had been committed to his lie for so long she knew he would try to deny everything.

Margo watched Sal's Town car pull into traffic and drive away. She realized that she had just been given her freedom, and she wasn't sure what to do with it.

CHAPTER 19

She showed her mother the ring and watched her clasp her hands, as if in prayer, and then cross herself quickly before reaching out to touch Gia's face.

"He's going to be a good husband, you are a lucky girl." Her mother hadn't had that luxury. The death of her father and the mental and physical abuse by her second husband had taken its toll on her mother; she looked old, haggard, and broken. Giovanna had kept the secret that would have pushed her mother over the edge. She knew one more tragedy would have been too much.

There was no mention of love, and Giovanna was grateful that she wouldn't have to lie about it. They were strict Catholics, and she was pregnant and seventeen. Love had very little to do with it. Her mother had loved her father and look how that turned out. She had been far more practical with her next choice, and her step-father had proven to be a good provider, but that was the only decent thing about him. Giovanna loved her mother but hated her at the same time for being so weak and helpless. She took the stairs slowly and told herself that she would not make the same mistakes her mother had. She would have a say in her destiny and love and protect her children from bad things and bad people.

Giovanna wasn't expecting her step-father to be waiting for her behind the bedroom door, and when he pulled her by the wrist and dragged her across the floor, she almost let out the scream that had been waiting for so long to burst out of her. Every time he had given her the lascivious stare, his eyes roaming over her, long before she had the curves of a woman, she wanted to scream. But it wasn't to be. She would take it in silence until it was over.

"So, you're really marrying him? What would he want with a slut like you?" She smelled the liquor on his breath and felt the droplets of his saliva on her cheeks when he hissed at her. She had stopped being his good little girl long ago. Once he had finally succumbed, he blamed it all on her. She had seduced him into taking her virginity, and she instantly became a whore. Yet, that hadn't kept him away. Indeed, he seemed more determined than ever to prove that he had been right all along.

Giovanna tried not to look at him. She could hide her disgust more easily if she averted her eyes. "I'm pregnant, and he wants to do the right thing." His grip on her wrist loosened; he was calculating.

"But it's not his." His smile was evil, and he was drunk enough that she knew that he'd get rough with her if she wasn't complacent. "You really are a slut." He yanked her dress up to her hips. "Wait until he finds out and discards you like the trash you are. Don't you dare think you can come back here. I'm not about to feed another mouth." He ran his greasy fingers up and down her body. He meandered up past her panties and began to rub her belly softly. "You should get rid of it."

"Stop it." She pushed his hand off her for the first time. Giovanna had never found the strength before, but now she was leaving. What else could he do in the two weeks that were left? She felt like a prisoner, marking off days on the wall of her cell. She wouldn't hear even the suggestion of an abortion. Not that she hadn't thought of it as well, but it was a sin that she couldn't have on her conscience. And the timing had accidently worked out in her favor.

"I'm having it." She was shaking from head to toe. God would forgive her for the rest of it.

"Does your mother know?" He was done with her belly and now his hands were pushing into her underwear. She didn't answer, and he gripped her chin tightly, his sour breath washing over her. "Does she know?"

She'd never pushed him this far and she wondered if he would hurt her. As if he could, after everything else he'd done—destroyed her innocence, threatened her, treated her like a common whore, but would he hit her or did he only save that for her mother and brothers? Her hands instinctively moved around her stomach. "She knows, but she thinks it's his."

"Got them all fooled, don't you?" He was satisfied and almost smiled as he turned her around quickly and pushed her forward so that her bare cheeks were exposed. She had discovered that she could shut almost all of it out; her participation meant nothing and she could close her eyes and tune out his grunts and sound of his weight shifting, the floor squeaking as he thrust in and out of her. Giovanna mentally removed herself from the bedroom and was a million miles away, plotting and planning; the escape from her step-father was just the beginning.

She had gone to her faraway place when her fiancé had bedded her as well. Men, she had only known two of them but so far, they all seemed to be the same. He was younger, handsome, and confident. He had been gentle, and it had never been a question of force, not like it had been with the man inside her right now. None of it would have mattered, though. The young man was going to pay for what he'd done as well.

He'd kissed her hand after sliding the ring on her finger and said something about how the two of them would learn to love each other and grow old together. It was like the old country; sometimes marriage was what was best. She had looked away, and the smile came involuntarily.

"Are you happy?" he asked as he slipped his arm around her shoulder.

How could he be so stupid? Or so blind? It didn't really matter, it was better this way. Let him believe what he wanted to, that she was just some dumb, scared girl that had gotten herself knocked up. She played the part perfectly and let him believe he was her knight in shining armor. Giovanna knew her revenge would take years of planning, scheming, and waiting. The waiting would be the hardest part, but she was willing to go the distance.

"Yes, I couldn't be happier," she murmured before letting him kiss her.

CHAPTER 20

It had been a week since her last conversation with David. Margo's anger hadn't subsided, and she was still pissed as she waited for her ex-husband at a coffee shop. What had been love, or at least what she had *thought* was love, had turned into hate soon after she had gone to prison, and then had dulled over the years. The hate was back now, and it seemed to pulse with a life of its own.

She remembered clearly the day that David had come to visit her in prison. Margo had been shocked when the beefy female guard had called her name, "Harris, you have a visitor." Margo had been more suspicious than elated at the announcement. It had only been a few months, but she was already used to the idea that David had cut her out. No visits, no phone calls, no letters, and her children seemed to be lost to her regardless of the pages and pages she sent to them weekly.

She sat on her side of the bench and stared at him through the glass, picking up the receiver when he picked up his. "You look good," he told her, sounding surprised.

Margo had a million questions, but all she really wanted to know was why the children had never been here to see her. "How are the kids?"

David nodded. "They're as good as can be expected." He looked around and took it all in. "They are afraid to come see you." The thought of frightening Abby and Thomas on top of all the other damage that she had already done was another stab in her heart.

Her chin trembled with the tears that she wanted to let fall. "Please tell them it's fine, nothing will happen here. Maybe if they come once, they'll see that it's not so bad. I need to see them, David." Margo was on the verge of begging him.

"Well, that's something I need to talk to you about." He had an agenda. He held up some papers in his right hand, gesturing to the guard. Once the guard set them down in front of Margo, she knew why David was here.

"You're divorcing me?" she sputtered. So much for "till death do you part." He couldn't even wait to see if her appeal was granted.

"It's the best thing for everyone." He spoke in a calm voice, but Margo could see his eyes shimmering with excitement, and she understood that this had been what he'd wanted since the day of her arrest.

"The kids need to get on with their lives, get back to normal, Margo. So do I. I would think that you'd want that for us." He didn't even hesitate to use her love for them against her.

"Fuck you, David," she hissed. "And what about me? When do I get back to normal?"

"That's not my problem." She had never seen him look at her with such cold eyes.

What had happened to the shy, tender-hearted boy that she had met? The sweet husband who doted on her when she came home from a long day?

There could only be one explanation. "Is there someone else?"

The hair on the back of her neck stood at attention as she watched it unfold in her mind's eye. While she was rotting away in a cell, day after day, her husband had a replacement woman in her house, with her children.

"Don't be ridiculous, Margo," David scoffed, "This is the best thing for all of us. Think of the kids. Their friends know about you being here." He rolled his eyes as if to say that Margo had clearly asked for this. "Abby comes home from school crying and isn't sleeping well at night. They need to be able to move on."

Under the guise of being a good parent, David had successfully cut her out of their lives.

She had signed; she hadn't even read through it all. David had custody of her children, and she had been promised liberal visitation once she was out and back on her feet, but by then, it was too late. The kids had been turned against her, and she knew who to blame for that.

Margo looked at her phone. He was over twenty minutes late, and she clicked her nails on the table. If only everyone adhered to Sal's timeliness.

It was fine. She had all the time in the world, and she had to admit that she was looking forward to seeing the expression on his face when she dropped her bomb.

She spotted David when he came in the front door and immediately felt the squeeze in her chest when he smiled and waved at her. The hypocrite, putting on a friendly face now after he had done so much to hurt her.

"Margo, you look great." He raised his eyebrows at her as he sat in the booth across from her. "How's the waitressing job?"

Smug prick. She could have killed him with her eyes. Of course, his world hadn't changed at all since she'd gone away. If anything, it had just gotten easier.

"I don't work there anymore."

"Oh, where are you working?" If David thought that she was going to play along with polite conversation, he had another thing coming.

"I didn't ask you to come here to talk about me." She tapped the envelope with one manicured nail. "I came to talk about these."

"And what are those?" He was intrigued.

"This is a game changer, David." She was going to play this close to the vest. Sal had taught her so much over the last few months.

"I have some very revealing photographs of you." Margo saw the panic slowly come over his face. He tried to hide it, but she knew him well enough to know that inside, David's heart was racing.

"I can't imagine what you're talking about." He cleared his throat as if he was dismissing her entirely. "Let's not forget, dear, that you're fresh out of prison, so I'm not sure what you think you know, but you have no credibility." David was going to stick with his act until the very end.

"I don't know, David." She bit her lip to hold back a wicked smile. "I think once people know how you spend your afternoons that you may find that *you* have no credibility."

She watched his hands tremble. He was less cocky when he asked, "What are you talking about, Margo?"

She had waited long enough and opened Sal's envelope. She pulled a photo out that was clearly her ex-husband, nude, with a larger man behind him.

"I'm talking about *that*," she pointed to his face in the photo. David was clearly lost in ecstasy.

"Or this one." She took out the next picture, David in between two men, on his knees and his mouth open.

"I've got a lot more where that came from."

David slouched over the table and covered his face with his hands. "Jesus, what have you done?"

Margo's temper flared. "What have *I* done? What have *you* done, David? Are you paying these men for sex, is that it?"

He wouldn't look at her and just shook his head. He was on the verge of tears. She could hear him sniffle and wondered what kind of person she had turned into, enjoying herself watching his pain.

"Why all the debt then, who do you owe money to?"

Sal had given her David's financial information he had dug up. She had sifted through his accounts, and Sal was right. At the rate David was going through money, he only had a few months left before he lost everything.

"It's Eric," he exhaled and laid his hands on the table, quiet and resigned. He would confess everything now. "I met him at the club. It's supposed to be discreet, you know, no cameras or phones," but apparently not everyone follows the rules. "He's probably in a lot of those pictures, but he knows that I'm not out."

David looked around to make sure no one else was listening, "He's blackmailing me and has been for a while. If I don't pay him he's going to out me with pictures of his own," her ex-husband's voice cracked.

She could have felt sorry for him if he hadn't broken her heart for this secret. "Jesus, David, just come out. What difference does it make?" She would have had mercy for him if he would have just told her long ago.

"Are you kidding?" he could barely breathe, and Margo saw the large vein in his forehead throbbing. "I can't come out. I'll be ruined, I'll be a leper. My career, my clients, my parents . . ."

The last one was especially painful. Margo knew that his parents would disown him once they knew, and she imagined that they were a big part of why he had shut the closet door long ago.

"I'm not ready to turn my life upside down for that," he whispered.

"I understand." Margo's voice was icy. "I totally understand about having your world turned upside down, David. But I don't see how you have any other choice though. You can't afford to keep paying this troll to keep his mouth shut, and here's a news flash: When you're outta money, he's going to out you anyway."

Tears silently spilled down David's cheeks. "I know you are probably enjoying yourself," he wiped his face, "and I deserve it, I guess, but please, just butt out. I'll handle this."

She had him right where she wanted him. "I told you this was a game changer, David, and I meant it."

Her ex seemed to be used to blackmail at this point and quietly asked, "What do you want, Margo?"

"First of all, I want the liberal visitation rights that I was promised with my children with no interference from you. God knows you will find something to do with your time." She couldn't help but throw the dagger at him.

"Done," he murmured. "Whenever you want, I really didn't intend to keep them from you, it's just been," he paused, the self-righteous parent act was not going to work with Margo any longer and he knew it, "hard on them."

"Because of *you*, David," she snarled. "You chose to make things hard for all us. Don't forget that."

David was crumbling right before her eyes, and she didn't care. She continued, "Second, you can't afford to keep paying this asshole. You, obviously, don't have the balls to bring this bullshit to an end, so I'm going to handle it for you. I'm going to meet with this jackass and the payments are going to stop. If that means you're out of the closet, then that's your problem."

"Meet with him?" She could see the fear in David's eyes. "No, Margo, you can't."

Eric, whoever he was, Margo had already decided, was nothing to fear, not when she intimately knew one of the most dangerous men in the city.

"I'm not asking you, David, I'm telling you." Margo was enjoying David's demise.

"Finally, you're going to be honest with the kids and tell them you're gay." Margo had grown up with secrets, and even after swearing that her children wouldn't, here they all were.

"No, Margo," he whined, "Don't do this, please."

"You don't have a choice, David." She had no idea what Abigail and Thomas would think, but she knew that neither of them were stupid. She suspected that they might know much more than they had let on.

"Is this payback, Margo? You know I'd never hurt the kids, "I love them." She was still simmering inside and hearing him try to use her love for the children one more time was enough.

"Yeah, I can see that, just how much you love them, David. You loved them so much that you've been lying to them about everything, ever since the day I was arrested."

She wished that they had met somewhere private so she could reach out and shake him.

"Just like you lied to me since I've known you. Our entire marriage was a fucking lie. Set up a meeting with your blackmailer," Margo was back in control and negotiations were over, "or I will."

As she left, she turned back once to see David slumped over in the booth. The old Margo would have felt nostalgic; the new Margo felt victorious.

CHAPTER 21

It was late for a client to be calling and Margo assumed it must be Sal until she saw the name on her phone. She should let it go to voice mail but didn't, "Hello, Marcus," she answered, trying to sound professional, "what can I do for you?"

"Well, you could start by kissing me again." He sounded a little drunk, his words slurred together.

What would Sal think about his sexy nephew calling her this late, especially to hit on her? He had told her that he'd let her go when the right man came along, but she doubted that he had Marcus in mind.

"That was a mistake, Marcus. We were caught up in the moment."

"Are you sure it was a mistake?" he asked her. It was a question that had been haunting her since she had found herself in his arms in the backseat. In truth, she hadn't been able to stop thinking about it.

If he had been anyone else, if he hadn't had the name that he did, if he weren't being groomed by her lover, it would have been so much easier. Sal had told her she was free to do what she wanted. Margo hadn't had time to test this, and she wasn't sure she believed it.

"Yeah, I'm sure." She paused for a moment and let herself imagine what it would be like to have the handsome, young man in her living room, on the couch, instead of just on the phone. “What do you think Sal would do if he found out?”

Marcus was silent, lost in his own imagination she assumed. He had known his uncle since birth and had a front-row seat for Sal’s tactics and power plays over the years. He would know better than Margo.

“I know he would be furious, especially with me.”

“No, especially with me.” Margo was quick to add, “You’re family, so you can basically do no wrong. I’m replaceable.” She swallowed hard when she heard herself say that. How true was it, and just how would Sal go about replacing her?

“No, he’s not like that, but he would be pissed.” Marcus sounded much more sober than when the call began. “What the fuck, what’s wrong with me?” he laughed.

“What do you mean?” She was picturing his face, his dark eyes, the mop of blond hair slicked back, his broad shoulders, and then there was that ass.

“Of all the women I could fall for, you know, it’s crazy.” The words seemed to have a life of their own.

“Fall for?” She tried to brush it off, but it carried more weight than she knew what to do with.

He didn’t answer; he was going to be a great politician, artfully dodging questions that he had no comment on.

“So do you love my uncle?” he turned the questioning around on her.

Margo wanted to have a quick answer. It was a direct question after all, and she should know either way. "It's not that simple, Marcus." It sounded disloyal, and she regretted saying it. "It's not black and white."

"I think love is pretty black and white." He was calling her bluff.

"Wow!" Margo chuckled, "You're kind of ruthless, aren't you? I wonder where you get that from."

"Seriously, Margo, do you love him?" Marcus wasn't going to give her an inch.

The man had changed her life. He had taken her out of the misery that had become her every day, given her hope, given her a future, and now that she was on the verge of reopening her case, she could very well have her career and her children back. She owed it all to Sal. Of course, she couldn't discount the sex; the man took her breath away.

"I do love him," she murmured, shaking her head at herself. "He is the first man I have ever known that I can depend on." Years ago, she would have said that about David, but he had lost her respect and trust.

"That's not very romantic." He was younger and had led a charmed life. "Does he make you happy? If he wasn't married to my aunt, would you be with him?"

"I don't think I'm really the marrying kind anymore, Marcus." He wasn't the only one who could evade questioning. "Considering that my last marriage was a complete meltdown."

"I heard something about that," he told her. "Not the details, I mean. Sal keeps secrets. He just mentioned your ex was in a bit of trouble."

Margo covered her eyes with her hand and winced. "Yeah, blackmail trouble."

"That's fucked up. I'm sorry." Marcus was just trying to comfort her, but just talking about David's mess made her anxious.

"Maybe you do need a kiss." Marcus was every bit as persistent as his uncle.

"OK, I'm hanging up now." She was firm. "You call me again if you get into some kind of a dilemma."

"That's not much of an incentive to behave myself," he said playfully.

She closed her eyes and remembered vividly the sensation of his lips on hers.

"I have to go, Marcus, good night."

She didn't wait to hear his response before ending the call. She may be free to fuck around, but she wasn't stupid. Even Marcus knew Sal wouldn't take kindly to the idea of the two of them together. Plus, what would the blowback be for an aspiring senator seen cavorting with an ex-felon?

Screwing Marcus would be one thing, but if Margo ruined Sal's larger plan for Marcus's career, that was business, and she didn't think she was prepared to face the fallout for that.

Margo went to the bedroom, stripped, and pulled the tee shirt that she wore as a nightie over her head. In the dark, she tossed and turned and tried to quiet her mind. She had no control over her pulse thumping in her throat and she finally admitted to herself that that she was turned on after talking to Marcus.

She could remember his touch, his hands on her skin as their lips melted together. Every nerve was alive as she recalled it, and the pleasure coursing through her body was undeniable. Her nipples were hard, and she groaned with desire.

Touching herself and thinking about the boy with dimples, she seemed to be teetering on the edge of insanity, but she did it anyway. When she came, she bit her lip hard to stop herself from calling out for Marcus.

In the morning, she was awakened by her phone buzzing and was surprised to hear David's voice.

"Sorry for calling you so early, Margo." He wasn't awake either. "I just wanted to let you know that your mom called the house late last night."

"My mother? Susan?" Margo was suddenly wide awake; she hadn't seen or talked to her mother in years.

"Yeah, she sounded pretty bad." David might be the enemy, but for years he had been a comfort when it came to her parents.

"Jesus, what did she want, did she say?" Margo could only assume that the woman had some motive for contacting her after all this time.

"I'm not sure; it was hard to understand her. Maybe she's looking for money?"

Margo's mother was a pill-popping drunk. She had been throughout her childhood. There had been many times growing up that Margo couldn't make out a word she said. She could only imagine how much worse it had gotten since then.

"Did she leave a number?" Margo had no idea how to contact her.

"Sorry, she didn't, but she said she would call back. I just didn't know if you wanted me to give her this number."

David was being considerate—for a lying, cheating prick, anyway.

"No, not this one. Not the work number." Margo had no clue what the woman wanted, but she didn't want her mother harassing her on her work phone. "I still have my other cell; if she calls back give her that number."

"Okay, got it," David agreed.

"So how's the other thing going?" David sounded as if he was afraid to know the answer.

"You mean Eric?" David was too spineless to set up a meeting but had given her Eric's number. She had called him herself, and the man was eager to meet with her, probably thinking his big payday had finally arrived. "It's in motion. I'm meeting with him today, and we're going to come to an arrangement."

"What kind of arrangement?" Margo could make out David sniffling. She wondered if he was crying and if she even cared anymore.

"I'll let you know when it's done." She was like ice inside when it came to this man. He had married her out of convenience. It was easier to lie and manipulate than to be honest, and now she wondered if he was even capable of telling the truth.

Margo dressed in a suit for today's meeting. She was all business, hair up, briefcase in hand, and a stern look on her face. A decade ago, this would have been a court day. Now she would sit in a coffee shop, scribble down notes, and listen to thugs plead their case. She closed her eyes and sighed. It wasn't the life that she had imagined, but it was a whole hell of a lot better than the alternative.

Thanks to Sal and watching him operate, she was at least confident of one thing thing . . . she was going to eat Eric alive.

CHAPTER 22

Eric was younger than she had imagined. Thin, small, his dark hair was spiked, and when he sat down, she immediately noticed his eyes were rimmed in black eyeliner. Margo didn't know if it was the make-up or the fact that his eyes were so cold as he stared back at her that gave her a chill.

"So you're David's wife," He wasn't asking, and Margo assumed that if he was clever enough to blackmail that he wasn't a complete idiot.

"Ex-wife," she corrected him, "and you're the young man with very expensive tastes." She wondered what he did with the money. Assuming that David wasn't the only closeted man that he had this type of arrangement with, the boy should have amassed a small fortune by now.

He smiled, and Margo realized that he would go on, after their little talk, regardless of what the arrangement was. He was untouchable because he didn't care about anything. She had met inmates like this boy; they had nothing to live for so there was no stopping them. She was determined to do what she could to intimidate him anyway, and there was only one way to do that.

"The money is stopping now, Eric." She made a point to look him in the eye. "David is done paying you. You can do whatever you like, but the gravy train is over."

"Oh really?" He crossed his legs and laced his fingers over one knee. "I guess you don't know as much as you think, ex-wife."

He was mocking her, and if they weren't in public Margo thought she could easily hurt this boy.

"What else do I need to know, Eric? Yes, my ex-husband is in the closet, but I'm sure that you knew that from the beginning." David hadn't been very careful with his secret sex life, but that was his own damn fault. "So he is going to have to face those consequences, but there will be no more money."

"Guess how old I am." The boy looked at her with an evil expression. He didn't seem desperate at all, and Margo wondered what she was missing.

"I have no idea." She cocked her head. "Twenty-five?"

The boy smirked, "Bitch, please, I'm only nineteen."

"What difference does that make?"

If Sal heard the way this boy was talking to her she could only imagine how he'd put an end to it. If Sal was here, this whole conversation would be headed in a different direction.

"The difference is," he raised one plucked eyebrow, "that the first time David hooked up with me was almost four years ago."

There it was. The card that he had been saving, and the reason why David had been so willing to pay. Visiting a gay sex club was a social faux pas in David's circle; sex with a minor would mean jail and being a registered sex offender for the rest of his life.

Margo could barely speak, and when she did, her voice was hoarse. "So when you met, you were only fifteen?"

Her first thought was of her son, and there were no other thoughts after that. If David had touched him, she wouldn't even need Sal to hurt him. Margo would kill him herself.

Her stomach was churning when she asked, "What were you doing in that club as a minor?"

His face looked older than his years, and she wondered if it hadn't been entrapment from the beginning. "When you grow up on the streets, you learn a thing or two." He fingered one of his necklaces. "Like who will pay and who won't. So I guess you'll let David know that I'll be expecting my payment after all, won't you? Or should I?"

It was a threat and one that she could do nothing about at that moment.

"Get the fuck out of here." She glared at him and clenched her hands into fists on her lap. Margo had never been one for physical violence. The lawyer in her wanted to settle arguments logically, but right now, the mother bear inside her wanted to tear this guy apart.

She watched him sashay out the door and to his car. Once Eric was out of view, she held her face in her hands for a long time. After everything that she had done, all of the struggling, her intentions had been to give her children a better life than she had. Now she was afraid she had failed them worse than she ever could have imagined.

Margo remembered the day clearly when her father had finally paid attention to her. Growing up, her parents had been far too dysfunctional to know what she was doing or even where she was most of the time. Her father was a drunk, and her mother preferred to pop pills over alcohol. They were poor and got by mostly with government assistance. They hadn't seemed much different than most of her friend's parents, and her first memories were of a desire to grow-up and get out.

She had grown up quickly, literally. She was almost five-nine when she was in middle school, and she was already a B-cup when most of her friends were just getting a training bra. One afternoon, Margo was naked, standing in front of the mirror, making a note of the recent changes when she heard her bedroom door creak open.

She screamed and tried to cover herself with her hands. Her father stood in the doorway, drunker than usual and leering at her.

"What are you doing, Dad?" Margo was in shock and suddenly more than a little frightened.

"It's fine, sweetheart, just fine," he slurred and walked toward her. "You're so fucking beautiful, you know that?" He was only inches away and Margo kept backing up, but there was nowhere else to go but the bed.

"Mom!" she yelled. Her mother was rarely coherent in the afternoon, and she didn't hold much hope that she'd

save her now. "Mom!" she screamed for her much louder the second time.

"Now why do you want to go and ruin it?" Her father reached out and touched her waist, running his fingers softly up and down her body. "Why don't you be a good girl and make your daddy happy?"

"Stop it! Get out of my room!" She tried to push him away but even in his intoxicated stupor, he was stronger than she and seemed determined to have his way.

She hadn't seen her mother enter the room. She just remembered the sound of metal on skull, and then saw her father crumble to the floor. Her mother stood there, her hands clenched around the handle of the cast-iron skillet that she sometimes made pancakes in, with a wild, crazy look in her eyes as she surveyed the scene.

"Get dressed, Margo," she whispered as she bent down to look at her husband.

Her father was bleeding profusely from the gash over his eyebrow, his face was white, and Margo noticed that he was trembling. She quickly threw her bathrobe on and tied it tightly; she would never undress in her bedroom again.

"Listen to me," her mother seemed incredibly lucid for this time of day and Margo couldn't begin to imagine what would have happened if she hadn't been. "If you ever touch her again, if you ever even look at her again, I'll cut your dick off. Do you understand me, you piece of shit?"

Her voice was unnervingly calm, but anger was written all over her face.

Her father grunted, and she slapped his face. "Answer me, do you understand me?"

He nodded, the blood dribbling down his face, coating his cheek with a red stain, "Yes, I'm sorry."

Margo noticed that the apology was to her mother and not to her. She would come to realize over the next few days that her father wouldn't look in her in the eyes and would never speak more than a word or two to her ever again.

Her mother rose up, kicking at him with her foot. "Get out of here, go wash up."

Once he was gone, she turned to Margo. "Men are fucking animals. All of them. Don't you forget it, Margo." She put the pan on the bed and had reached out and gripped Margo's shoulders as if she needed to punctuate the words. "They're all animals."

That had been Margo's mother-daughter sex talk. Now, as she looked out the window of the coffee shop, she marveled at how naïve she had been. No wonder she had married a gay man. Because of her upbringing, it was probably a miracle she hadn't been even more suppressed than she was.

The question was, did she really think that David was capable of hurting her son? Eric was a teenager when he seduced her ex, but he was no ordinary kid; obviously a hustler and probably more damaged than even she could imagine. Was she taking this too far?

David answered on the first ring, and Margo heard her voice, flat, emotionless, and cold when she warned him, "I'm telling you right now that I will find out, so don't even think about lying to me right now." Rage was coursing through her body from head to toe, and she had never wanted to hurt anyone as badly as she did right now. "Have you ever touched my son?"

"What the hell are you talking about?" Her ex-husband sounded aghast. "Wait, Margo, let me go somewhere more private." She heard him close a door. "I can't believe you would ask me that."

"I think it's a fair question considering that you like sex with young boys." Margo took a deep breath and hoped that the bile that churned in her stomach wouldn't rise up.

There was a long pause. "I told you to stay out of it," he whispered.

"Yeah, I can see what a great job you've been doing of handling it," she snarled at him. "So answer the fucking question, David."

"Jesus, God, no, Margo." He was on the verge of tears. "I'm gay, OK, that's what you wanted to hear, right? But that doesn't make me a pedophile." He was sobbing. "I made a mistake. I had no idea until it was too late."

Margo tapped her nails on the table. As much of a liar as the man had turned out to be, her gut believed him.

David wasn't what he appeared to be, but she had never known him to be a monster or a predator.

"All right, then, I'm going to have to give this a little more thought, David." She had assumed that shutting Eric down would be easy. Things had definitely not gone according to plan.

"I'm supposed to give him money tomorrow," her ex hissed. Margo might have felt sorry for him if this mess hadn't been entirely his own fault.

"Just hold off on that." She needed time to think and do some research. "Don't do anything, don't talk to him, don't talk to anybody, and David," she had to treat him like a client at this point, "do not go to the club right now."

"I won't," he mumbled.

Her cell phone buzzed after she had hung up with David, and she looked to see who it was. It was the first call she should have made, and now she regretted trying to handle Eric on her own. Legal research was her field; blackmail was more Sal's expertise.

"Tell me what happened, Cookie."

Margo didn't know where to begin so it all just tumbled out.

"It sounds like we both had a rough day," was all he would say when she had finished. "Let me pick you up in a few minutes. We need to have a little fun."

CHAPTER 23

Margo wasn't expecting to see Marcus in the backseat, and she immediately wondered what he was doing there.

"Cookie," Sal pulled her close, and his strong arm around her felt protective and solid, something she needed desperately at the moment, "I missed you." His dark eyes studied her face, and she tried to smile.

"I missed you too," It was true. Whatever had happened with Marcus, it was an accident, a chemical reaction. The feelings that she had for Sal were the one true thing in her life.

"Hello, Marcus," she nodded at him. She'd be professional and keep it simple. "How are you?"

"Staying out of trouble." There were his dimples again and she remembered their late-night conversation immediately. It brought a flush to her cheeks that she hoped Sal wouldn't notice.

"That's good, you know you don't want your uncle on your ass."

Sal's fingers were running up and down her neck, and even though it was the middle of the week, she hoped that he would break their Saturday routine.

"No, nobody wants that," Marcus laughed, and the two men talked politics until they turned into a driveway.

"Well, this is my stop. Margo, nice seeing you again." Marcus put out his hand, and they shook quickly.

"Be a good boy," Sal barked at him before he closed the door behind him.

"Where are we going?" Margo turned to Sal, their knees touching, his mouth was so close, and his eyes were full of a desire.

"Your place, Cookie," he whispered in her ear before his tongue flicked her earlobe.

They couldn't get there soon enough, and the minute she unlocked the door, Sal was behind her, his hands running down her back to her bottom as he pressed her up against the wall. "I've been thinking about you all day." He pulled the pin out of the back of her bun and her long hair tumbled down her shoulders.

She was trembling as his fingers clawed at the buttons on the front of her suit. He pulled the jacket off and grabbed the back of her bra, ripping it from her body.

Sal walked her to the bedroom as he unzipped her skirt. There was an unmistakable noise, almost a growl, as he threw her on the bed. "You look like you need to be fucked," he told her, making quick work of the pantyhose and grasping her by the damp crotch of her panties.

"Yes, I do." There was nothing gentle about this. He would take possession of her as he did everything else he wanted—quickly and completely. Sal ripped the panties in two, tossing them aside and spreading her legs. Before Margo could utter a word, his mouth was on her.

His tongue lapped up her crevice, tasting her with a moan, and then circling her clit, he knew what she craved. He knew it better than she did.

"Sal, oh my God," Margo reached out and grabbed the bed as if she needed to steady herself, the sensations were almost overpowering.

He slid a thick finger inside her, quickly filling her, and then sliding it out. She gasped, her thighs shook as his mouth-fucked her, keeping his tongue on her as he reached deeper and deeper in her throbbing heat. Margo felt a wave of longing wash through her, a need that she had never known before. She squeezed and convulsed as Sal inserted a second finger and pressed a spot that made her shiver.

His lips sucked at her and the tip of his hot tongue tormented her. His fingers curled and moved, and Margo was overwhelmed with pleasure. The pressure mounted inside. She could only whisper his name as the rush of her release set her body on fire.

Pushing her hips up, she heard the wet noises of his mouth slurping on her as he drained every drop of her first orgasm, drinking her down greedily, his fingers sliding in and out as he felt her peak again.

"Come for me, Cookie." He looked up at her, his face glistening with her juices as he continued to beckon inside, pressing on her once more until she spasmed on his hand.

When the last wave left her, Margo heard herself purr like a contented cat, and then laughed at herself. "Jesus, Sal, what are you doing to me?"

"Making you happy, hopefully." She watched him suck his fingers clean. "I think you deserve that."

She lay back and watched him undress. Shirt off, his muscles flexed and moved as he finished undressing. He was hard as a rock and just the sight of his bulging dick was enough to make her sigh.

"What about you, Sal?" She had never thought about his needs before and wondered if she was just entertainment or something more.

"What do you mean, Cookie?" he asked, hovering over her, hands on her hips, pulling her close and spreading her thighs.

"I mean, are you happy?" It seemed strange to ask. He got everything he wanted, how could he not be happy?

"I'm happy with you." His lips were on her neck, and Margo groaned as his teeth nibbled down her flesh. "You make me very happy."

Margo thrust her bottom up to meet him and felt the head of his cock touch her swollen lower lips. Every touch of him, every time she found herself in this bed with him, she fought hard to keep her emotions out of the sex, but today, it wasn't possible.

"I want to make you happy," she told him before gasping as he thrust inside her.

Sal kept his eyes on her. She could feel his pelvis grinding against her, his hands under her to pull her close. He was filling her up with every move, but it was his eyes that made her melt.

His expression—was it love? It had to be, it was something that Margo was completely unfamiliar with, but she knew this was new.

"Sal, yes," Margo panted, and when he sank into her, his mouth open, his tongue as deep inside as was his dick, she found herself running her hands through his hair as she pushed her hips up to meet him. He was thrusting faster as they kissed, sucking on her tongue and shuddering against her body. She came with a spasm and dug her fingers into his back as she felt him exploding inside.

He arched his back. Sal's climax continued, and when his head sank to the pillow, he stayed inside as he kissed her neck.

"My God, Sal, you did miss me." Her voice was shaking, but she resolved to try to keep the mood light.

"So what happened today, why was it a bad day?" Margo asked.

Sal rolled to his side and sighed. "Just a small problem really, nothing for you to worry about, Cookie." There was so much of his world that she didn't know about, and Sal would never tell her. "What did you tell your ex?"

Margo was no closer to a resolution, and it all came flooding back. "I just told him I needed more time."

"That's the thing about street punks and hustlers, Cookie." Sal was serious, his forehead crinkled. "You don't have time. I don't want you to get sucked in by all of this."

"What are you suggesting?" she ran her hand down his chest and felt his heart pounding. "What should I do?"

"Your life would be a lot easier without David in it."

Margo sat up quickly as the realization of what he was saying grabbed her. The moment of tenderness had passed, and a chill ran down her spine. No matter what else Sal was, to her or to anyone else, he had Mafia connections; he controlled and profited from organized crime; he was also a killer.

"What about family?" she could barely speak, and she definitely couldn't look at him.

"What's that?" He reached out for her, but she pulled away.

"What about family, Sal?" Margo wanted to scream, but instead, she clasped her hand over her mouth and just stared at him, shaking her head.

"What am I doing?" She hid her face in her hands, asking herself more than him. She had already ruined her kids' lives when she had gone to prison. Now she was going to leave them fatherless because of her own stupidity?

Scenes from her own childhood came rushing back, and she rocked herself slowly back and forth. "My mom and dad were both addicts." Margo never spoke about her childhood. "They hardly ever even knew where I was. If I hadn't gone to school they never would have known or cared."

Sal was sitting up behind her, trying to reach out for her when she shrugged away again. "I always told myself that if I ever had kids, I'd do better." All emotion had left Margo's voice. "But look at what a mess I've made."

"Cookie," he grabbed her and held her close; there was no getting away from him. Not only was Sal much stronger, but he was determined. "You're a good mother; you love them, and they love you. That's what family is." He ran his hand through her hair. "People that love you no matter what."

"Don't do anything, Sal," she told him. "I have to handle this myself. Promise me you won't do anything to David."

"Shh, it's OK, Cookie, come here." He pulled her back gently and stroked her hair. Margo was stiff in his arms. Her lover could easily destroy her family, and she found that the one man that protected her also frightened her.

She sat up. "Sal, I need you to leave." Her life, her job, even this goddamn bed—everything she had was due to Sal. What was she doing? The problem was that he could take it all away just as quickly as he had given it.

"I understand." He nodded, and she wondered if this was why the mistresses never lasted. She watched him get dressed almost as quickly as he had undressed, and he didn't say a word to try to defend himself or to change her mind. What would happen once he left?

"You call me when you need me" was all Sal said. No kiss good-bye, not even a long last look. He was out of her bed and maybe, Margo thought, out of her life.

The next morning her phone woke her before her alarm did, and Margo fully expected it to be Sal. "Hello?" she answered, her eyes still closed.

"Am I speaking with Margo Harris?" the man asked, and Margo was suddenly wide awake.

She sat up. "Yes, who is this?" Clients called her Miss Margo. Actually, the last time someone had used her full name was when Sal had been reading her file.

"This is Agent Richards with the FBI, ma'am." Her hands were suddenly so sweaty that she was afraid she would drop the phone. "I would like to meet with you to discuss a case I'm investigating in regards to Eric Flannigan."

This had to be bullshit. She tried to force herself to calm down. "I don't know an Eric Flannigan, sir."

"You met him yesterday, Miss Harris." The man waited for her to put the pieces together.

This was bad, very, very bad. The FBI had done their homework, and it was Margo's experience that they didn't waste their time unless they had a case.

"I didn't know his last name," she mumbled. There was no point in lying. They knew enough to put the two of them together. Margo would have to wait and see what else they knew.

"When would you like to speak with me, Agent . . . ," she paused. It was too much information all at once. "I'm sorry, what was your last name?"

How did they have her number, and how did they know that she had met with Eric? Did that mean that they knew the contents of their conversation as well?

"It's Agent Richards, ma'am, and I'd like you to come down to our office this morning, as soon as you can get here. Do you know the address?"

He was polite but firm. This wasn't an invitation. If she didn't make an appearance as he requested, he could obviously track her down easily enough. It would also make her look like she was hiding something.

"Yes, I know where you are." Her hands were shaking so much that she could barely hit the end call button. She knew the law, but she also knew that she had a lot to lose and a lot to hide.

CHAPTER 24

Agent Richards was tall and his handshake was firm. "Nice to meet you, Miss Harris. Please have a seat." He was built like a street cop. He had no soft gut like most of the agents who sat behind a desk. His dark blond hair had touches of gray, and his blue eyes had a twinkle.

Always attracted to the wrong men, she felt her pulse in her throat when she sat and looked at the size of the file that he was flipping through. This wasn't a coincidence; this was an investigation.

"How can I help you, Agent Richards?" Margo had resolved to keep her cool. She would act as her own attorney, and she wouldn't say a word that the man couldn't already confirm.

"How do you know Eric Flannigan?" he asked, his fingers pressed together. The FBI agent seemed friendly enough, but how many clients had she defended in the past who had been cornered by the police?

"He came to talk to me about a legal matter." She had to assume that the FBI must know what kind of work she was doing and prayed that they hadn't connected her with her employer yet.

"What kind of a legal matter?" He had a notebook out and Margo wasn't surprised he'd be taking notes. It was exactly what she would be doing if the chairs were switched.

"That's confidential." She knew she didn't have a leg to stand on, but there was no way she could tell him what the conversation had actually been about.

"Actually, Margo, you aren't an attorney, so there is no client privilege." The man knew more than she hoped, "So no confidentiality."

How could she protect Eric? What else was going on here? She decided to go on the offensive. "Why don't you tell me what this is about, Agent?" Margo barked at him. "I'm sure that Eric came to me with the expectation of attorney/client privilege regardless of the subject. Why would I break that?"

"I'm sure that Mr. Flannigan doesn't expect anything right now," the FBI agent tossed a picture on the desk, "since he was found dead last night."

There he was. The boy who had been so cocky, so sure of himself just yesterday. His smirk was gone and in its place was a hole through his forehead. Margo told herself to play it cool, but she felt sure that the man could hear her heart pumping madly in her chest. Clearing her throat, she could only say, "Jesus Christ, poor kid."

"That's right, just a kid," Agent Richards muttered. "And a damn good confidential informant too. A fucking shame that he died like that. Like a discarded animal. A bullet in the back of the head and one in the chest. Tell me,

Margo, you work with criminals, is that type of shooting familiar to you?"

"An execution," she whispered. Margo's mind was racing. Who else could it be? Had he ordered the hit before or after they made love? She couldn't imagine that Sal would dirty his hands, but what did she really know about him after all?

"That's right, an execution. So let me go over my time line with you." He flipped the notebook back a few pages. "Eric comes to see you, you're the go-to girl for Mazzillo's crew now, right?"

There was nothing illegal about that, although she couldn't help but feel disappointed that they had already connected her with Sal. "I do legal research for people that call me with all kinds of cases." Margo wouldn't give up Sal.

"But most of those people that come to you just happen to be people in Salvatore Mazzillo's organization, is that correct?"

Margo studied his face. Unlike most cops that she had dealt with over the years, Agent Richards looked sincere, as if he really cared; the worst kind of cop in this situation.

"Agent Richards, I'm sure that some of my clients do work with Mr. Mazzillo and some don't. Mr. Mazzillo has many businesses so a good deal of the people in this city work for him in one capacity or another." *But how many of them lived in apartments owned by him or went to bed with him?*

"True, Margo, he's got a lot of people that work for him." He tilted his head and smiled at her. "I can tell you were a great lawyer before you went to prison."

Her past was never that far behind her. "What do you want from me?" Margo would not let him see that she was alarmed.

"Let me get back to my notes." He read the page, "Now as I mentioned, Eric is a confidential informant and a little shady, but comes up with a lot of good stuff. So what is he doing coming to see you, Margo? He doesn't need legal advice from a waitress, so what was that conversation really about?"

He didn't need to go over his notes. The man probably had most of her life tucked away in that file and by now, had most of it memorized as well.

"Eric came to ask me about a run-in that he had with someone" . . . Never mind the fact that the someone was her ex-husband or that Eric had been lining his pockets with shakedown money.

"Was that run-in with Salvatore Mazzillo?" Margo felt relief. He was really asking, and that meant that at least the FBI had no idea what her ex had been up to and probably didn't know all of Eric's nasty little deeds either.

"No, there was no mention of Mr. Mazzillo." That was true.

Agent Richards leaned forward in his chair. "Margo, why are you protecting him?" Their knees were almost touching. There was something about him, something warm, something gentle, something that made her want to trust him.

"Protecting who? Eric?" Margo had been burned before—actually, every time she had ever trusted anyone.

"No. Sal," he pursed his lips; it was his tell, he didn't want to ask, "Because he's your lover?"

"Agent Richards, am I under arrest?" The FBI could have been following her ever since the first day she had gotten in Sal's Town car. The only thing to do now was to distance herself and protect her own family; it's what Sal would do.

"No, Margo, we're just having a chat." He gestured to the door. "You're free to leave at any time."

"Great, then I'm leaving." She stood up and wondered where she should go now. To the coffee shop? Her apartment? There was nowhere for her to hide.

"Margo, take my card." He handed it to her, and when she reached out for it, he held her hand in both of his. "Call me if you need anything. Please, listen to me when I say Sal Mazzillo is a dangerous man."

Margo knew it was true. He had hinted at killing her ex-husband last night, and she knew that he had the boy who had threatened to turn state's evidence taken out. What would Sal do if he found out who she was talking to right now? She forced herself to smile and pulled her hand away. "I'll be fine, Agent."

"Are you sure? He doesn't take break-ups well, Margo." Without another word she left his office and entered the first restroom she could find. Once inside she locked herself in a stall and quickly gulped for air. Her legs were shaking and her back was coated in sweat. Agent Richards had shaken her to her core. She composed herself before departing the restroom and FBI building.

She was walking to nowhere in particular when her cell phone rang. How could she see clients today, how could she go back to this life that she had begun to build when it was so precarious? She snapped, "What?" when she answered the phone.

"Well, I guess my uncle wasn't able to cheer you up after all." Marcus sounded as if he had been laughing when he called, and Margo wondered if he wouldn't sober up if he knew that the FBI probably had a file on him as well.

"I can't talk to you," He was family, and that made it even worse for her right now.

"Hey, wait, Margo, what did I do?" He sounded sorry, and she immediately felt bad. He hadn't done anything but been born with the wrong last name.

"You didn't do anything, Marcus. I'm sorry." She needed to watch what she said; cell phones were easy enough to tap. "Just a shitty start to the day, that's all." No mention of Sal, no mention of clients. She wouldn't give the feds any fuel for their case.

"Well, why don't I pop by and say hi?" The dimpled boy liked to play dangerously. He was willing to risk Sal's anger in order to hit on her, but it would be all about family once the FBI closed their net.

"I've got some errands I have to take care of today." She'd get a motel, something she could pay for with cash, something far away from the apartment and everything else that had become familiar over the last few months.

"You sure you're OK, Margo?" Marcus sounded suspicious, and she wouldn't tell him anything that could get back to Sal.

"I'm fine, just really busy. I've got to go." Marcus wasn't a client anymore, and they had no reason to speak. Neither his uncle nor the FBI would find their conversations appropriate. "I'll talk to you later," she promised, having no intention of speaking with him ever again.

She needed time to think, and the Motel 6 didn't ask questions. The man at the front desk with the cigarette hanging from his lip took the cash and handed her a key. When she closed the door behind her, her legs finally gave out as she sank to the floor and hung her head. She could punish herself for what she had done as much as she wanted to later; right now, she had to figure out what she was going to do next.

CHAPTER 25

When Giovanna woke up that morning, she knew something was wrong. The pain on her left side was sharp, and her heartbeat seemed to race and stop, and then race again for no reason. Her husband looked worried when he saw her hand clutching her round belly. "I'm calling the doctor." He rolled over and picked up the phone on the nightstand.

"No, it's okay, it's probably nothing." She knew it was a lie. She hadn't decided what she felt about this baby, and maybe the baby could sense it.

Her husband did what he wanted regardless; she had learned that much about him already. The doctor's office wasn't open yet, and their answering service took his call. "My wife is pregnant and is experiencing pain. I want to bring her in right now."

The woman on the other end of the phone didn't know her husband well, and Giovanna looked out the window with a smirk when he snapped at her, "I don't give a damn about your appointments today. This can't wait. I'm taking her to emergency."

He always got his way, and Giovanna contented herself with the thought that someday he would lose all of his power and privileges. She would get to watch as he was reduced to nothing. His carefully constructed empire wasn't indestructible no matter what he might think.

The doctor examined her and confirmed what she already knew: she was bleeding, her body was aborting the baby inside of her. She bit her lip in spite of the gentle tone he used when he explained, "Sometimes you can have some spotting the first couple of months, maybe even during the second trimester." He didn't want to alarm her, and no one seemed to want to call it what it was.

"Am I having a miscarriage?" She wasn't afraid, and she wasn't heartbroken. Her husband gripped her hand as if she was both, and she struggled to get into a sitting position. "Just tell me, please."

"We'll keep you for observation and keep you comfortable, but it looks that way." The pain was back, and she closed her eyes as it rode through her body. "You may feel the pain come and go; your body will begin to take care of things," he meant get rid of the baby. It was an awful thought, to have to lie here and know that it was slipping away. She was powerless to stop it; all of them were.

The nurse put an IV needle in her vein and patted her comfortingly. "That will help with the pain, dear, and I'll be back to check on you in a little bit."

Her husband was the one who couldn't accept it, He hadn't stopped pacing and fingering the medallion under his shirt. When it was finally over, the baby was gone and the cramps had finally subsided. He had a tear on his cheek when he kissed her hand. "Don't be sad, there will be plenty more babies."

Giovanna knew that she had changed forever at that moment. The years of living with her step-father had permeated her in a way that she had never dreamed. It hadn't been enough that he had destroyed her childhood; he'd changed her heart. She was frozen inside, somewhere deep down where no one could reach. She saw her husband's tear and felt nothing. She could only think of how pleased her step-father would be about her losing the baby.

The bastard was really going to get away with it after all.

CHAPTER 26

She called from the phone in the hotel room and it took David five rings to answer. “Hello?”

“It’s Margo.” Even if it wasn’t her cell phone, she wouldn’t say much. From here on out, she had to think like a criminal—or a lawyer. There wasn’t really much difference sometimes.

“Sorry, I didn’t recognize the number.” Even though her ex-husband was technically a criminal, she didn’t expect him to think like one. “How did it go with—” she cut him off.

“We need to meet. I’ll be at the house in an hour.” Anywhere public was too risky.

“Um, okay. The kids won’t be home until later. Is everything okay?” There was no time to go over the details.

“That’s perfect,” was all she said before hanging up.

It actually only took forty-five minutes. Margo took the bus and changed routes three times. It would be harder to follow than a cab, and she had bought a cheap sweatshirt and tucked her auburn hair into the hood. David peered at her as if even he didn’t recognize her.

“What’s going on, Margo?” he asked as she walked into her old living room.

"Did you ever bring men here?" She walked to the windows and closed the blinds.

"Really, do we have to do this now? As if I'm not going out of my mind." He stood, hands on his hips. "What happened with Eric?"

She placed a finger over her lips. There was no way of knowing how much the FBI knew, and it would be easy enough to have a CI plant some kind of listening devices here, especially if David had been careless with the types of guests he had brought home.

"Just answer the question; did you ever bring any men from the club here?" Margo prayed that she wasn't too late to keep him and her children out of this.

"No, never." He looked almost as frightened as she felt. "Why? Does he know where we live?"

How much to tell David, that was the question. As a lawyer, she would advise her clients to say nothing, especially to an ex-spouse after a nasty divorce. As an ex-spouse, she was going to go against her own advice.

"Eric is dead. You don't have to worry about him anymore." She saw the relief wash over him.

He sat down and exhaled loudly, "Thank God, I mean, that's awful, what happened?"

"Two bullets." Margo realized that her ex-husband knew nothing when she saw his eyes open wide.

"Who killed him?" He grabbed her hand. "What did you do, Margo?"

It was the first time she had genuinely laughed in a while. "David, come on," she shook her head. "It wasn't me, although that would probably be easier."

"Then who?" His hand was sweaty, and he seemed to be clinging to her for dear life.

"The FBI asked me the same question." She bit her lip. "I don't know exactly who did, but I have some ideas."

"What did the FBI talk to you about?" David was lost. She almost felt sorry for him at the moment. He was definitely in over his head, but so was she.

She asked her ex, "Do you know who Sal Mazzillo is?" It was a rhetorical question; she had come to learn everyone knew who Sal was. David shrugged. "Well, they think that he had something to do with Eric's death."

"What was Eric mixed up in?" David was getting a taste of his own medicine now, a lover, someone that he had trusted, suddenly finding out that it had all been a lie.

"Well, he was a confidential informant on top of being," she gestured at David, "whatever else he was."

"Jesus Christ." The realization of it all, the damage that he'd done, was clearly etched on his face. "Do they know about me?"

"No, I don't think so." The FBI seems to be focused on one target only. "Eric's little blackmail business must have been something he kept to himself."

"So what now?" He was pale white.

"Now, I think you're in the clear." Whatever else Sal had done, he really had cleared up the problem, at least for David. "But our agreement still stands." Margo pointed at him. "You have to tell the kids."

"Just the kids?" she knew what he was referring to; David wasn't ready to give up being the good boy for his parents. Margo hadn't seen her parents since she left for college; it was a bond she was unfamiliar with.

"Just the kids. Whatever else you do, I guess it's none of my business," she added in a stern voice, "unless you make it my business."

"I'll never do something this stupid again, Margo, I swear." David had taken such huge risks for so long; she wondered if he meant it.

"You want to stay and see them? I know they would like to spend time with you."

Margo looked around the living room and a thousand memories came back to her . . . the couch where she had spent so many long nights when she was writing a brief or nursing a fever, the chair in the corner where she had read to Abby and Thomas. Around the corner was the bedroom where she used to sleep next to this man that she hardly knew. "Yeah, I think I'll stay," she said.

Thomas ran to her when he saw her from the front door. "Mom!" His arms were quickly around her neck, and he kissed her with sticky lips. Abby looked at her from across the room, one hand on her hip, staring at Margo suspiciously.

"Hi, sweetie." She kissed Thomas back. "Hello, Abigail." She wished that her daughter would give her an inch, but she knew it had to be in her own time.

Abigail grimaced at her instead. "Hey." She shrugged her shoulders as if Margo barely mattered. "What are you doing here?"

"I wanted to come by to see you and your dad, and I need to talk to you guys." She ruffled Thomas' hair and patted the couch. "Why don't you sit down?" She watched as Abby scuffed her feet and took a seat on the very edge, as far away from Margo as possible.

David sat in the chair, looking at the three of them. Tears were already in his eyes, and Margo knew that this was going to be the most difficult thing he'd ever done.

"Kids, I just want you to know that I love you and would never do anything to purposely to hurt you. But I haven't been the best Dad, and I'm sorry. I've lied to both of you for a while, and I'm hoping that you'll forgive me and understand what I'm about to tell you."

He paused and one tear streamed down his cheek. "When your mom was in prison, she wanted to see you. And I wasn't visiting her when I told you that I was. I was having . . ." he looked over at Margo for help.

"Your dad was going on dates." She would save him. There was no point in the kids thinking worse of him than they would. "Your dad was dating, and he didn't know how to tell you." She could see David's relief and could tell he was grateful for her tact.

"I didn't know how to tell you guys because I didn't want to admit that I'm . . . I'm gay." There it was, a whole lifetime of shame, finally out in the open.

"How could you be gay when you were married to Mom?" Thomas squinted as if trying to figure it out in his head.

"Your dad didn't know he was gay when we got married, sweetie." Margo was hugging her son, and she had almost forgotten how good it felt to hold her children near. "It took him a while to figure it out."

Abby snorted, and Margo looked over. "I knew you were gay. I don't see what the big deal is." David raised his eyebrows. He was just realizing how smart his daughter was.

"So if Mom wanted to see us so much, then why didn't she call?" Abby was directing her conversation as if Margo wasn't there.

"She did call when she could, but I wouldn't let her talk to you, honey. But she wrote you letters." David stood up. "Hang on a second."

When he returned, it was with a plastic tote. It was so full that the lid barely stayed on and once he set it down, Thomas grabbed the lid and the envelopes spilled out all over the coffee table.

"I saved Mom's letters for you. I should have given them to you when they came, but I didn't. I was just being . . . just being stupid, and I'm sorry."

Thomas and Abby both gasped. Hundreds of letters from their mother, letters in which she had poured out her heart lay before their eyes. Margo remembered her heart aching daily as she would tell them again and again how much she loved them and missed them. David had betrayed her and turned his back on her in her time of need; maybe she could be the bigger person and find it in her heart to forgive him, if for only the kids.

Hours went by with her children opening envelopes and reading to themselves and occasionally out loud to each other, sometimes laughing, sometimes crying. When Abby sat down next to Margo, it was to rest her head on her mother's shoulder and wrap her arms around her waist. "I'm sorry for being mad at you, Mom," she said in a wavering voice.

Margo knew there was no holding back these tears, and she didn't even want to try. Now that she had her children back, she would fight tooth and nail for them. Sal was right. Family was the most important thing, and she hoped that he understood that she would do whatever she had to in order to take care of hers.

It was dark before Margo left, and David reached his hand out to her. "Hey, I deserved a lot worse. I just want to thank you."

Margo tilted her head to the side. "How about we put the past behind us and try to start over, for the kids sakes?"

He grabbed her hand. "I'd like that. I don't want to fight with you, Margo. I never thought you'd forgive me for, for . . . everything."

Margo shook her head back and forth slowly. He wasn't off the hook that easy. "I haven't forgiven you, David. I'm not sure if I can. Our entire marriage was a lie. How can I ever trust you again?"

"I know." David's eyes were sad but sincere. "But it wasn't all a lie. I did love you, and I still do. And what about the kids? They're the best thing that ever happened to us. I don't regret them for a second, and I know you don't either."

Margo sighed. She felt both physically and emotionally drained.

"When do you want to see the kids again?" He asked, zipping up her sweatshirt and putting the hood on for her. She missed the little things that David had always seen to.

Reality came back, and Margo's mind began racing all over again. The last few hours were wonderful, and she had needed them desperately, but she was no closer to a solution. Bringing the kids to her apartment was out of the question, and another seedy hotel room didn't seem to be any closer to normal.

"How about if I just see them here for now?" She didn't want to put David in a position of knowing too much, just in case Agent Richards came to see him next. "I'll call in the next couple of days." Margo turned to go.

"Take care of yourself, Margo," David called after her before he closed the door.

Chapter 27

Her voice mail was full, and she wasn't going to answer the calls or listen to any of the messages. None of the numbers looked familiar. At least Sal hadn't called, and neither had Marcus. She didn't know if that was good news or bad. The Mazzillo family was sure to stick together in a crisis.

It wasn't until almost three a.m. that the lightbulb went off in her head. At that time of night there was nothing that she could do about it, but Margo scribbled on the pad where she had originally written down all of the notes about her case. Clearing her name was her only way out, and if it worked, then she could walk away clean and start over—really start over.

She looked around the shabby room. She'd had enough of this. Months of working for Sal, and no matter how much better it had been than slaving away at the diner and the Laundromat, it was still not a life, living in fear, knowing that everything she had could disappear on a whim. Worse, she was too vulnerable. Sal had an army behind him. Who did she have except Sal?

Margo tried to shake off her feelings of loneliness and realized that it wasn't going to go away that quickly. It hadn't been all business, not for her, and she had thought as recently as yesterday, not for him either. The look in his eyes, his hands caressing every curve, his mouth on her—

she refused to believe that it was all just a transaction for him. He had a stable of prostitutes and probably countless other opportunities to get laid. Power was an aphrodisiac for most women, and Sal had power on top of everything else.

If she argued it like a lawyer, she would have to question, why her? What did Sal need her for? Yes, she had been a great attorney; even the partners had to admit that on occasion, she was brilliant, but there were other people out there that could fill her niche, so what had Sal chosen her for?

She still hadn't solved the puzzle by six a.m., and the sun would be up soon. Margo took a quick shower and threw the clothes back on from yesterday. If she were going to continue hiding out, she'd need supplies. Clothes, a toothbrush, some incidentals. She hoped that she had enough cash on her and wondered if her stash at the apartment would be there when she went back.

She opened the door—and came face-to-face with Agent Richards.

"Good morning." He held out a cup of coffee and flashed her a smile. "How are you, Margo?"

How had he known where she was, and why was he following her? Her heart was in her throat, but she was determined not to let it show. "Good morning." She grabbed the cup and took a long sip. "How long have you been out here?"

"Oh, all night. Thought I'd stretch my legs." Neither of them had slept. Who was chasing whom, and if the FBI knew where she was, wouldn't it have been just as easy for Sal to have her followed?

"Just you, Agent?" She would play it cool.

"Yep, just me. So what are you doing here?" He looked around and made a face. "Not the nicest place you could stay. I was thinking that you could afford much better."

"Hey, I work for a living." She wouldn't give him an inch. "I've stayed in worse places."

"Looks like you used to have a nice house though, Margo." The agent never took his eyes off of her. "Your husband get it in the divorce?"

Dammit, he knew about David. "Listen, what you're doing right now borders on intimidation and harassment." She couldn't make a case for either, and she was sure that Agent Richards knew it. "So whatever you think I'm up to, whatever you're really investigating, leave my family out of it."

"I'm not looking into your family, just keeping an eye on you." His smile seemed genuine. "I was worried about you after we talked."

Margo started to walk away. "You know, you don't need to worry about me. I can take care of myself just fine."

He took one step for every two of hers. His legs were long, and he looked to be in good shape.

"It's Jake."

"What?"

If Sal's people were watching her, then she could only imagine what Sal would think about her talking to someone he would clearly define as the enemy.

"My name is Jake." The agent seemed to be as doggedly determined as Sal, and Margo was caught in the middle. "I'm not here officially, and I didn't mean to upset you. I meant it when I said I was worried about you." He touched her shoulder gently, and Margo could not ignore the sensation of his fingers on her body.

She looked up and sighed. "OK, Jake, tell me what you want from me."

"Margo, I think you're a good person who has gotten herself into a fucked-up situation. It's probably not the first time, and it may not even be your fault, but I think you're going to need some help getting out of this."

For a man that had spent the night on a stakeout, he smelled good, and if it wasn't for the five o'clock shadow, she would have sworn he was fresh from a shower.

"I can handle myself." She couldn't trust him, and more so, she couldn't trust herself. Being attracted to him didn't change a thing.

"I just don't want to find out when it's too late that something happened," he scowled. "I think you deserve a happy ending."

It was an odd thing to say, especially considering that he didn't know her, and then Margo thought, perhaps she was completely wrong . . . Perhaps he knew her very well.

"I appreciate that, Jake." She had a busy morning ahead of her, and she was running on no sleep, so she couldn't afford to get sidetracked. "And I promise I'll let you know if I need some help." It was a complete lie, and he probably knew that too.

"OK, well, you have a good day, Margo." He nodded, and Margo didn't know if it was flattering or disconcerting that he was still watching her when she was halfway down the street.

Perfect—she would have laughed if the situation involved someone else. There's a whole bunch of men in the world, millions of them, and let's see, you marry a gay man, fall in love with an unavailable gangster, flirt with his nephew, and then have the hots for a cop who wants to take down the gangster. Margo needed to simplify, and Jake, regardless of perceived good intentions, was one complication too many.

She arrived at her destination and looked up at the building. St. Joseph's was a modern hospital, but the cross still towered over the sign. She hoped that Megan Dittmar was still inside and far more sober than she had been the last time that they had met.

The nurse at the front desk scanned the computer for her name. "Yes, here she is. Megan Dittmar. She's in room

923." The woman handed Margo a badge that she was to clip on her jacket, announcing she was a visitor.

Margo knocked on the door. "Megan," she called out. The television was on but no one was in the bed. Fine, she wasn't leaving. This girl was crucial to her plan and as much as she hated depending on anyone, let alone a junkie hooker, she was going to wait until she got what she came for.

Almost an hour had passed. Margo had flipped through all of the channels and turned the TV off in disgust thirty minutes ago and had taken to flipping through the girl's Bible that sat on her nightstand.

"Hey, what are you doing with that?"

Megan had arrived and hardly resembled the drugged out woman that Sal had introduced her to at all.

"I'm sorry, just killing time." Why had she started pawing through the girl's things? "I'm Margo Harris. I don't know if you remember me."

She extended her hand, and instead of shaking it, Megan grabbed her Bible back and sat down on the bed as she held it in both hands over her chest.

"I remember you," she nodded. "You were there that day with that man asking me questions, before I came here."

"Yes, exactly. So you do remember that day." Margo was relieved; at least the girl had some retention.

"I do, and I remember your boss trying to scare me." Megan's eyes flashed with anger, "and the other guys that he's sent here to check on me. You can tell him for me that I am working the program and God takes care of me, so there's nothing he can do to hurt me."

Margo wished for a moment that she could have that much faith in something—anything. "My boss doesn't want to hurt you, Megan." What else had Sal done that she didn't even know about?

"Well, maybe not, but he can stop checking on me. I'm not doing drugs, and I don't want to now." She crossed her legs and rocked back and forth. "When I think about the things that happened when I was on the street . . . just the things I can remember," she stopped and shook her head. She looked like she was about to cry.

"I'm sure it was awful." Just the time Margo had spent looking for her on the streets had been enough, and Margo was raised in the projects.

"So you're the lady that I testified against, right?" Megan's eyes were big. "What did you do?"

"That's the problem, Megan." Thanks to this girl she had lost six years of her life and damn near everything else, including her sanity, so there was only so much sympathy she could have. "I didn't do anything. My associate Jay . . . Do you remember him? He set me up and got you to help him."

"Yeah, Jay." Megan looked as if she was transported in the past. "He was a bad man, but in the beginning he was really nice to me. I thought he loved me and was going to take care of me."

Leave it to Jay to take advantage of some innocent girl, and then fuck her too.

"Wait a minute, Megan." Margo fished out her notebook and a pen from her bag. "Do you mind if I take notes?"

"Sure, it's OK. In NA, they say you have to make amends, do you know that?" Megan was rocking back and forth again. It seemed to comfort her.

"No, I didn't." Neither of her parents had ever seen the need to sober up, and Margo had avoided addicts the rest of her life, having had enough of them in her first eighteen years.

"Yeah, you have to make amends if you can, to the people that you've hurt." Megan sniffed. "Even though I didn't mean to hurt you, I guess I did. Did you lose your job?"

Margo almost lost her temper. Her tone was cold as she tried to reign in her emotions.

"Megan, I didn't just lose my job, I went to prison and that means that unless I get my case overturned, I can never practice law again. I can never be a lawyer, so I can never get my job back."

She had never said those words out loud before and once she had, Margo's reality caused anger to cross her face and flash in her eyes. Working for Sal had been a relief; at least she was using her brain again but the thought that her career, something she had worked so hard for, had been snatched from her and there was a distinct possibility that she could never get it back again.

The girl was moving back on the bed as if she were afraid that Margo might reach out and grab her. She had been traumatized on the streets. Whatever had happened to Margo, Megan had been treated like an animal, and Margo knew that she needed to be gentle with her. Her sobriety was new, and no matter how close to God she might feel right now, it was a slippery slope.

"I'm sorry, Megan, I'm not angry with you." She put her hands up. "It's the past I'm angry with."

"Let's focus on the future. Now, start from the beginning, tell me how you met Jay."

CHAPTER 28

It felt good to be here again, in the courthouse. It was a place that Margo used to feel at home in. It had been the place where some of the best moments of her life had occurred, and the absolute worst. She had been sentenced here, and when she looked at the table to the left side of the room, she could remember clearly rising when it was time, her knees knocking together, her palms sweaty as she clutched her hands at her sides, hoping and praying.

It hadn't been enough. Sentenced to six years, she hadn't gotten any time off for good behavior or credit for time served. Murderers and rapists had gotten better deals. Someone had wanted to see her stripped of everything; someone had been enjoying it much more than anyone should—and that person was Jay Cook.

This morning she was taking the first steps toward righting a wrong that would expose him for what he was, but Margo still wasn't sure if Jay was just petty and vindictive or if it was something more than that.

She was prepared for today. She had been impeccable with the details, writing the motion several times over. Margo couldn't afford to make even the smallest mistake. She would only get one shot at this, and her whole future hung in the balance.

When the bailiff called "All rise," she felt her legs shake as she stood and watched as the judge made his way into the room. How many times had she stood next to a client who had felt the same? The law had become so much more personal since she had seen its devastating consequences used against her.

"The Honorable Judge Vogle presiding, please be seated. Court is now in session," the officer announced, and Margo stared at the man behind the bench. Judge Vogle had been a friend and colleague at one time. He had worked in the state attorney's office, and they had ambitions in common. They used to work out plea deals over coffee in a backroom in this very building. She wasn't sure if this morning their previous relationship would help her or hurt her.

"09F142371, the State versus Margo Harris." The judge read her case number out loud, and when he saw Margo approach the bench, there was a warm smile that spread quickly across his face. Holding his hand over the microphone, he asked, "Margo, how are you?"

"Fine, Judge, thank you for asking." She wouldn't play up their past, not with the kid from the other side giving her a cold stare as he tried to assess the situation. What was he . . . One year out of law school, maybe two? He seemed to be far too young to be here, and Margo raised her eyebrow. Apparently the state wasn't going to take her seriously. She'd have to change their mind.

"And who are you, young man?" Judge Vogle pointed at the boy with the baggy suit and the buzz cut.

"Roberts, sir." He was young, and his voice was nervous. "Zachary Roberts for the state. This case has been closed for over seven years, Your Honor. The state doesn't see why it should be reopened."

"Margo, are you pro se?" the judge asked her, not seeing another attorney at her side.

"Yes, Your Honor, I'm representing myself." She heard the boy snort, and she fought back the urge to lose her temper. Calm and collected, she would take what she had learned from Sal and put it use. "I have new testimony to introduce, as I stated in the motion. The state's only witness in my case has recanted her testimony, and I intend to show that the case should have been dropped. I will be looking to overturn the verdict."

"Your Honor, how do we know that the witness isn't lying now?" the boy attorney asked. It almost sounded whiny, and both Margo and Judge Vogle fought back a snicker.

"Well, son, we'll have to listen to what Miss Harris has in the affidavit, and then I'll make my ruling as to whether or not I'll reopen the case. Why don't you ask your boss if he wouldn't rather send someone with a little more experience?" The judge shook his head and told the clerk, "Block out an hour after lunch for me, please."

Addressing Margo and the boy once more, "Motion granted. I'll listen to this new testimony at 2:00 p.m. today." He pounded his gavel and made it so.

Margo felt as if she could breathe again. It was a major hurdle that she hadn't expected to come so easily.

She knew the rest of the ordeal would be harder, especially now that the state attorney's office would be alerted to her presence. They had enjoyed watching Margo Harris go down. They would fight tooth and nail to make sure the guilty verdict would stick.

When two o'clock came, Margo realized that she had been right. The boy was gone, and in his place was the state attorney's second in command, a woman that she respected and admired for her fierce determination as well as her loyalty. Faye Russell wouldn't go down without a fight. She nodded at the woman when their eyes met. She had sat on the opposite side of the aisle from her before, and normally, she would have given herself better than 50/50 odds of winning. Today she wasn't that sure of herself.

Judge Vogle sat down and smiled at both women. "Ladies, we're here today to hear new evidence in Miss Harris' evidence tampering case. At the end of this hearing, I'll make my decision as to whether I'm reopening the case; however this isn't a trial." He looked over at Mrs. Russell as if to remind her to keep her attacks to a minimum. "So let's keep this friendly. Margo, what do you have for me?"

This was it. It was now or never, and Margo's pulse picked up the pace once more as she pressed play on the DVD player.

Megan had cleaned up well, but she still looked lost and more than a little frightened when she stared into the camera. Margo heard her own voice as they started. “Please state your name for the record.”

“Megan Dittmar.” She was nervously licking her lips and didn’t know what to do with her hands. It hadn’t mattered how many times Margo had coached her, it was clear that the girl had a tenacious grasp on her sobriety.

“Megan, did you testify in an evidence tampering case about seven years ago?” Margo watched as Megan nodded her head yes. “Please answer yes or no.”

“Yes, ma’am.” Even after watching the video over and over, Margo was struck again by the fact that Jay had ruined both of their lives. She wondered if either of them would ever recover.

“Do you remember who approached you about testifying in the case?” The girl looked confused, and Margo changed her wording. “Who asked you questions about me?”

“Jay, Jay Cook.” The girl shivered and rubbed her hands together.

Margo hoped that Megan would hold up for the rest of this ordeal. Just taking her statement had been difficult.

“Is this man you know to be Jay Cook?” Margo had slid a picture of Jay across the table at her.

Megan looked sad when she fingered his face. “Yes, ma’am, that’s Jay.”

"And what was your relationship with Jay at the time of the case?" Margo hated dredging up Megan's past in order to get what she wanted, but there was no other way.

Megan swallowed hard. "We were lovers. I thought he was going to marry me."

"So you were involved in a romantic relationship with Jay at the time that you testified?" The thought that Jay Cook had been romantic with any woman was laughable, but she couldn't call it what it was, pimping her out.

"I thought so, but I guess not." Margo hadn't known until she'd watched the video that Megan still had feelings for the man that had thrown her away like a piece of garbage. "I mean, if he cared, he wouldn't have gotten me hooked on blow, right?"

"Can you clarify what 'blow' is, Megan." Margo assumed everyone that had been alive in the eighties knew what "blow" was slang for, but she wasn't taking any chances. She was going to do this right.

"Blow is street talk for cocaine, ma'am." At that moment, it looked as if Megan would have liked nothing more than to return to her old habit.

"Why did Mr. Cook want you testify in my court case?"

"He said you were a bitch and needed to be knocked down off of your high horse. He said you were messing things up for him."

"Did Mr. Cook coach you on what to say when you testified in the case?" Margo had flipped the page on her notes; she would get back to Jay's despicable treatment of the girl later.

Megan sighed. "I was told to say I saw you messing with evidence." Her shoulders slumped. "I didn't want to do it. I knew it was wrong. I never saw nothing."

"Why did you do it, Megan?" This was the one answer that Margo needed for herself.

The first of many tears ran down Megan's thin, leathery face. Her time on the street had aged her, and cleaning up could only do so much. The damage was permanent on her body and her mind. Margo needed justice for herself, but she also wanted to see Jay pay for what he'd done to a young, naïve, insecure girl as well.

"I just wanted to make him happy. I didn't want to do it, but he got angry. He hit me and threatened to leave me if I didn't obey him." She wiped her nose with the back of her hand.

Margo continued with the questions. "What happened after you testified?"

Megan stared off into the distance before she answered. "Jay was really happy afterward. I'd never seen him so happy. We went out on the town and partied all night. We drank and did a ton of drugs. The next day he beat me up, called me a worthless whore, and kicked me out. He told me I should do the world a favor and kill myself."

The judge cleared his throat. "That's enough, Margo, you can stop it for now."

"Your Honor, I would like to point out that this is new testimony from a junkie prostitute." Mrs. Russell pointed at the monitor. "If every single addict that came through the system got to recant their story whenever they felt like it, then no verdicts would ever mean anything."

"I hear what you're saying, Mrs. Russell." Judge Vogle was a big man and his weight in the chair made it groan when he shifted. "But it appears to me that Miss Dittmar was sober enough when she was your witness that your office hung the whole case on her testimony, is that right?"

The prosecutor threw a look over at Margo that would have turned her to stone if she had been able. "True, Your Honor, but how do we know that she's not lying now? What has Miss Dittmar been promised in exchange for her testimony?"

"Nothing, Faye." Margo was fired up. She wasn't about to back down, not when so much depended on this. "I don't have anything to offer her besides an opportunity to do the right thing."

"You can let your witness know that I'll be filing charges against her for perjury and contempt if this case gets reopened." The state's attorney wasn't threatening; it was a promise, and Margo had known it was a possibility. Megan would have to be strong if she wanted to make things right.

"Considering that your office overstepped its bounds, and the way your predecessor tried this case, don't think I won't press charges for prosecutorial misconduct." It would be a stretch at best, but attorneys all knew that winning cases was like playing poker. It was the illusion of what was in the other's hand. "And a civil suit for damages is highly likely as well."

"Ladies, like I said earlier, today is just about hearing the evidence. We're not going to trial here." The judge had to keep them both in line. "And I've made a decision. I'm going to reopen this case."

Margo wanted to shout out in celebration, but she didn't even smile. It was a long way from being over, but she had drawn first blood and the state attorney's office would see that as a potential problem. She expected that Mrs. Russell would return to her boss's office this afternoon and a deal would be in the making by tomorrow.

"I'm going to give you a hearing date thirty days from now." Judge Vogle was looking at his calendar. "Is that enough time for both sides?" Margo was ready now and the extra thirty days would just give her time to go back over every detail.

"Your Honor, we're talking about a case from years ago. I'll need more time to go over the case file and review the details." Faye Russell was going to try to stall. It was tactical, and the judge knew it.

"I guess you better get busy then, Faye," he added insult to injury. "Margo is representing herself, and she's ready. You have two floors of lawyers and assistants. I'm sure you can manage."

As much as Margo relished that he had taken a stand for her side, she almost wished that he hadn't. Faye Russell was a pit bull, and once she latched on, she didn't let go.

The lines had been drawn; Mrs. Russell would now make this personal.

CHAPTER 29

Despite Margo's judgment call to hide out for the last three weeks in a motel, she had returned to Sal's apartment and was seeing clients again. If everyone she wanted to hide from could find her, what was the point?

Agent Richards had been the one to point it out, and as much as she had tried to keep her distance from him and view him as the enemy, he had grown on her.

"Margo, you know you can't disappear," he had said as soon as she let him in the dingy hotel room that was home for another night. "Well, you can, but," he paused; obviously, he didn't want to remind her of the predicament she was in, "you have your kids to think about."

"I don't want to disappear." Margo ignored Jake's cheap shot. A part of her was convinced that disappearing was exactly what she wanted to do. "I just have to figure things out."

Margo sat on the bed and reviewed her options. Jake sat next to her and the feel of him so close was distracting.

"What is there to figure out?" He saw everything in such clear terms. Agent Richards's world was still black and white; there were good guys and the bad guys. Margo just saw many shades of gray.

"I shouldn't even be talking to you, Agent." If she was so easy to find that the FBI could track her down, what could Sal's people do? She thought that she should assume that Sal knew that the man was here with her, right now. "I'm sure that Mr. Mazzillo would not like the fact that you're visiting me." Margo noticed every ripple and every line from his shoulders, which were wide and solid. She studied him through his clothes. The man was handsome and smart, a double threat.

"Is that for professional reasons or personal ones?" He reached for her face and gently stroked her cheek as he asked.

Margo pushed his hand away. "You know what? I'm tired of answering questions about my personal life, and I'm not helping you with your investigation."

"You don't have to help, Margo," he whispered. "I just don't want you to get hurt."

Jake's hand was on her cheek once more, and when she felt him drawing near, her brain screamed no!—but her body wasn't listening. Margo trembled with want as his lips collided with hers and his tongue reached out to caress the soft curve of her lower lip.

Before she knew it, her hands were in his hair, and she heard the deep, needy moans that escaped from her as she opened her mouth and tasted him. His tongue moved slowly, back and forth, drawing her out, bringing her closer, and memorizing the feel of her skin. His hands kneaded her flesh; his fingers were hot on her back, and then moved slowly down her waist as he lay back on the mattress and pulled Margo with him.

Their kiss grew deeper, and in a moment, Margo was on top of him, sliding her tongue in deeper, and then seizing his with her lips, sucking him into her mouth. Jake's strong hands were wrapped around her ass, and this time when he pulled her near, she felt the erection that had risen from between his legs. He was hard as a rock and thick, and when she felt the tip of his cock pushing against her hips, she instinctively wanted more.

Margo ran her hand slowly down the front of his pants, from the head of his dick down to his balls, and Jake gasped at her touch, "Jesus, that's not fair."

"Why not, Agent?" Her voice sounded a little wicked, and she couldn't hold back her smirk. She knew very well what she was doing. She had always kept herself in check, been the good girl, waited for the right time. Now she saw what she wanted, and she would take it. That was one more thing she could thank Sal for.

"Because," he pushed himself up off the bed to rub against her small hand, "I'm making it so easy for you, but Margo, I've wanted you since the first day I saw you."

Margo took her hand off his hard-on and returned to their kiss, pushing her tongue into his mouth, drawing his breath away, thrusting her body into him and feeling his chest crushing her breasts. She wanted to feel his skin instead of the clothes. She pulled away from their embrace and asked, "Really? Did you have a hard-on like this for me when I came to your office?" She grabbed him at the base of his dick through his pants and listened to him pant.

"Shit, wait." No matter what she wanted, he was bigger, stronger, and could easily push her off. Instead, Agent Richards sat up. "This is wrong, Margo. No matter how much I want it, it's not right."

"Why not?" She wasn't used to being rejected, and it was humiliating. Margo's face was flushed. How embarrassing for Jake to push her away.

"Margo, I'm on a case." He spoke between clenched teeth, shaking his head. "And you're an important part of that case. Besides, I can't look out for you when I'm replaying in my mind being in bed with you, making love to you."

"Would that be what it is? Making love?" She sounded a little bitter. She couldn't help it, she was angry. She didn't like being rejected. "Not just a good old-fashioned fuck?"

Jake sat up. His back was to her, and she could tell that he was struggling . . . not just to answer her question but to stop himself from changing his mind.

"No, Margo, you wouldn't just be a fuck. I've got to go." He didn't look back at her as he made his way to the door. "Put the deadbolt on when I go, okay?"

"Sure, whatever, Jake."

She did as he asked, and then found herself furious with him sitting on the bed, arms crossed over her chest, her breath coming in short, fast bursts. Sexual frustration wasn't a condition that Margo had found herself in until she had met Sal. Hell, she had gone for years without sex and barely given it another thought. It wasn't until she had gone to bed with Sal that she found that she craved it.

Sal. Just saying his name to herself in her head brought up so many feelings, not the least of which was longing. How could you want someone so much and know full well how toxic they were? What did she really know though? Wasn't Sal innocent until proven guilty?

She had spent at least an hour pacing back and forth, arguing both sides. She didn't know for certain that he had anything to do with Eric's death. That was all Agent Richards's doing. He had planted the seed in her head, and she had just played into his hands and assumed the worst.

Considering that Eric had a nasty side business that included blackmailing men with a lot to lose, he probably had a lot of enemies. Add that to the fact he was a confidential informant for the FBI and the likelihood of him meeting his demise by the hands of almost any criminal on the streets grew exponentially.

On the other hand, she was almost positive that Sal had taken care of the Bollin kid; he had almost admitted it when he had given her that speech on loyalty. Then there was the suggestion that her life would be much easier if David were out of it. Had he meant that David should die, or was he just suggesting a move? Was she on the cusp of cooperating with the FBI and betraying her lover because of a suggestion?

She was no closer to a solution this morning as she sat in the coffee shop than she had been then. Sal hadn't called her, not even once, and Margo felt almost like Megan Dittmar this morning. No matter how bad he might be for her, she needed a fix.

So far, she had met with two low-level dealers who had both been caught with enough product to be facing charges, but in both cases, the police had used force, and in one, the young man still had a fist-shaped bruise on his face that he swore the officer gave him. Margo would need to see his booking photo, but if that was the case, it was an easy walk.

Her next client was walking in the door, and Margo was more than a little surprised. "Max" was not another young thug with his hat on backward and his pants pushed down low. Without a doubt, Max wasn't a he at all. The girl was petite and blond. Her curves were outrageous, and every man within a three-mile radius had their eyes all over every inch of her real estate as she clicked across the tile toward Margo in her five-inch stilettos.

"Miss Margo?" she asked and flipped her long, almost white curls over her shoulder before offering her hand.

"Yes, that's me." She shook the young lady's hand. "Are you Max?"

"Yeah, it's short for Maxine." She crinkled her turned-up nose. "I always hated my name, and I used to go by Summer." It would fit her, Margo decided. "But Sal convinced me that Max was sexier." She giggled and sat, her jacket was open and her enormous breasts were on display through the low-cut dress she wore.

"That Sal, he's crazy."

"He is," Margo nodded and told herself not to ask, not to go there. It was jealousy that was prompting the question; it was unprofessional to even have the thought, but she did it anyway. "So how do you know Sal?"

"Oh, I've known Sal for a long time." The girl's full lips curled into a smile. "Ever since I was a kid, my mother used to dance in one of his clubs."

"Oh." Margo wondered if Sal saw the girl as a friend or if there was more to it.

"So you're a dancer?" She had the body for it, and Margo couldn't help but notice all the eyes that were still lusting in the girl's direction.

"No, I hated dancing, I'm an escort."

Sal had girls like this around him constantly, and Margo had never realized until just now how easily she could be replaced; in reality, she might not even be in his thoughts at this point.

"So, Sal sees you professionally?" If the girl knew that none of these questions were pertinent to her case she would tell Margo to go fuck herself.

"God, no," she giggled. "Sal is almost like my dad. I mean, if he wanted to have a go, of course I would." She shrugged. He was still her boss regardless of what other role he played in her life. "I guess he's handsome . . . for an old dude."

It was a wave of relief that washed over her. Margo could hardly admit it, but it was the truth. If she cared enough to feel almost sick with jealousy, didn't that say something about the feelings she carried for the man?

"So tell me why you're here to see me, Max. What's going on with you?" She was ready to get back to work, pen in hand and jotting down notes.

Max had a custody dispute with the father of her two children. He was threatening to use her profession against her and take the kids away.

"He knows I'm a good mother; he knows that I love those kids." The girl's tiny hands were clenched into two small fists. "If I didn't love them, would I be doing this?"

She was drop-dead beautiful and blessed with a body that inspired lusty thoughts, but at the end of the day, she was a single mother working a job that she hated so that she could provide for her kids, something that Margo could relate to all too well.

Abigail and Thomas had accepted her back into the fold, but it still wasn't fair that it had been a question to begin with, that they had been ripped apart in the first place. She had come to terms with David's poor judgment and selfishness, but nothing could make up for that lost time.

Margo clicked her pen back and forth. "Max, tell me about your ex. What does he do, who does he hang out with, where does he go?"

If there was one thing that Margo had learned over the last few months, it was that finding your opponents' soft spots was sometimes as easy as following them. She was determined not to let Max lose custody.

Margo told Max, "We need to find your husband's dirty laundry and air it. What about drugs, drinking, gambling?" She kept taking notes. Over the past few months Margo had learned more about the importance of investigations than she had in her entire time in law school.

Margo had enough information to get started, and she looked over at Max. If she hadn't pushed herself in another direction, she could have very well ended up in the same position as the buxom blond. Actually, if it weren't for Sal's help, things could have been so much worse.

"One last thing, do you think you could get another job, just temporarily?" She knew she was asking a lot. "Just in case, as a Plan B?"

Nothing would pay Max like the escort position did and Margo knew that she needed to provide for her children. "I just want you to be able to tell the truth if you have to go to court."

"Do you think it's really going to go that far?" The girl was scared and rightfully so. The legal system was set up to screw people over in her position.

"I don't," but Margo didn't want to leave her vulnerable to be ripped apart in court. She had gone from jealous to maternal and for some reason she reached out and patted Max's small hand.

"I am sure that you're an excellent mother; it's just the court system . . . They look at women like us as easy targets."

"I can try," Max nodded and sniffed again. "I've waited tables before. It's just so hard, and I don't get to see my kids as much."

It was the harsh reality for so many women in the same trap. Legitimate jobs paid next to nothing. Margo remembered clearly how her feet and legs had pulsed with pain after working long hours with little to show for it.

"I tell you what, let me see what I come up with. We'll hold up on the career change unless we need it." Margo checked the time. "I'm going to get started on this right away, and I'll call you later in the week."

Max pulled out a handful of crumpled hundred dollar bills from her purse. "Sorry, let me straighten them out."

"Hey, no." Margo pushed them back toward her. "You don't owe me anything."

"But I want to pay." The blond had been burned by getting things for "free" in the past, Margo was sure.

"I'm working your case as pro bono." Margo smiled, and then realized that the girl didn't understand. "This is a favor for you. You shouldn't lose your kids; let me help you out, okay?"

Max hesitated, and then stuffed the money back where it came from and smiled. "Sal was right about you; you're a good person."

After the blonde left, Margo replayed the words in her head. If Sal thought she was a good person, wouldn't he be surprised to know that she had been contemplating talking about him to the FBI? And if she were really a good person, would she be lying to Agent Richards as well?

The more complicated things got, the more she realized that life wasn't black and white; it really was many shades of gray.

CHAPTER 30

It had been a long afternoon and Margo needed an adult beverage. She stopped in at the bar that was two blocks away from her apartment and was pleased to see the place was dead. It was just what she needed; somewhere quiet to help her relax and sort everything out.

She ordered an old-fashioned and felt the whiskey burn in her throat as she swallowed. Never much of a drinker, she felt the warmth run through her immediately and smiled to herself. She had always been on the go, her whole life. She worked to get through school, worked to get ahead, and now she was working her ass off for Sal's criminal clientele. She almost felt guilty when she tried to relax.

Not that there had been much relaxation lately. The last time she had really let go was the last time Sal had taken her to bed. His strong hands ripping at her clothing, ravishing her with his fingers and tongue and taking her forcefully.

Margo had thought in the beginning that it was just because her sex life had been so limited, so lukewarm, but after being his lover for the last few months, she thought it must be him.

Sal was a man who was used to taking what he wanted, and he had wanted her. It seemed that it had been just as easy for him to stay away though, and Margo had to admit, it hurt her ego. Had she really expected him to beg her to take him back? Did she think he was the kind of man that sent flowers and penned poems? Was the heartache felt only by her, or did he miss her?

Margo finished her drink, ordered another, and flipped through her notebook. Relationships were not her specialty; actually, she was a novice in that area. Obviously, if she wasn't, she wouldn't be tearing her hair out wondering if Sal was mooning over her when she was the one who had put the distance between them.

Then there was the fact that she had totally succumbed to Jake's fear tactics—the one man she shouldn't even be talking to, much less fucking.

"Do you mind if I sit here?"

She looked up when she heard the question and saw a dark-haired young man in a suit take a seat two stools over.

The place was virtually empty. "Help yourself." She waved her hand and looked back at her notes. She needed to stick to work. She had too much riding on her future to fuck things up now.

The Jake-Sal debate would have to wait until another day or work itself out. Margo needed to stick to what she knew.

"Drinking alone?" the young man asked, and she sighed when she looked up again. He was interrupting her. Didn't he get that?

"Yes, I'm drinking alone, and I suggest that you do the same." This was much more comfortable for Margo, putting men on ice and shutting down their advances. She'd done this her whole life, and tonight was going to be no exception.

"Wow, so I take it that you had the same kind of day that I did." He was persistent, and when Margo closed her notebook, she saw that he had rugged good looks and a nice smile.

She didn't know if it was the effects of the second cocktail or not, but she smiled back.

"That's better." It was an actual grin now, and his eyes gleamed with mischief. "I think you should relax for a little bit and enjoy my company."

Margo laughed. "Well, you're cocky, aren't you?"

"I have to be, I'm in sales." The man put down his drink and offered his hand. "My name is Hugh."

"I'm Margo." She shook his hand and turned to face him. Not bad. She was checking him out. Well-built and definitely in his thirties. The smile, the hair, the dark blue eyes, he was the total package, and she reasoned, at least he wasn't a gangster or a cop.

"What made your day so shitty?" she asked.

"Lost a deal, something I had been working on for two months." The disappointment was clear in his expression, "And it was my boss's fault, but the cocksucker is blaming it on me."

"That blows." She was about to finish the second drink, and Margo knew that she'd had enough if she was going to remain comfortably buzzed rather than drunk.

"Was it on purpose?" She didn't really care, but she was trying to keep up her end of the chitchat.

"Who knows." Hugh shrugged, and she watched him slide out of his jacket and loosen his tie.

"Excuse me," he gestured at the bartender, "can I get another round for me and Margo?"

"No, I'm good." She put her hand up. "I'm a lightweight."

"Come on, drink with me. You'll make me feel better."

There was no denying the look in his eye, and she knew exactly where this was heading. But Margo had always stopped herself right here—on the edge.

"Sure, why not?" Tonight she needed to forget. She needed something more potent than whiskey, something more satisfying than arguing back and forth with herself. She needed something that would blot it all out, and Hugh was clearly available.

"Tell me about your day," he smiled and patted her hand. "What do you do?"

She assumed that he didn't really care, and she wasn't going to give him the full story anyway.

"I'm a lawyer." It was close enough. "I have a client that I'm worried about." Margo reached up and pulled the clip out of the back of her hair. She felt her long, auburn waves tumble down her back. The move was not lost on Hugh, and his eyes traveled to her cleavage before returning to her face.

"Are they in trouble?" He had almost finished his drink already, and she had made up her mind. Could she just tell him what she wanted? She had never been so straightforward with a man.

"I tell you what, Hugh, the last thing I want to talk about is work." It was true; in fact, Margo didn't want to talk at all. "I live a couple of blocks away. Do you want to get out of here and go to my place?"

"Wow!" He licked his lips greedily and nodded, "Hell yes!" He sucked down the rest of his drink. "Looks like my luck just changed."

"Funny how things can shift so quickly, right?" She had packed up her notes and rose, feeling the effects of the alcohol rush through her.

"Did you drive, Hugh?" She stared at his ass and wanted to reach out and feel what she hoped her fingers would be wrapped around in a few minutes.

"I did." He put his arm out for her, and she took it quickly before he saw her wobble.

Once they were inside her front door and Margo had slammed it behind her, she watched him pause, as if unsure of how this was going to play out. To the left was the living room and more polite, strained conversation; down the hallway was the bedroom.

"Bedroom's that way," she pointed and once they were inside it, her hands ran down his chest, feeling the curve of his muscles and his heart racing in his chest.

"Damn, you're sexy." His hands were in her hair, and he pulled it back and kissed her neck, soft, tender kisses that quickly turned into hard nibbles.

She moaned, turning her back to him, pushing her hair to one side to give him her throat, his fingers of pleasure were running down her body the harder his teeth grazed her skin. The man unbuttoned her blouse and reached into her bra, freeing her left breast with his fingers as he continued to nibble on her. He pulled hard on the pointed nub, and Margo whispered, "Yes," as he kept the pressure coming, twisting the engorged flesh and sinking his teeth into her throat.

"You like it rough, don't you?" He wasn't asking, and he used both hands to push her skirt up. Her bottom was exposed and he pushed her down, her head on the bed, still standing as he fondled her between her legs.

Margo was soaking wet, and he answered his own question, "You do. You're a bad girl, and you need to be fucked hard." The man reached down the front of her panties, and she gasped, feeling her inner thighs tremble as he parted her lips and touched her where she ached.

She closed her eyes and pictured Sal. Sal's fingers were magic on her body, soft, and then hard, sweet, and then almost violent, he would bring her to the very brink of a release, and then keep her there and make her beg for more. The two fingers that were sliding into her hot, tight opening were Hugh's, but in her mind's eye it was Sal fingering her, and she arched her back and bit her lip to keep herself from crying out his name.

"Damn, baby, you're so wet, I love it." The man was working his two fingers in and out of her. He was rough and fast, and Margo let her hand wander down to meet his. She would guide him to what she wanted. Pulling his fingers out, she held his hand in her own and slid him up to her clit. She rubbed his fingers around her swollen bud and bucked her hips under him as she closed her eyes once more. It was Sal's hand; he knew her and what her body needed from the very first time.

She pushed herself back and forth and rolled her hips, feeling the solid erection pushing up against her cheeks. "Fuck me," she murmured and reached behind her to unzip him.

Sal wouldn't have waited; he would have plunged deep inside while keeping her on the verge of a sticky, sweet orgasm with the pluck of his fingertips.

The man's cock was out, and the head of his dick rubbed against her pussy and he wet himself with her juices, all the while she rocked herself and rubbed his fingers around her clit. Margo could feel the flutter of desire coursing through her. It had been far too long. She couldn't wait another second.

He thrust inside and buried his cock deep in her with one aggressive thrust. Margo pushed back and his mouth was on her back, his teeth sinking into her tender flesh and the sound of his balls slapping against her ass grew louder.

She screamed in ecstasy. “Yes, harder,” it was all she wanted, to be filled up and feel the vibration of her need run down her body.

The man did as he was told, pushing himself all the way in and pulling almost completely out, their skin coming together, and then apart, the smell of him, the touch of his fingers, the sting of his mouth, Margo convulsed as she became only a sensation. The pleasure was about to peak, and she squeezed her wet walls around his dick seconds before she started to come.

He was crying out, “yes!” and “fuck!” and then a name, “Dixie!” and Margo didn’t care as he tensed and latched on to her hips with both hands as he pumped her full of semen.

As the last of her climax rushed from her, she sank her head back against his shoulder and heaved a long sigh.

The man slid from inside her and once Margo collapsed on the bed, she felt his weight on the mattress next to her. There would be no kisses and no need for them; actually, she would never see or speak to Hugh again, and she found it oddly comforting.

This didn’t need to be analyzed, this could just be what it was; sex.

“So who’s Dixie?” She shouldn’t ask, but it was too late to take it back now.

"Did I say that?" She turned her face and watched him grimace. "Dammit, I'm sorry."

"No, don't be." Margo wasn't about to confess her own fantasy. "Is she your wife?"

"Ex-wife, and she broke my heart." It might have been the first truthful thing he had said since they met less than an hour ago.

Margo nodded. How many faceless strangers did it take to heal a broken heart? "What happened?" He might as well confess it all now.

"I came home a day early from a business trip and caught her in bed with a guy who lived up the street. She was fucking him in our bed." He paused, waiting for her to comment, and then added quietly, "The worst thing was that it turned me on."

"Why is that the worst thing?" Maybe having two lovers was really the best of both worlds, and she'd just keep things purely physical. Hadn't she learned anything from Sal?

"It's humiliating." His cheeks were red as he recounted it. "I was so pissed, but I had such a hard-on. She said it was pathetic, that I wasn't really a man."

"She wanted you to fight for her?" At the end of the day, Margo wasn't sure if men or women had evolved much past the traditional roles.

"Maybe." The man rolled over on his back. He seemed to be completely comfortable telling her his secrets now.

"She thought I couldn't take care of her sexual needs anyway because of a fetish I have."

"Oh yeah? What is it?" Margo might as well know all of it now.

"Well . . . It's embarrassing." He shrugged. They would never speak again; it didn't seem to matter if she judged him or not. "I like to eat out a women's ass. It's probably weird, but I fucking love it. My ex was repulsed by it and wouldn't let me do it to her."

Margo was curious. Her oral sex experiences had mostly begun and ended with Sal. Every touch of his mouth on her body was a sensory explosion, and there was no time like the present to discover if that was his prowess as a lover or her lack of experience.

"Do you want to do that with me?" she whispered. The man had never even taken his clothes off, and she was still mostly dressed as well. She'd never really just fucked before. She wondered if this was customary.

"Would you let me?" The heat was there in his eyes. It was obvious that he wanted to do it, and Margo wanted to surrender to her curiosity, surrender to the hot and wet pleasure she craved.

"Yes," she nodded, and his body slid down the bed, reaching for a pillow and making his way down her back with a line of closed-mouth kisses.

"Stay on your stomach," the man said, "just raise your hips, let me put this pillow under you." Margo raised up her bottom, and he parted her legs, his tongue was instantly on her slit, lapping up the remnants of the orgasm that he had left behind.

His tongue weaved along every bit of her skin, and when she felt his fingers pry her cheeks apart, she almost squealed and forced herself to take a deep breath as he lapped at the delicate skin there. Her nerves pulsed with every touch, and when he slipped his tongue inside her ass, she gasped. Margo let him have her there, and her hips seemed to follow his tempo, rising up to meet him and pushing into the pillow as he withdrew.

She was lost in the feeling of being taken, the wet noises of his tongue as he darted in and out of her, his hot saliva running down her crack, dribbling below to make a puddle beneath her. Margo had a need, still unfulfilled, and when she pushed up to let him open her again, she slipped her fingers under her mound and began to masturbate.

It was obvious in a few moments that he was masturbating too; she could hear the slick noises of his hand around his cock, sliding back and forth, the same as he probed her with his tongue. Margo sighed and made slow, wet circles around her needy clit. She wanted Sal. She could feel the greedy, gripping want for him on every inch of her body.

Once more, she was in his arms. It was Sal behind her, over her, inside her, stroking her, controlling her climax, and pushing her to say his name and beg for more. As she rubbed herself faster, her body shivered, and she suddenly felt a finger inserted into her ass.

Margo cried out, a little bit from shock but mostly from pleasure. "Oh my God, yes! That feels soooo good."

Hugh tentatively and slowly moved his finger in and out of Margo's ass.

Every nerve ending seem to be standing at attention in her body and she cried out, "More, more!"

The man removed his finger and spread her cheeks wide with his hands before he licked her crack and buried his tongue in her ass.

"Yes, no, no, more, more, I want more." Margo was panting and on the verge of hysteria with need of being filled up.

His tongue was obediently replaced by two fingers that he buried up to his knuckles. He expertly moved his fingers in and out of Margo's ass with quick, fast thrusts now.

Margo responded by squealing like a schoolgirl and pushing back into his thrusts. She turned her head to look at him and saw he was completely focused on her ass while he absent mindedly stroked his dick.

Margo felt like she was having an out-of-body experience. On one hand, she could see she was completely out of control and caught up in wild, primal desire, and on the other hand, she knew exactly where she was, what she was doing, and what she wanted to happen next.

She was moaning with every thrust of his fingers. "More, more, I need more. I want you to fuck me with your cock."

He pulled her hair and forced her to meet his gaze. He had a snarl on his lip when he spat, "Only bad girls take it in the ass. Are you bad girl?"

His fingers continued their steady pounding inside her.

"Yes," she said in a deep, throaty voice, "I'm bad. I'm a very bad girl. A bad girl that wants you to put your cock in my ass, take me, and fuck me."

He removed his fingers, and she felt the tip of his cock at her entrance. He slowly pushed the head of his cock inside her and paused. He gently entered her a little at a time until his cock was buried within her.

Margo bit her lip as she initially felt some discomfort, but about halfway in it was replaced with pleasure. He started out slow, but was soon fucking her fast and hard. He pulled her hair, and she looked back to see his other hand on the small of her back and his dick rhythmically moving in and out of ass. Margo was so turned on, the visual pushed her past the point of no return and she moaned loudly, tensed, and then let go, her release violently spilling from her. She felt the man's tongue fill her as her clit pounded in waves and she felt her orgasm rock her body.

Her eyes were shut, and she was a million miles away when he rested his head on her lower back. She purred and sank into the bed, no longer drunk. Her body was drained, and moving from this position seemed almost impossible.

She heard him stirring behind her and felt one last kiss on her backside. "I better go," he told her, and she heard the jingle of a belt and when she rolled over, there he was, the man she had picked up in the bar, and she wondered if she'd even remember his face later.

"I'll walk you out." She didn't know the protocol for this type of thing and wondered if they kissed goodnight. Did they pretend that it wasn't what it actually was?

"Thanks for the nice time, Margo." He looked apprehensive, as if he wasn't well-versed on the rules either. "Do you want me to give you my card?"

She shook her head no and patted his arm. "I had a good time too."

She was spent, and she had no regrets, but if she had learned one thing tonight, it was that Sal was not a meaningless fling, and she missed him more than ever.

CHAPTER 31

There had been something about the boy from the moment Sal had brought him home. He had stirred something inside her that she had thought was missing or at least broken beyond repair. It was more than maternal instinct, it was an understanding of grief, of loss, of pain that a child should not experience and is not equipped to deal with.

She held his hand in hers as she walked him to the bedroom that would be his. It was a spare room that had a pull-out couch and the walls were bare. There had been no time to prepare it properly for the boy. Giovanna shook out the sheet she would use to make up the couch. "I'm sorry about the couch, but it will just be for tonight. We'll get you a bed and some furniture tomorrow. We'll go shopping, and you can pick out whatever you want. Would you like that?"

The boy hadn't spoken yet and wouldn't do anything but nod. He was understandably in shock; his whole world had just been turned upside down. He had only learned of his parents deaths a few hours ago and hadn't had time to process what was happening. Giovanna understood. It hadn't really been that long ago . . . She could remember when her father died like it was yesterday. She had been numb, and when the relatives, the friends of the family, and all of the virtual strangers had tried to console her. The only thing she had felt was rage. It had never left her; it was what drove her, she had just learned to control it and conceal it with smiles and secrets.

She knew better than to try to console him. She sat next to him on the couch and held his hand. "Nothing anyone says will make the hurt or the pain go away. I know because I lost my father when I was just two years younger than you. A lot of people are going to say things to try to make you feel better, but you won't. Other people won't know what to say to you, how to treat you. They will be uncomfortable and feel sorry for you. This will eventually pass."

"How did your father die?" the boy asked her.

Giovanna smiled tenderly and combed her fingers through his thick, sandy blond hair. The blond came from his mother, but the rest of him, his dark eyes, his dimples, his mannerisms were definitely Mazzillo genes.

"My father was murdered. He died in a public restroom in a pool of his own blood." It felt good to talk about it with someone, like finally ripping off a scab that wasn't completely healed. It was a relief.

The boy looked up at her. "Why did someone murder him?"

Giovanna sighed before she answered. "Money."

There were other factors that had played a part in her father's death, like greed, power, someone's overinflated ego and the borderline psychotic loyalty to family, but she knew it all ultimately came down to money. It was the simple answer.

"You'll learn soon enough, money is what makes the world go around. Money corrupts people, and they will do terrible things for money. The more money that is involved, the greater a person's sins will be. People will sell their souls to get money and to keep it."

"Do you know who murdered him?" The boy rested his head against her shoulder. He was too young for all of this, just as she had been. Giovanna vowed to herself that the boy would feel safe and loved, unlike her childhood. She would protect him and make sure he was prepared to deal with the reality, the benefits and the sins that came with the Mazzillo name.

She kissed the top of his head. "Yes, I do. But we can talk about that another time."

Later that night, she tucked him in the makeshift bed and pulled the blankets up to his chin. "Do you want the light on?" she asked him. He might be family, but she knew nothing about him really.

He shook his head no and waited until it was dark to ask, "Am I staying here with you now?"

Giovanna spoke softly, "Yes, you are. Your uncle and I can't replace your parents, but we are family, and family takes care of each other. We want you here, and we will take care of you. You are a part of our family now." For the first time in a very long time, her words and intentions were true and sincere.

CHAPTER 32

McKinley, Patterson, Conley, and Cook, Margo read the new name. Jay had made partner, and now he was on the letterhead. She scrolled down the screen as she read. Since Margo had left the firm, he had rocketed up and was their shining star. His client list was impressive. He had brought in high rollers, big names and big companies. She was sure that he had dazzled them all, and with Margo out of the way, it would have been much, much easier. He was never the lawyer that she was.

Jay was more of a used car salesman. She had labeled him that years ago, and it still stuck. He used cheap tricks, manipulations, slights of hand, and showmanship, rather than research or work. Margo remembered years ago when she had been putting in fifteen-hour days, preparing for a trial for two weeks, when she looked up and saw him standing in her doorway. It was dark, she was exhausted, and he was smiling, shaking his head at her. "Margo, Margo, Margo, when are you going to stop working so hard?"

"When I can get by on bullshit, like you, Jay." She had never backed down to him since they had first met, and it wasn't about to happen now. He might have everyone else in the office bamboozled, but Margo could see right through him.

"It's not bullshit, it's called giving people what they want. You should try it sometime, Margo, it's like magic." He looked in the windows behind her and preened, running his hands through his hair and strutting as he walked closer to her. Jay had always thought he was handsome. Margo didn't agree, but she had kept that to herself.

"Why don't you loosen up and have a little fun?" He was behind her and when his fingers touched her neck, Margo froze as if he had turned her into stone.

"Don't touch me, Jay," she muttered, flipping a page and hoping that the less attention that she gave him, the faster he would leave.

"Just giving you a neck rub, Margo, you're so tense." His breath was on her throat, and she felt sick to her stomach. He reeked of alcohol and cigarettes, and his touch was loathsome.

"Seriously, knock it off, Jay." Margo moved out of his grasp. It was too late to deal with him on top of everything else. "Why don't you go to your office and do some fucking work for a change?" Her voice was angry, and the volume was rising. Instead of spending time with her children, she was tucked away at her desk.

"I'll do some fucking for a change, how about that?" He grabbed her hand and clasped it to his crotch, pushing his erection against her palm. "You need some more dick, Margo, you know that?"

"I swear to God, Jay," she tried to pull her hand away, but he was too strong, "if you don't get out of here and stop this right now, I'll have you brought up on charges. This is sexual assault, just like the perverts who rub themselves on women on the subway."

"Jesus, Margo, why are you so goddamn uptight?" He let her go and stormed off. "I meant what I said, you need some dick."

Before he left she said in a calm voice, "I might need some dick, but that tiny little thing you were rubbing in my hand sure didn't feel like anything I could use. And I better not ever feel it again."

He had stared at her with rage, his mouth open, and she noticed that his fist was clenched at his side. Jay, on top of all of his other faults, probably abused women too. It would fit the profile. All the women in the office either fucked him or he had labeled them "frigid" or "dykes." It was only a matter of time until the partners saw him for what he was: a liability.

It had been almost a decade since that night, and Margo shook her head as she continued reading the article. They still hadn't figured him out, or if they had, no one cared. He brought enough money to the firm that they were willing to look the other way. There was something else there, there had to be. Margo could almost smell it when she was missing something.

She decided to look at the cases that he had been taking since she'd left the firm. A quick search with his last name in the courthouse online system would tell her. One firm name popped up at least twenty times, "Great American Eagle," a company that she'd never heard of. When she searched the company name, she read through their Website and still had no idea what the company did.

The president and CEO of Great American Eagle was Vladimir Slivka, a name that she thought sounded familiar but couldn't remember why. Once she typed in his name, the page was covered in blurbs, *That's right* . . . Margo bit the pen as she quickly scrolled through the images and articles. Vladimir Slivka, migrated from Russia almost twenty years ago, and according to the crime wave that followed him, had brought the Russian mob with him.

It was mostly conjecture, nothing had ever stuck, and even the murder charge had been dropped when the only witness had "disappeared." Mr. Slivka had been very quiet for the last few years; it seemed as if he had become a respectable businessman. Margo smiled to herself, just like Sal.

She had gotten to a point in her research where she had exhausted what she could do legally. Any road from here was at least shady if not downright illegal and there was only one person she could call.

"Cookie, how have you been?" His voice was warm, and she could immediately picture his face on her pillow instead of on the other end of the phone.

"I've been okay, Sal, just working." Margo's heart drummed in her chest as she remembered the vivid fantasy she had two nights ago with the stranger from the bar. If only she could just tell him how badly she missed him, it would make things so much easier.

"Me too, Cookie, but I miss you." Her body automatically responded to his words as if his mouth were on her as he spoke them. Sal's powerful arms around her, his thick fingers running down her spine, sending an electric spark through her, Margo tried to stop herself but it was almost impossible.

"I miss you too," she murmured and wondered if he knew what he was doing to her.

There was a pause and she thought perhaps she had lost the call. "Can I see you?" Sal asked.

She could say no, she could press end call, she could tell him this was a professional call and change the subject, but in the end, she had known before he answered what she was really asking for.

"Yes, Sal." Margo didn't care that it was weak of her. She hadn't been able to stop thinking of him since the last time they had spoken. Didn't that mean anything? No other man had ever had this kind of hold on her and she was famished for his presence.

"When will you be home, Cookie?"

She could play hard to get, but what was the point?

"I'm at the coffee shop." Margo assumed he had kept close tabs on her. "Do you want to come and get me?" She tried to keep the excitement out of her voice.

It took him almost no time to arrive, and when she watched him exit the back of the Town car and open his arms for her when she exited the restaurant, nothing that she had thought mattered; it had solved nothing. It was uncharacteristic for Sal to kiss her in public, but there, right in front of anyone who was paying any attention, he kissed her greedily, scooping her up in his arms and devouring her lips with his own. She sighed into his mouth when his tongue slowly delved along her mouth, his hands gripping her ass as he pulled her even closer and sucked the air out of her lungs.

When he released her, Margo was shaking and could hardly catch her breath.

"Let me take you home, Cookie." He took her hand in his and once the door was shut behind them, she was firmly back in Sal's world, and she couldn't think of anywhere else she'd rather be.

In her bedroom, he sat on her bed, still dressed, not making a move, just looking her in the eye. "I want to say something to you, I've been thinking about it since the last night we were together."

She was unfamiliar with this look. His dark eyes shone and looked vulnerable. She couldn't tell if he was sad or this was something darker. What did Sal know about her activities since that night?

"Sure, Sal, I'm listening." The hair on her arms had risen, and she held her breath.

"I would never do anything to hurt you or your kids, Cookie, you have to know that." He exhaled slowly and raised his hand to her face, stroking her cheek tenderly. "I love you."

The words broke from her—there was no stopping them, and she heard herself repeating them back, "I love you, too," before she melted in his arms. A long, soft kiss began as their fingers busied with the other's clothes.

Margo heard him sigh as their tongues touched and she unbuttoned his shirt. His well-muscled chest was bare, and she wanted to explore every inch of it with her mouth as well. Wearing only her bra and panties, Margo eased Sal back on her pillows as she pressed her mouth to his throat, down the center of his chest, her fingers unbuckling his belt as she buried her face in his skin.

Once his pants were off, she wrapped her fingers around his throbbing dick. Even through his boxers, the touch of him was almost burning and the necessity of having him inside was tormenting her.

"Take your panties off," Sal moaned as he freed himself from the last of his clothes. "Get up here and sit on my face." It was a command and one that she could hardly wait to follow.

Margo was facing the headboard as she lowered herself down on his mouth and threw her head back with a howl as Sal lapped up her slit and tasted her wet heat. "Yes, Sal, oh yes." She pushed back and forth against him and felt her thighs clench around his face as he continued to pleasure her with the tip of his tongue flicking her bud. She reached back behind her, holding his enormous cock at the base with her index finger and thumb and heard the noises that burst from him as she squeezed him tight.

His tongue worked on her faster the harder she held him, and when she brought her hand up to the wet tip of his dick, she felt his precum drip from his slit. Margo shuddered and bucked, rubbing herself against his mouth and feeling his lips suck her clitoris in, his tongue keeping its perfect, heart-stopping rhythm that he always kept so perfectly.

There was no way to stop it. A rivulet of her desire for him poured from her, and her bud felt as if it would burst with her impending pleasure. She cried his name over and over as her orgasm rocked through her. "Sal, oh God, yes, Sal, I missed you so much."

She was his, and she only wanted more—more of him, more of his touch, more of his skin colliding with hers. She felt the wetness sliding down his cheeks as he lapped her up and drank her down.

"Cookie, I missed you too," he murmured as he rolled her over, hovering over her, his face was glistening with her juices, and he shared it with her as he kissed her once more. "I can't stop thinking about you," he told her as he took her, hard and slow, thrusting to the bottom, and then pulling back until she begged and tried to clutch at him to keep him inside.

Sal pounded at her, picking her legs up and pulling her thighs to his chest with every single drive into her core. Margo was crying from the want that was bubbling up inside and reaching her hands up to him, running them down his chest, feeling the sweat on his skin, smelling him, staring into his eyes that contained a heat she had never known.

They came in unison this time. Sal flooded her with a torrent of his hot need, and she felt every spurt at her center, squeezing every drop from him, covering him with her own pulsating orgasm. Margo never remembered feeling this way before and didn't know if it had been his body or his words or the fact that she had been so parched for him, but when she felt him collapse on top of her, she pulled him near and trembled as they kissed.

CHAPTER 33

"So Jay represents Vladimir Slivka and his front company?" Sal had his arms around her and their mouths were only inches apart as they talked.

"Yes, he's been very busy with them, twenty cases or more since I left the firm and probably thousands of billable hours." She still didn't know what the connection was to her or if there even was one. She just smelled that she was close, close to something major.

"And you think he wanted you out of the way? You think the firm is in on it?" Sal was close, but she didn't know what she was looking for either so Margo had to throw up her hands.

"I'm not sure, I don't even know if it matters. I'm just grasping at straws probably." Her mind was still busy even though her body was spent. Her legs were curled around his, and everywhere his fingers touched her, her skin was like putty under his caress.

"I have Megan's testimony, so I'm not even sure if I need anything else."

Was it just a need for revenge at this point? She would blow Jay's credibility out of the water once the court heard that not only had he forced the girl to perjure herself, but he was fucking the witness and feeding her drugs.

"It would be good to know if there was another reason though, besides just that he was pissed off that you told him he had a small dick." Sal chuckled at that one, "Although for a lot of guys that would be enough." His hands molded along her waist and were moving up to her breasts, and then crushing her into his body again. Margo felt his cock stirring once more, and she moved down his body. She had a hunger for him, wanting to run her tongue along his girth and feel him harden in her mouth.

Her phone buzzed on the nightstand, not the phone that Sal had given her, the other phone. Who in God's name would be calling her?

"Cookie, that's you." He handed her the phone, and she suddenly remembered David's message.

It had been such a long time since she had talked to her mother, she was hesitant, but she answered. "Hello?"

"Margo, is that you?" She sounded weak and far away.

"Mom?" Margo sat up so she could hear her better. "It's Margo, is that you, Mom?"

"Yeah, it's me." She was coughing; it sounded wet and she gurgled into the phone, "I hope you don't mind, your husband gave me your number."

"No, I don't mind." Margo felt no emotion hearing her mother's voice.

"Are you okay? You don't sound so good." Her mother had been using her many imagined ailments as an excuse to pop pills and self-medicate for so long, Margo wondered if a real illness had finally caught up with her.

"Yeah, I'm okay, just a little under the weather." Her mother's voice was raspy.

Margo got right to the point. "So why are you calling me, what do you want?"

"I just wanted to hear your voice, find out if you were doing okay." Margo thought her mother's voice sounded sad, maybe even a little desperate.

Alarms were sounding in Margo's head; something wasn't right. She hadn't talked to her mother in over twenty years, and now the woman was tracking her down to see how she was? "Mom, what's really going on? Is something wrong?"

"Ah, the doctor said I got something wrong, but what the hell does he know?" Her mother sounded weak. "These damn doctors, they won't even give you anything good anymore; it's like they want you to suffer."

Her mother had abused pills before it was fashionable, and Margo wondered how many she'd taken before she had called.

"What exactly do you mean something's wrong? What did the doctor say?" She waited for an answer and just heard wheezing.

"Mom, hello? Where are you?" She heard a series of coughs on the other end before her mother gasped, "I'm in the hospital. Hold on," she muttered.

Margo heard more coughing, hacking, and wheezing. She wondered what the hell was really going on. As she waited for her mother to come back on she felt her pulse accelerate.

"Are you there?" Margo asked. There was no answer. "Mom?" It was the story of her life. When she needed her mother, she was nowhere to be found. She was about to hang up. She was probably in the hospital for something stupid like falling down the stairs again and cracking a rib before passing out.

Margo thought about all of the times as a kid she had to make excuses for her mother's bad behavior and poor judgment. "Mom, I'm hanging up now," she called out, not sure if she even cared at this point.

"No, I'm here," she rasped. "I'm here, sorry."

"What hospital are you in?" Maybe she would get some factual information from a doctor instead of the bullshit her mother would try to peddle.

"I'm at Bowman."

Bowman General was an old, run-down hospital in the old, run-down neighborhood she had grown up in.

"OK, well, I'm going to come see you in the morning, Mom." She was speaking loudly in the phone, overcompensating for her mother's lack of conversation.

"See you later, Jellybean." Her mom was fading, and she didn't know if she had hung up or passed out.

Margo felt a little sad when she lay down once more. Sal would do anything for family; he would protect them or die trying. As much as his methods at protection scared her, she had never had that growing up. She wished that she'd grown up feeling loved, safe, and secure.

"What's wrong with your mother, Cookie?" He ran his hand down her cheek and lifted her chin so they looked each other in the eye.

"I don't know, she's in the hospital. She doesn't sound good."

Margo knew that Sal had the details of her life but wondered how much of her early family history was tucked inside her file.

"My mom is a hypochondriac pill popper who washes everything down with a fifth of whatever she can get her hands on. She's just a junkie, I guess." She hated to use that word, but it was more than appropriate. "I haven't talked to her since I left for college."

"You really are all alone, aren't you?" Sal didn't approve. "Life is short, Cookie, and everyone needs family. Kinda sounds like your mother might need some family right about now."

"I'll go see her tomorrow." Margo didn't like thinking about her mother needing her. The woman's addiction had drained her almost dry by the time she left home. "It's probably something minor. It can wait until the morning."

"Did she hurt you, Cookie?" She hadn't thought about her mother for a long time. It wasn't hurt, it was something else.

"She didn't physically hurt me; she just cared more about getting high than taking care of me. She was never there for me when I needed her. I was on my own."

"So she didn't hit you? Did she make sure you had food? A warm place to live?" Margo made a face at him.

"I'm just saying that maybe she did the best she could. You know, Cookie, not everyone is as strong as you."

She hated giving her mother an excuse; her mother had given her hundreds growing up. "I guess you're right," Margo relented.

"Why don't you go see her now?" Sal asked.

Margo groaned. She was still in heat, and she wanted more of him. More of his hands on her skin, more of his wicked tongue that brought her to a boiling point along every curve.

"I'll go in the morning."

Sal raised his eyebrows at her, and she clung to him but knew he was right.

Margo sighed in defeat. "All right, I'll go."

"I'll drop you off, Cookie." He was staring at her face, his dick pulsating against her thigh. "I can wait for you." He gave her one last kiss. His tongue circled hers, drawing it out, bringing it into his mouth for him to suck on slowly. "I do love kissing you," he admitted when he relinquished his grasp.

Her pussy twitched with desire, and it took every bit of her self-control not to mount him. Instead, she peeled herself off the damp sheets and redressed.

She locked the door behind her, then they walked to his car. “I just realized your driver sits here and waits for you when we’re together.”

Sal shrugged, “Yeah, it’s his job.”

“Don’t you feel kind of weird? I mean, he knows everything you do.” Margo had never gotten comfortable enough to forget there was another pair of eyes on her when she was in Sal’s backseat.

“Joey’s OK. He’s loyal. He’s been with me for a long time, and I trust him,” Sal told her when he opened the door for her.

Margo looked out the window and thought about who else might be watching them. Did Agent Richards have them under surveillance; was he eavesdropping and listening to their conversations? Was someone else? Was she just being paranoid, or had she been naïve, taken too much for granted?

Just because Sal was wonderful to her didn’t mean that he didn’t have enemies everywhere. Did she really think that she could be intimately attached to him and never have his world touch her?

“I’ll ask around a little about the Russian.” Sal would get more answers than she could, and Margo reached for his hand and laced her fingers around his.

"Thank you. Like I said, it could be nothing." She doubted that it was nothing, but it could be nothing that she could use. Hopefully, Megan was enough to bring Jay's house of cards down.

"I don't think it's nothing; besides, the Russian's on my turf." Margo didn't want to hear anything else. They were getting dangerously close to the frightening aspect of their relationship that she hadn't come to terms with in her mind.

"Jay's an asshole, and he's definitely not above doing illegal things,"—like putting together phony charges that got her out of the way—"but I don't think he has the balls to be behind anything this big."

"Cookie, a guy like Slivka needs someone like him . . . spineless and weak." Sal would have firsthand knowledge of what gangsters needed. "He's easy to control."

"Really?" Margo tried to picture Jay being an errand boy for a ruthless killer, but she just couldn't.

"Not like you." Sal was smiling at her. "You're a firecracker."

Their lips met briefly when the car pulled up to the curb in front of the hospital. "Go see your mother." Sal stroked her hair before his driver opened the door for her. "Call me later."

She promised she would, and as Margo turned back to wave good-bye, she saw Sal watching her and wondered how much of that was his affection and how much of it was just habit.

CHAPTER 34

The woman at the front desk looked up and smiled. "How can I help you?"

"I'm here to see Susan Harris." Margo hated hospitals, especially this one. The place looked as if it were sagging around them. Even more run-down than she remembered during their numerous trips here as a child, when her parents had need to be bandaged and stitched over the years. It smelled familiar, and it was making her nauseous.

The woman looked somber when she turned from the screen. "She's in 1289. Take the elevators to the twelfth floor."

Margo punched the button in the elevator and read the sign. The twelfth floor was cardiology. She swallowed hard. This looked more serious than she had thought.

The room was dark when she entered and a shape was in the hospital bed, so much smaller than she remembered her mother being. Margo flicked on a light near the bed and could hardly contain her horror. Her mother was asleep, mouth open, wheezing with each breath. Oxygen tubes in her nostrils, and other wires and tubes came from under her gown and inside her arm, connecting her to a machine that beeped. There was a large Band-Aid on her neck and one on her hand. She had greenish, fading bruises on one of her arms and face. Margo was dumbfounded. How long had her mother been here, and how sick was she?

She pulled a chair next to the bed and touched her bony hand. Her mother had never been a big woman. She had always seemed almost dainty, and when Margo had reached her adult height, she stood a good six inches above her. What she had lacked in size, however, she had more than made up for in swagger.

Her mother had been defiant since Margo could remember. When the school would send home a letter or the landlord would deliver a notice, Susan was bent on rebellion.

"Don't be a sheep, Margo." If her mother had told her that once, she'd said it a thousand times. Now that she thought back over her childhood, she was sure that her mother's biggest disappointment in her daughter was that she had been such a good kid.

Margo's freshman year in high school her mother constantly harassed her. "You gotta live a little, Margo," she would slur. "Why don't you go out and just have a good time?"

"I have homework to do," she would hiss at her mother. She had taken to calling her by her first name, "and I have to go to work, Susan."

"Oh my God, my own daughter is a Goody Two-shoes." Her mother's bathrobe fell open as she lolled in the doorway. That time she had been wearing clothes underneath, but so many times before, Margo remembered being ashamed at seeing her mother's naked, sagging flesh.

"How come you're not like me at all, huh?" Although she hadn't thought of the day for years, it was all coming back as if it had happened yesterday.

"What do you mean, Susan? A drunk? Should I take pills all day? Would that make you proud?" Margo had snapped, and when her mother stared at her, her mouth open but silent, Margo remembered feeling victorious, even if it had been a cheap shot.

"I'm sorry that I'm not good enough for you." Susan's chin had trembled as she attempted to hold back her tears. "I suppose you wish you had a different mother, right? Someone who baked cookies and went to PTA meetings?"

"Get out of my room!" Margo couldn't win the argument. If she said no it was like giving Susan her way once more. If she said yes, she was afraid that the woman would dissolve into hysterics right there.

"Come on, Margo," her mother was in the mood to fight, which she often was, and Margo watched her draw her shoulders back. "Tell me, tell me what a bad job I've done with you." She was slurring her words a bit, and Margo knew she should just gently lead her to bed so her mother could pass out there with a tiny bit of dignity.

She hadn't done that though; instead, all of the words that she had kept down for so long were fighting to erupt from her mouth and Margo stared at her and screamed, "Yes, you're a terrible mother! You shouldn't have even had me; you should have given me up for adoption. Anything would have been better than living here with you and *him!"*

Since the attempted molestation, Margo had never called him Dad. He was "him" or "your husband" when she spoke about him to Susan. She hated him for being a disgusting pervert, but she hated her mother more for being so weak. Susan didn't have to have this life. Margo could tell that she had the intellect and the will to have done so much more. Susan had chosen this lifestyle and chosen to give in to the demons that fueled her addiction. Margo felt that it had been a grave injustice.

"Well, I'm sorry that I'm so awful, Margo." Her mother had taken the verbal assault and didn't even try to defend herself. She remembered watching Susan hang her head and look down at her open robe and tie it quickly as if she had just realized how offensive it may be.

"It probably doesn't matter to you, but I always loved you. I'll leave you alone." She shuffled off down the hall and went to bed. Margo wouldn't allow herself to feel guilty for how she felt, and she hadn't gone after her to apologize.

The next three years, Margo had been like a ghost. She hardly ever came home, choosing, instead to do her homework at her job or at the library . . . anywhere but there. She volunteered to work holidays and weekends, any excuse to stay away from home. When she did make an appearance, it was quick and quiet, tip-toeing across the living room on her way to her room, washing some laundry or making a sandwich. The few times that she saw Susan face-to-face, they exchanged superficial pleasantries and didn't look each other in the eye.

Margo had figured her tirade had been forgotten before her mother even passed out that night, but Susan chose her high school graduation day to remind her of it. Her mother had come to the ceremony. She was clean, and her hair was combed into place, something that Margo hardly remembered seeing. Her mother had worn an old dress that she'd had since Margo had first gone to kindergarten, but it was ironed, and Margo remembered watching her mother fidget in it, obviously uncomfortable and wishing she could have worn the old robe instead.

They walked down the hall together as she left high school for the last time. Margo was going away to school and had an internship that started that summer. She was leaving home for good and had no intentions of ever returning. When they reached the bus stop, Susan pulled an envelope out of the purse she had carried. "This is for you."

Margo peeked inside and saw the bills. None of them were new. It was old money, and the creased envelope smelled musty too. The cash was in no apparent order; here a twenty, there a ten, even an odd hundred dollar bill had been stashed away. "What's this for?" Margo asked when she had finished counting it. It was a little over a thousand dollars, a veritable fortune in their household.

"Your college fund." Her mother looked sad. "I know it's not much, and you're getting scholarships, but maybe it will help. I always had high hopes for you, Margo, even though I've been a shitty parent for you."

Margo should have reached out and hugged her. She should have thanked her for doing her best and never completely succumbed to her addiction for Margo's sake. Instead, Margo had pressed her lips together and said nothing.

When the bus arrived, her mother got on first, and Margo sat two rows behind her. Margo had felt nothing. Two days later, Margo left home, and she hadn't seen Susan again until tonight. She bent her head as she hovered over her mother's hospital bed and wondered if she would have the opportunity to make up for lost time. Did she deserve to right the wrongs of her past?

Margo hoped so, now that she had been on the other side, rotting away in prison while her children grew further and further distant from her. Had she been any better of a mother than her own had been? At least Susan had been there every day, even if she was self-medicated and incoherent by the time Margo came home from school. Perhaps she had been a bad example, but wasn't a bad example better than disappearing for six years?

Her mother thrashed around in the bed and was mumbling a bunch of gibberish. Margo feared she was going to dislodge the wires connected to her. She started tapping Susan on the arm. "Mom, Mom, wake up." She shook her gently by the shoulders, and her mother finally came to.

"What are you doing to me now? Can't you just let me die in peace?" she grumbled and rubbed one eye.

"Mom, it's me, Margo." She held Susan's bony fingers in both of her hands, trying to warm her. Her mother's skin felt like paper and she thought that if she hugged her, she looked as if she might disintegrate.

"Margo?" her mother peered at her as if she were a stranger. "Am I dreaming?"

"No, Mom, it's me." She tried to force a smile but looking at the sack of bones on the bed was painful.

"How do you like my suite? It comes with room service." Susan was trying to downplay the seriousness of her situation with humor, something that she'd done for Margo's sake many times before. "Did we talk on the phone or am I imagining that too?"

"Yes, Mom, you called me a few hours ago." If it hadn't been for Sal insisting that she come, she would still be wrapped up in his arms. She was grateful Sal had prodded her into coming.

"What happened, Mom? Why are you here?" she asked. She also wondered how long she had been here, how long before she could leave, and where was her father? One question at time.

"My ticker tried to give out on me, but no such luck. As you can see, I'm still here." Her mother smiled and squeezed Margo's hand.

"How serious is your condition?" Margo asked, bracing herself for the worst.

"Oh, who knows. These stupid doctors, they just make stuff up." Her mother waved off the question. "Tell me about you. I haven't seen you in so long."

Margo didn't know where to begin. "Well, I'm doing good. The kids are good." She reviewed the details and discarded them one by one: She was divorced. No. The kids just recently gave up hating her and they had called a temporary truce. No. How about she had been set up in her job and spent time in prison? Definitely not that one. She was sleeping with a gangster and defending criminals in his organization. Again a no. She was running out of news.

"What are their names again, your kids?" Margo had told the kids very little about her family on purpose. She thought she was protecting them but realized now she was just being selfish on so many levels.

"Abigail and Thomas." When her mother got out of here, Margo needed to introduce the kids to their grandmother. She had a lot of making up to do, and she hoped that she would have the chance to make things right.

"Nice, Abigail is a good name. Thomas is a saint, so that's not bad either," her mother shrugged. "And David, that's your husband's name, right?"

"Yes, David." It wasn't a secret that she could keep for long though; the kids would slip. "But he and I are divorced."

"Oh? That's too bad," her mother wheezed and held her chest; her thin hand trembled in Margo's as she began to cough again. Her eyes were wide as she gasped for air.

"What can I do for you, Mom?" Margo had jumped out of the chair and hated feeling helpless. Her mother pointed at the red button on the bed rail, and Margo pressed it again and again.

A woman in scrubs came running in. "Susan, hold on, we're going to have to get you back on the ventilator." The nurse had pulled the clear tubes from her mother's nostrils and a mask was pulled over her mouth.

The coughing stopped and she watched her mother's chest move up and down regularly once more. Her eyes were watering from the coughing and it was almost too much for Margo to bear. The nurse looked over at her, eyebrows raised. "And you are?"

"I'm her daughter." Margo felt her mother's hand slip from hers and watched as she closed her eyes.

"Oh, I didn't know she had one." Margo knew that it wasn't meant to be malicious and felt that she deserved it even if it was. "She's not going to be able to talk while she has this on, so you might want to get some coffee or something." The woman was flipping through her mother's chart and wrote something down.

"She's here because of a heart attack?" Her mother had never answered and Margo needed some answers.

The nurse looked up from her mother's chart. "Oh, sweetie, she came in for cardiac arrest, but we found a lump on her breast. The doctor did tests and a biopsy. She has stage two breast cancer. We are working on getting her heart stabilized so she is strong enough to undergo surgery." The nurse made a face. "You should talk with the doctor about treatment options."

The nurse left and closed the door behind her. Margo was sure her flippant attitude was simply a case of being surrounded by illness and death every day and becoming immune to it, but Margo felt a mixture of emotions; disbelief, shock, and fear churning in the pit of her stomach.

CHAPTER 35

It had been a sleepless night, and Margo had haunted the hallways, making numerous trips to the vending machine for coffee. She had looked at her phone, her finger hovering over Sal's number too many times to count. He had asked her to call when she knew, but what she wanted was to run to him and feel his strong, comforting arms around her. Margo had started to depend on that, feeling as if Sal could take care of anything, and it frightened her. She didn't want to depend on anyone, especially not a man.

The doctor had finally arrived and knocked as he entered. "Mrs. Harris, good morning." He looked surprised to see Margo there. "Hello, it's nice to see a visitor." He looked as worn and tired as Margo felt.

"I'm her daughter, Margo." She put the cold cup of coffee down and extended her hand. Her mother had been in and out of sleep all night, but they hadn't talked. She was still hooked up to the ventilator. "What can you tell me about my mother's condition?" Margo was sick with worry, guilt, and hopelessness.

"Well, it's serious, very serious. Years of drug and alcohol abuse has damaged her heart, but we're getting that under control. The bigger concern now is the cancer."

"How far along is it?" Margo asked, bracing herself for the worst.

The doctor ran his hand through his mop of graying hair. "The good news is we have caught it fairly early. It hasn't spread to the lymph nodes and throughout her body."

"Is a mastectomy required?" Margo asked.

The doctor shook his head. "No, we have caught the tumor early enough."

"And the bad news?" Margo held her breath.

The doctor looked at her over his rimless glasses. "We need to remove the tumor as soon as we can, and there are always risks associated with surgery for patients in good health." Margo understood. Her mother was at risk in surgery fresh off her heart attack, but without the surgery the cancer would spread and kill her.

"And after the tumor is removed, what then?" Margo was going to think positive.

The doctor sighed, "I would recommend aggressive radiation at the very least and maybe chemotherapy, depending on the outcome of the surgery. However, your mother's insurance will only cover the cost of her surgery."

"Are you kidding me?" Margo asked incredulously.

The doctor shrugged his shoulders in defeat. "Insurance covers reactive not proactive in cases like this."

"So the difference between life and death is a matter of money." Margo was thinking out loud, but the doctor held out his hands and again, shrugged before saying, "I'm sorry." It was a sad fact that the man was used to the poor, which made up most of the hospital's patients, and they were given only what care they could afford.

Margo absorbed this information before continuing. "If money wasn't an issue, what are the options? What would you do for *your* mother, Doctor?"

He tilted his head and Margo could tell he was reassessing her. "I'd get her out of here and put her in Pleasant Valley Center for Cancer. It's a private hospital that specializes in cancer prevention, treatment, and rehabilitation. Cancer is all they do, and they are very good at it. They have a high survival success rate, but they're not cheap."

"How much money are we talking about?" Since working for Sal, she had been saving money. She had a cash nest egg stashed but feared it would be too little, too late.

The doctor looked her in the eye. "I'm not really sure, but if I had to guess, I'd say you're looking at hundreds of thousands of dollars."

Margo's heart sank, but she kept her poker face. "How would I go about getting her transferred?"

"They have an evaluation process, but I have some contacts there. If you're serious about this I could make some phone calls and cut through the red tape." The doctor smiled at her gently, and Margo was grateful for the hope and sincerity she saw in his eyes.

"Thank you, Doctor, I would appreciate it."

He clicked his pen and wrote something in her mother's file. "Leave your number at the nurses' station and someone will be in touch with you soon."

Margo thanked him again but was already lost in thought. She had no options but to turn to Sal now. She hated having to depend on him, and she didn't want to owe him any favors. She bit her lip. This would be yet another string keeping her attached to Sal, but she was out of options, and this was literally a matter of life and death. Margo vowed to herself that if she had to work for Sal for the rest of her life to pay him back, she would.

Her phone buzzed and jolted her back into reality. She was going to have to reschedule her appointments for today. The call was from David, and she answered, "I'm at the hospital with my mom."

"Oh, Jesus, Margo, I'm sorry. What happened?" Her ex-husband had never met Susan but heard enough stories to understand why Margo had left home and never looked back.

"She's had a heart attack and while she was here they discovered cancer." Margo gave him the details that she had just received from the doctor.

"Shit, well, now I feel even worse that I'm calling," David let out a long sigh, "but I thought you would want to know that the FBI came to the house last night. Agent Richards is who I spoke with."

Fuck! Margo closed her eyes and felt her empty stomach curling on itself. "What did he want?"

"Apparently Eric kept records." The kids hadn't left for school yet, and David was barely audible. She heard him close a door and he continued. "My name was in a book, and he kept track of the money I gave him." David's voice was trembling, and Margo understood his fear.

"What did the agent say?" This was not the time to say anything to her ex about her history with Jake.

"He danced around Eric's death being a mob hit and asked me if I knew Sal Mazzillo, which I don't and I told him so. He didn't ask anything about you."

David was a mess, and she wondered if either of them had slept a wink.

"I just want this to be over with. It's like this nightmare just won't go away. Should I get a lawyer, Margo?"

David had nothing to do with Eric's death, but he was in a sticky situation. Out to his children, that had gone pretty well, but David was still closeted with the people at work and his family. Having his name in the paper along with the allegations would be hell for him.

"Can you afford a lawyer?"

David was only a month or two away from financial ruin thanks to the boy who had blackmailed him.

She didn't need to remind him of his financial situation. Margo could almost hear David calculating things in his head. "Not really, but I can't afford for this to go public either."

"Let me think about it." Margo wasn't above using her female wiles to protect her family. Let Jake divide the world up into bad guys and good guys. She was pretty sure that flirting with him for purposes other than the fact that he turned her on was some shade of gray. It was where she lived lately, and as she looked over at Susan, she suddenly understood her mother's world much better. Hopefully she would have time to tell her that. "Did he ask you any other questions, was he talking about charging you?" What did Agent Richards have besides a ledger that had led him to David?

"He was just asking me about when I saw Eric at the club," David didn't even want to mention the place by name, "and when the blackmail started, when was the last time I saw him, the last time I spoke to him, but nothing about me being in trouble. Just said that Eric's list might go public, and then my name would be out there."

So Agent Richards didn't have anything; he was just leaning on David for something, something that would tie Eric to Sal. He hadn't gotten anything from Margo so he was expanding his reach. It was what she would have done if she had been in his position, but right now, he was a threat that needed to be dealt with.

"Sit tight, David." Margo needed real coffee and some fresh air to clear her head. "Don't do anything; don't talk to anyone, not even the FBI. If they come over again, tell them you're not answering any more questions without your attorney present." It was the advice she would give a client.

"Just keep me posted, Margo, about your mom too." David was trying to be considerate, even though Susan was a stranger to him.

"I will," she promised.

She found a courtyard outside designated for guests and smokers. She sipped her fresh coffee and wished for a cigarette. She smoked a little as a teenager to fit in and had occasionally indulged in the habit when she was stressed over exams or work but it had never been a necessity. She had quit smoking the day she found out she was pregnant with Abby, but the craving hit her suddenly and she watched the passersby, mostly hospital employees, blowing smoke rings. "Excuse me," she asked a young orderly who was sitting a few feet away, "can I bum a cigarette off you?"

He smiled. "Sure." He fished one out and lit it for her. "Visiting someone?"

"Yeah," Margo said as she blew smoke with a contented sigh, "my mother. She's got cancer."

"Sorry to hear that." The young man probably heard the same stories day after day. "Is it terminal?"

Margo just shrugged.

He nodded. "Good luck," he said to her before returning to work.

Margo remembered telling Sal that she had made her own luck. That was exactly what she was going to do now. She took out her phone and called her lover. She knew that he would be up and his day would be well underway.

"Cookie, how is your mother?" Sal wanted to know when he answered.

"Not good. I'm glad you talked me into coming last night."

"I'm so sorry, what's going on?" Sal echoed her concern.

Margo repeated what the doctor had told her and ended the story with, "It's going to cost a grip to get her the best care. I have some money saved, but I doubt it'll be enough to make a dent on the total. I don't know what to do."

"Well, I'll tell you what we're going to do." He had already taken charge, and Margo wished he was next to her instead of just a voice on the phone. "You do whatever needs to be done to get her transferred to the cancer center, and I'll worry about the rest," meaning the money which she didn't have.

Margo felt a huge sense of relief mixed with caution. There was no such thing as a free lunch. As much as she cared for Sal, she feared she might be tying her future to him indefinitely.

"Sal, I don't know what to say but thank you. This is a huge favor, and I want you to know I appreciate this and will make things right. I'll pay you back." Margo meant it. All of it.

"Cookie, when I say I'll handle the rest, I mean it. I'll cover the cost, and I don't want you to give it another thought. I got it." Sal's tone was stern.

Margo wondered if the money was going to be a loan or a gift.

She sighed. "I'm worried about, um, the details." The FBI had her name as well as her husband's now. How long would it take for Agent Richards to have something that did stick? Receiving a large amount of money from Sal would raise red flags and look suspicious. "I can't have any problems right now. My case is being reopened, and . . .," she paused, her paranoia told her that certain things shouldn't be said on a cell phone.

"Go, take care of your mother." He was firm. He wouldn't listen to her anymore. "Keep me posted and get some sleep, Cookie, you sound like hell." Sal was always concerned about her taking care of herself.

"I look like hell too." She was trying to be flippant, but any attempt at humor fell flat, she was being pushed to her limit.

"Impossible," he told her before ending the call.

The next call was more difficult and Margo couldn't help but wonder if Agent Richards didn't already know who her first call had been to.

"Margo, how are you?" The man had a smile on his face; she could hear it in his voice.

Margo, on the other hand, was frustrated and scared, and she snapped, "What are you doing, harassing my ex-husband?"

He was slow to respond. "Oh, so you heard about that?"

"Of course I heard about it." Was he playing dumb or did he really think that David would keep it a secret? Based on David's past, she could see why he was betting on the secrecy.

"Well, your husband's name came up during my investigation, just as yours did. I'm getting to the bottom of this, Margo. Eric might not have been citizen of the year, he might have even been on the fringes of what's legal, but he didn't deserve to die, especially not like he did."

"On the *fringes?"* Let Jake pull that on someone else. "Blackmail is just on the fringes for the FBI, is *that* what you're telling me? Your CI was a piece of shit. Every man's name in Eric's little black book is just one more person who wanted him dead." After she thought about it for a moment, she added, "And every single person that he ratted on as a CI for you, I'm sure *they* wanted him dead too. I don't have to tell you how long snitches live in prison, do I, Agent Richards?"

"No, you don't, Margo." She was seething, and his polite singsong tone was pissing her off.

"So do you understand how ridiculous this is, this wild goose chase?" It wasn't a wild goose chase at all. If Sal didn't actually kill Eric, he had someone do it for him. "You need to leave my husband out of your investigation." As much as this had been brought on by David himself, this seemed to be above and beyond.

"I can't do that, Margo, you know that . . . Unless you have something that you'd like to tell me." The man was relentless, and even if Margo respected him for it, she was a little frightened because of it.

"Like what?" She could argue both ways; she was a damn good attorney.

"Like some information on your boyfriend."

The man who was going to save her mother, or at least try.

The man who had just told her that he loved her.

"Are you asking because of your investigation, Jake?" She used his first name to remind him of what had happened between them, "or is this personal? Are you jealous?"

"Not at all, Margo." She didn't believe him. "Last night, you were seen entering your apartment with Mr. Mazzillo and approximately an hour later, you exited together. What happened, Margo, only an hour?"

"Fuck you, Jake," she said with as much venom as she could muster. "Like I said, is this personal?"

"Yeah, well, maybe it is." He sounded rattled, and Margo pictured his face as his voice rose. "And it will continue to be personal until Mr. Mazzillo is dead or behind bars for the rest of his life."

This was something beyond work. It was beyond even the chemistry they shared. This was borderline obsession. "Why do you have such hard-on for Sal? What did he ever do to you, Jake? Whoever took out Eric saved all the other victims from having to do it. This case is old news, so why do you care?"

He spoke quietly; he had pulled himself together now. "I have a score to settle with Sal Mazzillo, and yes—it's personal."

"That's a dangerous place to be, Jake." Margo felt a little sorry for him. She didn't think the agent stood a chance of winning against Sal.

"Tell that to my partner." He wasn't flirting anymore . . . he wasn't even pleasant. "Call me when you want to cooperate with this investigation, Margo, or don't—whatever. Maybe you're right, why should I care?"

He hung up and Margo shook her head. What was Jake after? What had happened to his partner? Most importantly, what would it take to protect herself and her family? She was caught in the middle between two men, both dangerous in their own rights. She had too much at stake to be a trophy for either side.

CHAPTER 36

Margo had gone home to take a shower and was in the kitchen making herself a sandwich, her wet hair dribbling on her tee shirt, when her doorbell rang. She took a bite on her way to the door. "Who is it?"

"I got a delivery for you, Miss Margo." Her heart was in her throat, and she could hardly swallow. The only people who called her Miss Margo were clients from Sal, and absolutely none of them knew where she lived, or at least were supposed to know where she lived.

"What kind of a delivery?" She didn't have her cell phone, and she looked around for something to use as a weapon.

"I have an envelope. I'm just here to drop it off. Mr. Mazzillo told me you'd be expecting it." That was a relief. If Sal had sanctioned it, she must not be in any danger.

The fact that the FBI was probably outside watching her every move was still alarming, but she couldn't do anything about that right now.

She opened the door. The man had a hat pulled down low. She couldn't even see his eyes. "This is for you." He handed her a legal-sized envelope and turned away, walking quickly before she could say another word to him.

Margo put the deadbolt on and promised herself that from now on when she was home she'd make a habit of it.

She carried the envelope into the living room and opened it. She began scanning the contents and gasped, covering her mouth quickly. Inside was account information from a Swiss bank in Geneva. There was a typed note that stated five hundred thousand dollars had been funded by an anonymous cancer survivor in the name of Susan Harris and Margo was the legal executor of the account. The full amount was to be wired to Pleasant Valley Center for Cancer. Additional funds would be deposited if deemed necessary by the cancer center. There was only one stipulation: Any money not used for Susan Harris's treatment was to be donated to another cancer patient in need. In other words, pay it forward.

Margo was speechless and began to pace in her living room. Five hundred thousand dollars—it was a lot of money. It would take years living in this apartment to make enough money to pay Sal back. Would Sal charge his mistress interest? If so, then she would be in debt to him even longer.

She shook her head. Maybe she was looking at this all wrong. Sal was a rich man, and he cared about her. It wasn't about the money. He had scraped it up in just a couple of hours. Margo wondered if she was over thinking the situation. Maybe it was simple . . . it was a gift, and Sal did it out of the goodness of his heart. He put family first, and maybe this was his way of telling Margo to get her house in order and put hers first as well.

Margo cracked her blinds and looked out, scanning for anything out of the normal to indicate the FBI's presence.

She knew it was just a matter of time before Agent Richards dug up something that might stick.

The FBI was watching her, but then again, so was Sal. How else did he know that she had come home? Margo had never been under scrutiny like this before, even when she'd been on trial. The stress was getting to her, and that had been before finding out that her mother was knocking on death's door.

Her phone rang and she wondered if it was her mother's doctor calling with some good news. "Hello?"

"Is this Margo Harris?" a pleasant female voice asked on the other end of the line.

"It is," Margo replied. "Whom am I speaking with?"

"Miss Harris, my name is Carrie, and I'm an admittance officer for Pleasant Valley Center for Cancer."

"Yes, yes, good morning." Margo bit her lip.

"I have good news about your mother, Susan. We are willing to admit her as soon as we get some paperwork and loose ends taken care of. I was told you were the contact for payment?"

"Yes, I am," Margo answered.

"We will bill your mother's insurance for whatever we can, but we require a minimum good faith deposit of fifty thousand dollars up front." The woman paused. "Do you have the funds?"

Margo smiled. Sal had good timing and had definitely held up his end of their deal, and her mother's doctor had held true to his word as well.

"Yes, I have the funds," Margo replied breathing a sigh of relief.

She made an appointment to meet with Carrie in a few hours to sign papers and transfer the money. Her mother was far from being out of the woods, but this was a positive step in the right direction. Things were moving fast, and Margo felt as if a huge load had been lifted off of her shoulders.

That feeling didn't last long.

The next time her phone rang, it was Megan. The girl sounded like a scared little mouse. "Margo, are you there?"

"Yes, I'm here, Megan, what's wrong?" She needed the girl to stay focused and strong through the upcoming court date.

"A lady just came to see me. She's some fancy lawyer." Megan was still in the habit of blanking on details, and Margo didn't know if it was the drugs or if she'd always been that way.

"Was she from the district attorney's office? Was it Faye Russell? Was that who came to see you?" Margo knew the woman was pissed about their appearance in front of the judge, but she didn't expect her to strike so quickly.

"Yes, that's her. She is very mean," Megan sounded like a small child as if she were rocking back and forth, and Margo could only assume the worst. "She said that I could go to jail because I lied before on the stand." She started crying as she spoke.

"Megan, listen to me. That's just a threat; it doesn't mean anything." That wasn't entirely true, but Margo didn't want to talk about that possibility right now. "She's just trying to scare you. Attorneys do this kind of stuff, but you're not going to fall for her bluff."

Margo realized she needed to get Megan out of St. Joseph's and moved to an unknown location. She was fragile and easily influenced; she would break under the pressure of the defense team's pretrial tactics if they kept hounding her.

"But I think she really means it," Megan whined. "What should I do? I can't go to jail. I was in lockup a couple of times, and it was real, real bad."

"Megan, you are not going to jail. I will do everything I can to protect you and keep you out of trouble." Margo had to be nice to her. She needed her—even though the truth of the matter was that she still wanted to choke the shit out of Megan sometimes. Turning over a new leaf was commendable, but nothing would ever give Margo six years of her life back.

"I can't go to jail." The girl was now sobbing, and Margo heard a noise in the background that sounded like dresser drawers opening and closing.

"What are you doing, Megan?" It didn't matter how long she'd been clean; she was still a junkie as far as Margo was concerned, and therefore a liar.

Another scraping noise was louder than the first, and then something fell to the floor. "I can't stay here. I have to get out of here."

"What?" Margo was about to explode. The girl was threatening to run. Her entire case was dependent on Megan's testimony. "Don't Megan, don't you dare. Stop whatever you're doing and sit down right now!" She was as angry as she sounded.

"Don't yell at me," the girl sniffed piteously. "She scared me. I don't want to go to jail, and I don't want to be here anymore."

"You listen to me right now, Megan." Margo tried to stay calm, but it was almost impossible. "You can't leave. Even if you were done with your program, you can't leave."

"Yes, I can. Other people leave all the time." Megan's tone had turned defiant.

Margo hadn't wanted to resort to threatening the girl, but she felt as if Megan was giving her no other choice.

She spoke in an icy tone. "You're not like them, Megan. You can't leave because you made a deal with Mr. Mazzillo. Do you remember him? Do you remember the deal?"

"Yes, I remember." She sniffed and more tears started. "What difference does it make, why does he care what I do?"

"He cares because he knows how important this case is to me." Margo should have been ashamed of herself, but she wasn't. She had too much riding on Megan to let it slip away. "You have to stay at St. Joseph's, and you have to stay clean. When my case is over, you can start your life over. You'll be clean, you'll have a job and place to live. A fresh start. Won't that be nice?"

"I don't wanna work for your boss. I don't wanna hook anymore." Megan continued to sob.

Margo realized that Megan assumed her only job skills were on her back. "Megan, my boss is not a pimp. He's not going to put you back on the streets."

"He's not?" the girl asked.

If Megan left St. Joseph's she'd be back on the street and Margo could bet money that she'd be snorting or shooting drugs within twenty-four hours or less.

"No, he's not. Mr. Mazzillo is a business man."

Megan thought about this and tentatively asked, "What kind of job can I do? I'm not very good at much."

"We can talk about that later." Margo would tell her she could fly unicorns if that's what it took to keep Megan compliant.

"I just want my life back," Megan sobbed.

Jesus, Margo had had enough with the tears. She closed her eyes. It hadn't been that long ago that she remembered lamenting those very words every day for the first year of her sentence. She could barely find the strength or the will to get out of her bunk to eat or bathe. What was the point?

"Do it for your kids," her cellmate had kicked the bottom of her mattress. "Get up off your lazy ass, white girl, and fight for your kids."

This entire mess was all because of Jay Cook. Why he had been threatened by her, why he had gone after her? She didn't know why. Jay was the reason her life was in shambles and the source of all of her pain and misery. Megan, she was just the puppet that had gone along for the ride and really, at the end of the day, Megan was fucked. Margo was tough: she would recover and be fine, but it was the principal of the thing.

"I want my fucking life back—" Margo stopped herself. She had to be gentle or there was no guarantee that Megan wouldn't leave despite Margo's threats. "Just take a deep breath," she was telling herself as much as the girl. "Let me see about getting you released from the program and moving you somewhere else, somewhere that nobody else knows about besides me. Okay, Megan? Give me a couple of days."

"No. A couple of days is too long." She was really pushing Margo to her limit. "I want to leave now."

"Where would you go right now, Megan?" Margo couldn't wait to cut her loose at the end of this. She almost didn't feel sorry for what had happened to the girl at this point.

Megan was quiet. "I, I don't know," she stuttered.

"You don't have any place to go, do you, Megan?" Margo needed her to realize she had no other options.

"No, I guess not," she mumbled.

"And, Megan, if you were on the streets tonight, how long would it be before some pimp or some John recognized you? How long would it be before you were using again? Or even worse, how long before Mr. Mazzillo found you?" Might as well give her a good dose of reality.

"I don't know, not long, I guess." Margo could hear defeat in her voice.

"I don't want anything bad to happen to you, Megan," Margo said. "You've worked so hard to get clean. I don't want to see all that go down the drain."

"I don't either," Megan admitted.

Margo breathed a sigh of relief. She had to keep Megan together, yet fearful of the unknown on her own. But what was she going to do with her? Where could she keep her and keep a watchful eye on her. She needed to handle this problem on her own without Sal's help. Just the fact that Megan knew that she and Sal were connected was probably not a good thing. She definitely didn't need it coming up in her court case, and then there was always the complication of the FBI lurking in the shadows. They had an immediate opening for a replacement confidential informant.

"You can you trust me, Megan. Give me a couple of days, let me find someplace to put you that's nice and safe. Where no can bother you, okay?" Margo needed the girl to stay put for now and do as she was told.

"OK, but not more than two days, Margo, I mean it." Megan didn't have the ability to play hardball; her options were limited.

"Okay, Megan, no more than two days, you have my word." Margo had to figure this new problem out fast. Regardless of everything else going wrong in her life right now, the girl had to be moved to the top of her priority list. Megan was the key to unlock the door for setting the story straight and Margo getting her life back.

CHAPTER 37

They went to church on Sundays, and the boy sat between her and her husband. He was quiet but fidgeted the whole time, swinging his legs back and forth under the pew. When he hit the bottom of the bench with his feet, she placed her hand on his leg and shook her head no.

When the service was over she made her way to the front of the church to light a white candle in remembrance of her father. It was a ritual she had started when she was fourteen and had begun to think about avenging his death and the life that had been stolen away from her.

The boy watched her light a candle, and she beckoned him to come closer. "Do you want to light a candle too? For your parents?"

Over the months he hadn't talked about them much, but Giovanna knew that didn't mean he hadn't stopped thinking about them.

"Go ahead," she encouraged him.

They both stood quietly, watching the flame sputter until it took hold.

"Don't ever forget them or how much they loved you." It was all a part of what he was and who she was molding him to be. "Or who took them away from you."

The boy looked at her with trust in his eyes. "The priest says that we should forgive those who have hurt us."

Giovanna was impressed, the boy had been paying attention after all. He was smart and studious, he made good grades in school, was liked by his peers, and was athletic. She knew that he said little but watched everything. His dark eyes shone with excitement when he learned something new. He would be formidable when he grew up, of that she was sure.

She had heard the priest's words too and had chosen to set them aside a long time ago. "Some people deserve forgiveness, my darling, but others don't. Even God sends people to hell when they have done something unforgivable. Shouldn't we let God decide?" Giovanna had chosen to help God's hand a long time ago. Whether those who had sinned would be forgiven in heaven or not was no longer her concern.

"Did you forgive the person who killed your father?" he asked her.

She had taken his hand as they turned to leave the church, the sound of their steps in unison echoed in the almost empty-space.

Her husband was waiting by the car and she couldn't take her eyes off of him when she answered.

"No." ***

Amy Morford grew up a country kid in Northern California who from an early age loved to read and appreciated the companionship and loyalty found in dogs. After graduating from California State University at Sacramento with a B.A. in Psychology, rather than analyze human behaviors she steered her interests to understanding dogs. Over the years Amy has assisted owners in training companion dogs, sport dogs, and working breeds.

Amy has published numerous books that touch on behavior issues, caring for, and training dogs and puppies. Amy's goal has always been to assist dog lovers and owners with raising and training a well-mannered and good tempered pet. With the right skills and patience, a happy, healthy, and well-adjusted companion and friend can be had from any dog.

Amy became inspired to use her dog knowledge and expertise to write a children's book series about a dog named Pup Pup based on her German Shepherd, Cozmo. Before Cozmo's greatly anticipated arrival Amy's great-niece, three-year-old Scarlett, had a ton of questions: What will the puppy eat? Where will the puppy sleep? How big will the puppy get? Will the puppy be nice? The questions rolled in, so Amy created the Pup Pup Series to educate children on the responsibilities and companionship that comes from owning your first dog. Amy firmly believes that if taught early, children can grow up to be responsible and lifelong pet owners.

While writing the Pup Pup Series, Amy discovered a creative outlet for writing fiction. It's this new love of writing that's produced her first novel, Sincerely, The Boss. In pursuing the adult fiction market, Amy's discovered a latent talent she didn't know existed. Already planning future titles and plotlines, Amy's set on making her new readers lifelong fans.

From Inmate to the New York Times Best seller:

Three-time New York Times Bestselling author Wahida Clark has become one of the most sought after Urban Literature authors of this generation and is one of only 4 Urban Lit authors to appear on the New York Times bestseller list.

Wahida Clark has an amazing story. Tenacity, vision and sheer determination are what brought her to where she is today.

Clark began writing her first novel while serving a 9 ½ year prison sentence, including 9 months in solitary confinement, at the Lexington Prison Camp in Lexington, Ky. While behind bars, Clark inked a publishing deal with a major publishing house, wrote *and* released 7 novels and laid the groundwork for her publishing company, Wahida Clark Presents Publishing. Released in June of 2007, today Clark is signed to Cash Money Content, the publishing arm from iconic record label Cash Money Records, home to multi-platinum hip-hop recording artists Nicki Minaj, Lil Wayne and Drake. To date she has released 13 successful novels including THREE *New York Times* bestsellers. Her own publishing company, Wahida Clark Presents is one of the fastest growing independent publishing houses in the country. In just 4 short years, WCP has earned nearly 1 million dollars in sales, has 26 titles currently in stores across the country and has a roster of 14 established urban authors.

Her Novels

Wahida Clark has sold more than 700,000 novels to date including TWO New York Times bestsellers with Cash Money Content. Her latest novel, in stores April 23, 2013 is the CMC release, "Honor Thy Thug," the follow up to her *New York Times* bestselling title "Justify My Thug" (2011, CMC) which debuted on the list at #19, only two weeks after release. "Payback Ain't Enough" (also from CMC), made its debut on the *New York Times* Extended Bestseller List at #27 in 2012 and is the follow up to Payback With Ya Life" (2008). Payback With Ya Life was one of only four urban fiction releases to appear on the *New York Times* list.

In 2005, Wahida Clark was crowned the Queen of Thug Love Fiction by the reigning Queen of Hip-Hop Fiction, Nikki Turner. She has since become known as the Queen of Street Literature. Per Professor Vanessa Irvin Morris of Drexel University School of Library Science's *Readers Guide to Street Literature*, "Wahida Clark is the creator of the Thug Love Fiction genre which is a sub-genre of street lit. She is also the first street lit author to pen a series, thus establishing the trend. Wahida's style of writing has become the *template* for urban literature. When you read her novels, they are so real you are convinced that you either know the characters; you want to know the characters; or you *are* one of the characters!"

Clarks bestselling novels include: Thugs and the Women Who Love Them (Part 1 of the "Thug

Series"), Every Thug Needs a Lady (Part 2), Thug Matrimony (Part 3), Thug Lovin' (Part 4), Justify My Thug (Part 5), Payback is a Mutha (Part 1), Payback With Ya Life (Part 2), The Golden Hustla and Sleeping with the Enemy. She has also edited her first anthology, What's Really Hood!: A Collection of Tales from the Streets.

Her Business

A naturally business-savvy woman, Clark followed the invaluable advice of jailhouse mate and multi-millionaire Queen of Media, Martha Stewart, who she consulted with on her business plan for Wahida Clark Publishing. Clark and Stewart also both participated in the facility's career day event. Wahida chose to speak on publishing and being an author. Stewart spoke on the basics of starting a business and business trends. Clark's Wahida Clark Publishing opened its doors in 2008 and today is home to 14 successful and award-winning urban lit authors.

CPSIA information can be obtained
at www.ICGtesting.com
Printed in the USA
LVOW03s1426090517
533874LV00008B/600/P

9 781944 992200